The Neighborhood

A Novel

The Neighborhood

A Novel

First Edition

By David E. Feldman

<u>Table of Contents</u>

For Mom

Who really did put her "best food forward."

Prologue

The neighborhood is about four fictitious families in Valley Stream, New York in 1973. It's a book about people in the place and time in which I grew up. It's also a book about racism, and transcending challenging change, so I thought it made sense to write a bit about Valley Stream's history and my own family's place there before beginning the story proper.

When I was six months old, my family moved from Sheepshead Bay, Brooklyn, to Valley Stream, where I would spend the next seventeen years. Both my parents were teachers. My father, Lawrence, was a fine jazz and classical musician who turned to teaching high school music once we children were born and the family needed financial and familial stability. My mother, Enid, was a reading teacher. Both my parents were highly literate and took great interest in social issues, particularly the challenges faced by those less fortunate than us. My parents were influenced by FDR and Eleanor Roosevelt and, perhaps, by my father's family's poverty. Politics were very much a subject for discussion in our home. My parents were activists who participated in social justice organizations, such as Amnesty International. They were also deeply involved in the Ethical Humanist Movement, which they referred to as the Ethical Culture Society, or simply the Society, which still is on Old Country Road in Garden City.

We lived in a little corner of southeast Valley Stream, bordering what was known as the Yorkshire section of Lynbrook, where the streets had names like Piccadilly Downs, Tottenham Road, and Northumberland Gate. We lived next to the William L. Buck School, which, I had heard, had been a strawberry patch once upon a time.

The neighborhood was middle class and entirely white, but for a few Latinx and Asian families. I remember people of my age speaking with what we now know to be racist language; these words were used casually, as references to people of color; other offensive words were used among young people I knew to refer to people of just about any heritage.

While I'm sure that none of them would think of themselves as racist, I often heard the most derogatory terms for Black and Latinx people, and also Jews. While I was and am Jewish, many of my non-Jewish friends at the time thought of that as an unfortunate accident of birth, a handicap of sorts. I was Jewish, but I was referred to by them as a "good Jew." I remember hearing this as an apology on my behalf.

I heard a lot of derogatory slang about Jews. Italian Americans and Irish Americans were not exempt from the seemingly casual bigotry that was very much the norm in certain circles that included many of my friends at the time. I suppose you could say that bigotry is never casual, but that is the way it was expressed—casually, and in passing, as opposed to being hurled as epithets, though there was that too.

By the time we moved to Valley Stream, the village had been divided into the sort of post-WWII parcels of land that soon populated most of Long Island. Rather than the strawberries that had once flourished in our neighborhood, one would find shaded streets beneath canopies of sturdy oaks and maples, brilliant yellow forsythias in springtime, scarlet roses, and fragrant honeysuckle, which we used to carefully pluck, and from which we pulled a bit of stem to reveal a droplet of delicious nectar. My mother said that her parents' yard on East Ninth Street in Brooklyn was overrun with honeysuckle, which I never did see or taste, though I visited my grandparents' home many times. Even now, the smell of honeysuckle peels away more than a half century of time and delivers me to the Valley Stream of my 1960s youth.

We spent our afternoons, weekends, and summers in the streets, playing Red Light, Green Light and Giant Steps, or running races and riding our bikes.

• • •

Many of Long Island's towns are named after the indigenous tribes who lived here in the seventeenth century: Canarsie, Rockaway, Merrick, Massapequa, Nissequogue, Seatauket, Patchoag, Manhasset, and Montauk. When these indigenous people lived here, they lived in largely peaceful coexistence with the white settlers who followed and eventually crowded them out.

Given the geography, most of the indigenous people were fishermen. They traveled by canoe and caught their seafood with bow and arrow or hook. Even the farmers—who grew corn, beans, and squash—fished, as they needed fertilizer for their vegetable crops and variety for their dinner tables.

Long Island's indigenous people had a deep understanding of how to put our weather and soil to use. They hunted turkey, raccoon, rabbit, and deer in the forests and meadows that blanketed Long Island before the white developers came.

Early European explorers included Giovanni da Verrazzano, who arrived in New York Bay in 1524, followed by Henry Hudson in 1609 and Adriaen Block, a Dutchman, in 1615. Valley Stream was bought from the Rockaway Native Americans, who were Lenapes, by the Dutch West India Company in 1640.

• • •

For my story, it is fitting that Peter Stuyvesant became director general of what would become New York City—not because he was, like my own father, severely handicapped, having lost the lower portion of a leg to a Spanish cannonball, but because he was known to have bigoted views and this is a story about bigotry, among other things. He particularly despised Jews.

Robert Moses was responsible for much of the development of the New York metropolitan area. He favored the building of highways as a means of transportation, and his highways were a prime contributor to the suburbs of the time being nearly all white.

The Federal Housing Administration's *Underwriting Manual* specifically recommended highways as a way to segregate the suburbs. Funding for housing and highways meant funding for segregation. Black neighborhoods were barred from infrastructure funding. Highway overpasses were constructed so that cars could pass beneath them, but buses could not. Much of America's Black and Latinx populations were too poor to own cars in the early twentieth century and were restricted to living in neighborhoods on the outskirts of cities, to long rides on public transportation away from the vibrance of the cities, yet out of reach of the affluence of the suburbs.

Like so many other Long Islanders, I moved here from Brooklyn. My mother's family lived in Flatbush, my father's in the Bedford-Stuyvesant area of north Brooklyn. My mother's parents were Morris, who emigrated from a little town called Schtabze, in what was known as Russia-Poland, just after the turn of the twentieth century, and Nettie, who was born here. Morris's father was Papa Max, who used to ride horses, often with Howard, my mother's brother, and later, with Ruth, Howard's elder daughter and my first cousin. Morris had a brother, Max, a handsome man—both brothers were handsome—who owned the Palladium Ballroom for a time in New York City and helped to introduce Latin jazz to New York. I think of my Grandpa Morris as looking a bit like Humphrey Bogart.

Morris owned a factory in the garment district of New York City. I remember a visit there when I was a child, and walking among row upon row of sewing machines. Family legend has it that he prospered in part because of his less-than-ethical or less-than-legal means of finding the cloth his factory needed during the Second World War. He and Nettie were observant, though not orthodox, Jews—what would be called Conservative today. My grandfather went to *shul* on Saturday mornings, and when I visited, which I did several times a year when I was a boy, I went along. Because neither of my parents practiced, and the services were conducted entirely in Hebrew for adult congregants, I found the experience boring and confusing; at that time, I had no understanding of nor interest in Jewish religious practice.

I found my grandfather gruff, disapproving, and more than a little bit frightening. As I grew into my teens and let my hair grow long, as was the fashion in the late '60s and early '70s, he was critical of my appearance and tried to convince and even bribe me to cut my hair.

My grandmother was loved and admired by everyone in the family. She still is. Grandma Nettie was, along with my sister, Cynthia, a shining light of my youth. Grandma had a clean, sweet smell, which may have come from perfume or any number of her tiny bars of soap, some of which were molded into the shapes of seashells, and which she kept in small brass or silver dishes in the bathrooms. She was forever kind and generous, never critical or cruel. My idea of nurturing grew from my experiences as one of her grandchildren. She adored us all and we all adored her.

The breakfasts we had on the weekends I stayed in my grandparents' home on East Ninth Street between Avenues I and J were magnificent Jewish feasts of fresh bagels, round rolls, nova, belly lox, herring, cream cheese, and butter. I do not remember cakes or *rugelach*, but we may have had them. In those days, people often put out small bowls of candy, mixed nuts, or cashews. Grandma often offered guests candies from boxes of chocolates, which had a second level, below the first, to my and my brother and sister's delight.

I remember the smell of the Brooklyn streets—a unique mingling of cooking smells wafting from apartment windows and food shops, the subway smell rising from the iron gratings on the sidewalk, and bus and car exhaust all joined together into the strangely homey smell of Flatbush, Brooklyn.

I never knew much about my paternal grandfather, whose name was Barney and who was a tailor—a *schneider*. Unlike my Grandpa Morris, Barney sewed with his hands, not with machines—one article of clothing at a time. He was, according to my father, not a nice man. He keeled over in *shul* one *Shabbos*, dead of a heart attack at fifty-nine. I don't know much more about my father's mother, Clara, except that my father loved her very much and spoke of her as loving and kind. I remember her as a gentle, sweet, extremely elderly woman, who, even in my earliest memories, was frail and ill. I remember her visiting and my being told that we had to be very quiet because she was resting.

My father's family was extremely poor, yet his parents—particularly his mother—were somehow able to pay for music lessons for at least four of their five children. The eldest sibling was Molly, a talented pianist who, despite terrible dementia late in life, retained her ability to play the piano. I think of Molly as having the same easy smile, light complexion, and freckles as Lawrence, my father. Molly endured painful personal tragedy; she loved a man, a musician, but was forbidden to marry him because he was not Jewish. The man she married, Harry, was a taxi driver who liked to joke around and was often sarcastic. As a boy, I thought he was funny because he thought he was funny. My parents did not think much of Harry, probably because they loved Molly so much and saw in Harry her unfulfilled love for her beloved musician.

While her marriage and unfulfilled love must have been difficult, the true tragedy was the loss of her only child, who, like my father, suffered from polio, and died by suicide as a teen. A great-aunt on my mother's side had two sons who also died by suicide, and my mother's maternal grandmother jumped off the top of the house after having a botched breast cancer operation that my mother referred to as mutilation. I don't know if any of these lost lives had anything to do with clinical depression, but that awful illness runs through my family and was briefly responsible for a terrifying low point in my own life.

• • •

The 1840 census lists about twenty families, most of whom owned large farms, as inhabiting the area that is today Valley Stream. Rockaway Avenue's Valley Stream Village, as we called it, was known as Rum Junction because of the prevalence of bars in the area. Northwest Valley Stream was Cookie Hill, the northeast was Skunks Misery, and the west was Hungry Harbor, perhaps named for the poor squatters who lived there, and which is still the name of a road there.

Robert and Ellen Pagan emigrated from Scotland in the 1830s, settled in the Town of Hempstead, and for the sake of convenience, established a post office at their home, where Robert was named postmaster. The post office needed a name, and Pagan chose Valley Stream—and the name was accepted by the U.S. Post Office in 1843. The nearest religious services were in Lynbrook, several miles to the east, so Ellen Pagan established Valley Stream's first congregation, also for convenience sake, when she hired a Methodist minister to provide services at the family home.

By the 1850s, the primary roads in Valley Stream were Hempstead Turnpike (which connected the village to Jamaica), Mill Road, Sand Street, and Dutch Broadway—all names for the same road at different points. Merrick Road was built at about that time and named because it connected Jamaica to the west with Merrick to the east. Valley Stream's growth accelerated after Merrick Road's construction, as families settled and businesses sprang up along its route.

Rail transportation to the area began about a decade later, and a new branch, to the Rockaways, was constructed. The convergence of the Far Rockaway and Babylon railroad lines just east/southeast of the Valley Stream train station formed an iron canopy beneath which I and my teenage friends congregated, drinking beer and planning our nefarious exploits.

Just one year before my father's birth in 1926, Valley Stream became an incorporated village, which was also the year the developer William R. Gibson began building homes in Valley Stream, many of which were inhabited by immigrants and their families. Gibson believed there to be a need for a railroad station to serve the families living several miles south of the Valley Stream rail station, and he built what would be named Gibson Station, which retains that name today. I spent much of my teen years in the Gibson Station area and the neighborhoods between the Valley Stream and Lynbrook stations.

. . .

In the early 1970s, our south Valley Stream neighborhood was populated by the families of Italian, Irish, German, and northern European immigrants, along with some American Ashkenazi Jews—most of whom were from the Russia/Poland area, and a smattering of Asian and Latinx families. Many of these families included young couples with school-age children, who could often be seen and heard along the streets and sidewalks as they played, rode their bicycles, or roller-skated. Grade school children played games like Giant Steps; Red Light,

Green Light; potsie; or hopscotch, and skipped rope in the springtime, summer, and fall, and went skating at the Grant Park ice rink in the wintertime.

Many teenagers paid attention to their schoolwork, while others paid more attention to cigarettes, pot, pills, and other drugs. Quite a few managed to do both. Athletes who played high school sports—wrestling, basketball, and football, in particular—were admired. High school fraternities were the focus of much social activity. Groups of older teens rode around in souped-up cars.

Boys gained entry into many of the fraternities by being "nominated" by a member, then "interviewed," which included various forms of hazing and, usually, a hell night. Fraternity hell nights could be vicious beatings administered with wooden paddles, some of which had holes drilled through the flat striking surface to keep the air from cushioning the blows as they struck.

Chapter 1

John Welles Jr. was known to his friends as J. J. In 1973 he was sixteen years old, as were most of his friends. His schoolmates thought of him as average in most ways. He was neither particularly tall, nor short, nor fat, nor thin. He was not a lettered athlete, nor was he athletically inept. While J. J. was not bad looking, he despaired of ever having a girl-friend. He surreptitiously watched couples make out just off school grounds at South High's Jedwood Place entrance with envy. He stared at the girls in his classes and as they walked along the streets to and from school with secret lust. He thought most of them were beautiful and very much out of reach.

J. J. hadn't planned to cut more than one or two classes today, but he saw Ernie Derico and Jimmy Kelly riding their Sting-Ray bikes with Jimmy's dog, Lucy, running alongside; Jimmy rarely went anywhere except for school without Lucy. Both boys were drinking cans of Schaefer Beer. J. J. was on foot a short way behind them. He called to Ernie, who stopped his bike, turned, and waved. Jimmy had stopped as well; a six-pack of beer was swinging by one of two empty plastic rings from Jimmy's handlebars. Lucy waited patiently until J. J. trotted up to the other two boys. She sniffed J. J. and, remembering him, trotted back to her owner.

"Hop on," said Ernie to J. J.

"Pinball?" J. J. asked.

"Sounds good," said Ernie.

"Let me get my bike."

"Sounds good to me too," said Jimmy Kelly, who went along with just about anything Ernie said or did; the boys sometimes referred to him as Ernie's shadow. He poured a little beer on the ground for Lucy, who loved beer. She lapped it up eagerly and looked up, hoping for more, but Jimmy knew not to give her more. His father had yelled when he'd caught Jimmy giving Lucy beer, which he had said was poi-sonous to dogs. Jimmy didn't believe him but only gave Lucy a little at a time, just to be sure. "Soon, Luce," Jimmy said.

J. J. swung a leg over the banana seat on Ernie's Sting-Ray, and off they went. As always, Jimmy had a transistor radio in his top pocket, which was tuned to one of New York's three rock stations. Jim Morrison was singing "Riders on the Storm," and as they rode he seemed to be singing about them, born into this world to be actors out alone.

As they bumped along Roosevelt to Brooklyn Avenue, then to Woodlawn and Bismark Avenues and the blocks surrounding Horton Avenue that composed their neighborhood, J. J. was thinking about Ernie's sister, Debbie Derico. The combination of beer and thinking of Debbie was a comfort to J. J.; the combination quelled his ever-present anxiety. He had doodled "J. J. + DD" all over his notebooks, then changed the *D*s to capital *B*s to disguise his feelings. At lunch one day, Mario the jock had asked him if he liked Barbara Bailey, a tiny, quiet girl with auburn pigtails, who was in none of his classes. After that, he scribbled over all of the *BB*s.

Now Morrison was singing "Love Her Madly," again connecting with J. J.'s thoughts and imagination. He loved when life and music came together like that.

His friends waited at the corner while J. J. went to his garage to get his bike. He never knew when his father, who drove a cab part-time out of the train station, would be home. J. J. had never been able to find a pattern in his father's work schedule, so he was careful to scout his home before entering during school hours, while his friends waited far enough away to remain unnoticed should his father show up.

His father was working, so J. J. went into the house, past his mother, who was watching an old movie on TV and drinking vodka mixed with some kind of juice. She drank for much of the day, which was fine with J. J. since she rarely bothered him when she drank, as long as he wasn't disruptive, meaning as long as he didn't get between her and the TV or the living room window—another of her favorite haunts—or make too much noise.

He grabbed a couple of Fig Newtons and headed out the back door to the garage, where he grabbed his bike and wheeled it out to the driveway, stood it on its kickstand while he closed the garage door, and headed to the corner, where he met up with his friends.

"Ted's?" said Ernie. Ted's Sweet Shop was a candy store about four blocks southwest, on Rockaway Avenue, where the main attractions were two pinball machines. Ted would let them hang around and play pinball as long as they bought something now and then. J. J. and his friends were partial to egg creams and black cherry sodas, which were made with syrup mixed with carbonated water from the fountain.

As they rode, they passed the houses of people J. J. knew, his parents' friends, or people he had heard about—the Ashfords, the Scalesis, and the Storch family. He stopped just shy of the Storch home, where a small crowd had gathered and was silently watching something. The Storch family had moved out Saturday—three days earlier.

Ernie and Jimmy Kelly saw that J. J. had stopped riding, and they made U-turns with their bikes and came to a stop alongside him. "What's happening?" Ernie asked.

"Dunno," said J. J. as he edged his bike forward until he was abreast of one of the older boys from the block—he thought the boy's name was Richard but wasn't sure. "What's going on?" he asked. Richard, if that was his name, put a finger to his lips and nodded toward the Storch house. J. J. angled so he could see the house between the bodies of the assembled crowd.

At first, he didn't notice anything. A beige station wagon was in the driveway, its rear door open, and family members were carrying suitcases, lamps, musical instruments, and other belongings from the car into the home. A moving van was parked in front of the house, and three men were busy hauling furniture from the van to the screen door at the front of the home, which was propped open.

A family was moving in. A tall, balding father, a hefty mother, and two older adults who must have been grandparents. The grandfather had gray hair and a matching brush mustache. The grandmother was thin and frail, yet projected strength. She looked the watching crowd directly in their eyes. The mother was a large woman with prominent cheekbones and a generous mouth that pouted slightly. She wore red lipstick, and her hair was pulled back. As she carried clothes on hangers over her arm, she paused and surveyed the crowd that had gathered to watch. She smiled.

"Whoa," said Ernie.

"Yeah, whoa," said Jimmy Kelly.

Lucy said nothing.

No one in the crowd spoke. They just watched silently. No one returned the mother's smile.

A girl of about J. J.'s age emerged from the house and headed for the car. She wore a red-and-white checkered blouse with a collar and jeans with the cuffs turned up. Around her neck, she wore an orange kerchief. She had short brown hair with a reddish tinge, a sprinkling of freckles, a short, wide nose, and an amused mouth. She looked over the crowd as her mother had, caught J. J.'s eye, and smiled. J. J. was startled and smiled back. He felt himself blush. A boy of perhaps fifteen made several trips to carry stacks of textbooks into the home. He was chubby and wore black horn-rimmed glasses.

Once the family was in the house, the crowd began to talk amongst themselves and disperse. The boys rode around the side streets for a while, not speaking. Lucy stopped to pee now and then.

They made their way to Ted's, bought candy bars—Milky Ways for Ernie and Jimmy, Three Musketeers for J. J.—got change for three dollars, with each boy chipping in a dollar, and set about playing pinball in earnest. They played with a little more intensity than usual, as their minds were on the event they had just witnessed. All three boys understood that they had seen something important—too important for them to fully understand its significance—but they could feel an intensity within the gathered crowd, and, not understanding, they turned their attention and focus toward pinball, frantically using their flippers to keep the silver ball from draining at the bottom of the machine.

Once their quarters were gone and their candy was eaten, J. J. headed for the door. "Later, guys. Gotta go."

"Later," said Ernie and Jimmy Kelly in unison.

Lucy said nothing.

• • •

On the ride home, J. J. thought more about Debbie. He was feeling stressed, though he wasn't sure why, and thinking about Debbie was his go-to at times like these. He was sure she was interested in him because she ignored him so completely that there was simply no other explanation. No one so utterly ignored another human being who was right there in front of them without a reason, and he had decided that the reason was that she liked him. He knew he was stressed about having to present his algebra homework to his father. Algebra was worse than Spanish 2. With Spanish 2, he at least understood the language a little bit. Algebra was so foreign and seemed so out of reach that J. J. despaired of ever passing the course, not to mention his father's muster. His father had hired a tutor, and now J. J. had to present his homework to the tutor, as well as to his father. He was expected to have at least a bit of a handle on the week's work by Friday, and the tutor, whose name was Mr. Bulgarian, would either approve and support his efforts or would shake his head and launch into an explanation of math that was far beyond J. J.'s ability to understand.

When he opened the door and stepped into the vestibule, he found himself faced with the impossible prospect of explaining his algebra work to his father, who, he suspected, understood the math even less than he did, yet expected correct answers. A wave of chilly tension ran up the front of his chest and lodged in his throat; he struggled not to gag. He tasted bitter bile, opened the door, and hurried to the bathroom, where he knelt on the floor in front of the toilet and vomited, his body heaving as he gulped for air.

He washed his face and rinsed out his mouth and walked to the entrance of the kitchen, where he waited and listened. From somewhere to his left, he heard the kind of mindless, easy-listening music that could be heard at the mall and knew his father was home, probably at the kitchen table. He continued listening and heard the soft tinkle of ice cubes somewhere to his right; his mother, he now knew, was sitting at the living room's bay window with the first of her afternoon vodkas, watching the birds, the children on the block, and the neighbors. He would have liked to have gone up to his room, but that would mean walking past his father, who was sure to ask about the algebra.

"We'll be eating in ten," his father said, and J. J. knew he was busted. "Start your algebra now. Finish it and show me after dinner."

J. J. walked into the kitchen and found his father reading the paper with his good eye. Well, he probably wasn't reading but was thumbing through the paper, looking at the headlines, stopping to read a sentence or two when a story caught his interest until he got to the comics, where he relaxed with Charlie Brown, Snoopy and the Peanuts gang, Blondie and Dagwood, and Hagar the Horrible. From what J. J. could tell, his father liked Hagar best, probably because he was rather like Hagar. J. J.'s father rarely spoke, and when he did, it was in short sentences, often composed of single syllables, which were either orders or complaints.

J. J. knew enough to listen, pay attention, and do whatever his father asked of him, or at least to look as though he were. His father's cab-driving job required very little speaking. He knew his father received a pension from the Army, but that was all he knew about his father's service. J. J. had tried asking about it, but his father refused to speak about his years in the service. J. J. knew he had been part of the invading force in June of 1945 at a place called Utah Beach that had been added to the war effort at the last minute. It was the western-most of the D-Day landings, but that was all he knew, except that his father had been hit in the face with shrapnel, which tore out his right eye and most of his right cheekbone, leaving a gouged valley that disappeared behind the patch he always wore. As little as his father said about his World War II experiences, he said even less about his injury. Nor did he speak about what life was like with one eye, something J. J. was curious about, though he had never dared to bring the subject up. The only time he had was when he was about six and Robert, one of the neighborhood boys, had asked if his father "got blinded in the war." It was then that J. J. learned never to bring up the war or his father's service. His father had responded to the question with a rage that was out of proportion to a question asked by a child. Since then he had developed a terror of his father that he suspected was a reflection of his father's war experience. J. J.'s father seemed to him to have two gears: silence and rage.

"What's for dinner?" J. J. asked.

His father didn't answer.

"Pot roast," his mother replied from the living room.

"Algebra," his father said.

"Algebra's for dinner?" J. J. cackled a laugh, which was cut short by his father's withering look—a look that accurately augured an impending storm, as lightning did the coming thunder.

His father crumpled his newspaper with one fist, slammed it on the tabletop, and used the other hand to push himself up, until he glared down at J. J., bellowing, "Talking back again? I'll teach you to talk back to me!" His voice flashed with rage, his fists clenched, and J. J. backed quickly away until he pressed against something soft. He reached back and found his mother's hand on his shoulder.

"He's starting his homework now, aren't you, J.?" This, J. J. knew, was as far as his mother was prepared to go in defending him. No one stood up to his father when his storms came.

"Sorry. I'm sorry!" J. J. stammered, and he was. Anything to tamp down his father's anger, which inevitably left him cowering. He had regularly wet his bed until the age of twelve, when he began exploring the contents of the bottles of alcohol he found in a cabinet in the living room as a means to quell his constant anxiety and frequent terror.

He slid from beneath his mother's hand, hurried to the stairs, and ran to his room, where he opened his algebra text and scanned the day's reading, then opened his notebook and wrote out the first problem. He thought hard about how to answer but soon gave up. He had never understood how numbers could be multiplied by letters. He understood what one plus one was, but what was one plus X? He gulped several times and let the shaking that had taken over his body subside.

He read some more and wrote out a few problems and his best guesses at their answers. After a few minutes, he heard his name called, and he ventured downstairs, careful to avoid looking at his father. Instead, he met his mother's gaze, acknowledged her nod, and sat down, waiting for his father and then his mother to take portions of the roast, the potatoes, and the carrots.

His mother caught his eye. "Your sister's out," she said, reading his mind. "She'll do the dishes later, after she eats."

J. J.'s mother did not slur her words when she drank, no matter the amount. Alcohol seemed to wake her up. Before her first drink, which was sometime after lunch, Connie Welles was lethargic, even depressed. But she came somewhat more alive with her first vodka and juice, and by her third, she had a focus that took over the home for the evening, as long as J. J.'s father was at ease. The Welles household ran on one of two energies: John Sr.'s trauma-fueled rage or Connie's alcoholic haze.

On the rare days his mother didn't drink, the Welles home was usually quiet, the only sound the rustling of John's newspaper—unless something triggered his trauma and rage.

J. J.'s mother got up and brought her glass first to the freezer, where she cracked some cubes from a tray, then to the counter next to the sink, where she splashed from several bottles. J. J. thought to ask where Joanne was—not so much because he cared about his sister's whereabouts, but because turning his parents' attention away from himself made for a safer evening. His father folded his newspaper and slid it next to the small black-and-white TV that sat on the dark pine side table that filled the space between the counter and the dining room table.

At that moment, J. J. heard the screen door latch give two metallic clanks as the door was pulled open, and his sister cruised through it and into the house. "Hi, Ma! Hi, Dad!" she called as she breezed into the kitchen and plopped down at the table.

"Hands," J. J.'s father said, with his searchlight stare.

Joanne had medium-length black curly hair, and dark-brown eyes accented with blue eyeliner. She wore a navy-blue collared blouse and blue jeans. Three thin silver bracelets jangled on her right wrist. She went to the kitchen sink, turned on the water, and poured a little dish soap onto one of her hands. When she was finished, she dried her hands on the beige dish towel that hung over one of the cabinet doors below the kitchen sink, then returned to her seat and waited as the food made its way around the table. She was last to be served because she had been last to the table.

The family ate silently, cowed by their patriarch's outburst, each fearing to be his next target.

"I've got dishes tonight," Joanne volunteered. "A Negro family moved into Storches' house. Can Laurie Derico come by?" She looked at her mother. "I know—after my homework—to listen to records?" She glanced at J. J. to see if he had noticed the pace of their mother's drinking tonight. She saw that he had.

Joanne was a dark-haired perpetual motion machine, always talking, walking, thinking, creating—and all of it at high speed. J. J. had long since stopped trying to keep up with her. He was quite certain his sister was crazy.

Their father's eye swept over his family and the food on the table. He said nothing.

Four vodkas enabled Connie Welles to keep up with her daughter for at least a few hours. She hadn't touched the food on her plate, but had been sipping regularly from her drink—but now she stopped, glass poised and shaking slightly several inches from her mouth. She answered her daughter's pronouncements in order. "Yes, that's right. No, I did not know. And you may, once your father looks at your homework." She lifted the main dish and held it out to J. J. "Have some more, J." Then she turned to Joanne. "Did you say a Negro family?"

J. J. nodded. "She's right. Me and Ernie and Jimmy Kelly watched them moving in."

His father's eye moved to J. J., but he didn't speak. J. J. wondered what he was thinking.

"Ernie, Jimmy Kelly, and I," he said.

J. J. couldn't help but giggle. "You were there too, Dad?"

His father slammed his fork down and briefly closed his eye. "Dinner," he said softly, his rage coiling, "then algebra."

J. J. sighed. "Daa-aad." His father held up a finger for silence. His eyes widened.

Chapter 2

John Welles knew that his son, J. J., thought he was too hard on him. John thought so too, but he believed that discipline was a necessary precursor for maturity and character; he had only a vague perception of his anger, which, when he was aware of it, frightened him and caused him to emotionally dissociate. He thought his son was a pain in the ass and tended to talk back with a fresh mouth that ran on for too long and with too little respect. Yes, maybe he occasionally got a bit too angry with him, but the boy needed to be kept in check; he was asking to be yelled at and maybe even for a smack now and then. Perhaps more. John's grandfather had taught his father, his father had taught him, and now he was teaching J. J. the value of regular hard work—the value of discipline. If you didn't have it, you deserved what was coming to you. That was what John had learned from his father, lessons he now passed on to J. J.

But what John did not remember was that he had learned discipline, not from his father, but from the United States Army. He had joined up as soon as they would take him following Pearl Harbor, though they'd made him wait until his birthday in 1942. Just about all the boys he knew had joined up. Most he had never seen again. They either were killed or went on with their lives in some other place, with other friends. He had also forgotten how frightened he'd been at boot camp. Before joining up, he and everybody else was gung ho to fight, but much of that had been on the surface—for show. He landed in Europe and on the second day had his face torn up and left eye lost to a land mine's shrapnel. He'd had no idea of what he was getting into. Boot camp had been overwhelming. His tendency toward anxiety—however buried it might have been—was a detriment in the Army's no-nonsense environment. If he would have known what to expect, he might still have gone, given what was at stake, but he would have known enough to be far more afraid of the fighting than of boot camp.

The years following the war had been dominated by hospital stays and surgeries. Some combination of these experiences and a desire to avoid talking about his injury led him to shy away from social situations. He had been lucky that Connie had been a friend of his sister's, or he might never have married. She was witty in a slightly bitter way that John had found attractive, she had a way of looking directly at him that was sexy and rare, and she was not put off by his injury but seemed somehow attracted by it.

She hadn't been happy about having to work; even now, she thought his part-time cab-driving job wasn't enough, and she was right, but she didn't walk in his shoes. She hadn't been where he'd been and seen what he'd seen. She thought the Army should have taken better care of him. Right again, but so what? Over the years, her wit had turned to sarcasm and then to real bitterness with no trace of her former humor, as she found comfort in the bottom of her ever-present glass of vodka, juice, and ice, with the occasional slice of lime.

John knew his son wanted his approval, and he thought he occasionally offered it, but the boy didn't listen. The boy avoided work. He couldn't understand algebra, which every kid his age apparently understood. John didn't understand algebra either, but since he was a veteran and not a student, he rejected the fact as irrelevant. He reminded J. J. just about every day to do his schoolwork and his chores, which weren't very much—making his bed, clearing plates after dinner, washing dishes twice a week, and, now that he was fifteen and strong enough to push the mower, mowing the lawn on Saturdays.

He had hoped J. J. would have joined a sport at school. He had no illusions about football but had hopes for wrestling. Valley Stream South High had a pretty good wrestling team that was coached by good men. A sport and attention to schoolwork could keep J. J. out of trouble—keep him off the streets and away from the fraternities, which John believed to be a bad influence. Drinking clubs that got into fights was the way John Welles thought about fraternities. That they might bring young men together and offer mutual support did not occur to him, or if it did, he considered the idea a naive pipe dream.

The Welles family could not afford a dishwasher or a power mower on John's meager VA pension and the few dollars he earned driving a cab, but he did not mind. Pushing a mower and washing dishes by hand were fine by him; they were good for a person, especially a person with demons like his. Keeping busy and focusing on a task kept his demons in the background, where they lurked and grew, waiting for moments when his mind was triggered to strike. They also struck as he was trying to go to sleep, or in the middle of the night when he would awaken covered in a cold sweat.

He had loved his time with J. J. when his son was a baby, but somehow, now that the helpless baby was becoming a young adult, a gulf between his expectations and his son's resistance to them had sprung up and grown between them. When J. J. had been a baby and then a dependent toddler, their mutual love had taken John away from his monstrous memories, but now the boy was more of a responsibility than a joyous diversion—an albatross—and John's memories had roared back like a black wind. And that wind had become a cavernous black hole—a thing that sucked the life from the world of living into its bottomless vacuum. John wanted to make the black hole go away, but he didn't know how, and so he had given up trying. Now he fought it when he could with awareness and by staying busy, and by not letting himself get sucked into it. He fought it by walking around the neighborhood and noting everything he saw, to keep his mind focused. He fought it by reading newspapers, and by pushing his children to do better. He did not fight the black thing by spending time with Connie. Connie, he somehow believed, had become an ally of the black thing.

The thing consisted of the war, his memories of the war, what the war had done to him, the buddies he had watched suffer and die, the persistent images of their torn, bloodied bodies, and the toll all of this had taken on him. The black hole was all of these and more—or perhaps less since it was the utter vacuum it left in the wake of all things— as its insatiable maw inhaled them all.

The war was a horror that thrived in his mind even now, twenty-eight years later. At least, he thought, he hadn't been in the Great War and his son in World War II. He had no illusions about J. J. surviving on a beach in France in 1945.

He sighed and forced his mind to its tasks, diversions like the downspout that was coming loose on the northeast corner of their house, the bare patch on the strip of grass along the street on the south side. He would take a metal rake to it, sprinkle it with seed and cover it with dirt, then train the hose on it until the bright green shoots struggled forth.

He missed Mike Storch. Mike had been their only neighbor who had been in the war—other than Greg Jordan, who had been a medic and well back of the front lines. Not that John and Mike spoke about the war. They didn't. But they both knew, and that was a comfort of sorts. John never spoke about the war with anyone, except once with Connie early in their marriage, and that had been a painful disaster. Conversation about the war ignited a fuse to a bomb of terror and rage that was beyond his control. Mike Storch had been there and seen things that bound them together, yet they never discussed any of them. John knew and he knew that Mike knew, and now Mike was gone, and there was just a little less shared experience to keep the black hole at bay.

He could hear Joanne's record player upstairs, a woman's voice singing, "It's too late, baby now," and he remembered what she had said earlier. A Negro family had bought Mike Storch's house.

Chapter 3

Laurie Derico served the Taylors, the last customers on her side of the diner. His was a turkey platter with mashed potatoes and green beans, and gravy on the side; hers was a Cobb salad. Both had Tabs. She had chatted with them, nodding agreement at their concern about the rumor about the Negroes moving in and in their minds taking over. Laurie had not heard anything about this, but customers at Dericos' expected their waitresses to be up on local gossip (which they called "news"), to share their opinions (which she did, since doing so was good for her tip), and to be gracious (which she always was).

She glanced at Maria as she brought the Taylors their check. Laurie could see from Maria's expression that she understood that, since it was eight o'clock and there were no new customers on her side, Laurie would be off for the night, and Maria, who was sixteen years old, four months pregnant, and needed the money, would handle the rest of the night until closing at eleven o'clock.

Laurie slid the check beneath Mr. Taylor's plate, which still held a sizable amount of turkey, his entire portion of green beans, and very little mashed potato. The butter was long gone. She smiled.

"You have a great evening, Mr. Taylor, Mrs. Taylor."

"And you, young lady," said Mr. Taylor, arching a shaggy white eyebrow. "Be careful going home. This neighborhood's getting worse every day."

"That's right," echoed Mrs. Taylor, her blue eyes wide, a forkful of salad poised between her plate and her mouth, which was ringed with slightly smudged pink lipstick.

Laurie knew exactly what they were referring to. "Thank you, sir. Thank you, ma'am." She ducked her head and headed back into the kitchen, whipping off her apron. She heard her mother calling to her over the whoosh of hot water as she filled the soup tureens to soak before closing.

"Going to Joanne's?"

"Just for an hour." Laurie pressed her lips together and looked politely at her parents. Her father waved as he headed from the kitchen to the dining room.

Her mother smiled and aimed the spritzer, pressed its trigger, and squirted a weak stream of hot water in Laurie's direction, but it fell far short of her. "Nine thirty, young lady, or else."

"I know. I did my homework when I got here." She slung her big brown pocketbook with its heavy copper buckles carefully over her shoulder. She didn't want to spill what was inside. "I might help Joanne with her homework if there's time." She had no intention of doing this since Joanne was a far better student than she was, but she knew that saying it would make a good impression.

"Okay, then." Her mother nodded, and Laurie hurried out the kitchen door, bounded down the back steps, alternately walked, and skipped to the Welles house, which was just under a half mile away from Dericos' Diner, not far from Gibson Station.

She rang the bell, waited, and when J.J. answered with a sullen, "Hi Laurie," she peered around him to see if Joanne was downstairs.

"Sister here?"

He turned. "Joanne! Laurie Dereeeco's heeeere!" he called.

"Stop yelling!" John Welles's voice yelled from beyond the hallway.

Joanne ran from her room and down the steps that were just inside and facing the front door in a one-and, two-and, three-and cadence. "Hey, Laur!" She pushed open the screen door.

"What's up?" Laurie answered as she entered the house.

"Long story," Joanne said, rolling her eyes. "Long story" was their code that said there was exciting news. "We'll be upstairs, Mom!" She turned, started up a few steps, then waited for Laurie, who had stopped to wave to Joanne's parents.

"Hi, Mr. Welles, Mrs. Welles," she said, in the polite voice she reserved for parents and customers.

"How are you, Laurie?" asked Connie Welles, who leaned against a counter, swaying slightly and looking down into a glass, where she swirled clear liquid and ice. "How is your family?"

"All good, Mrs. W."

John Welles sat stiffly at the dining room table, staring straight ahead, despite having a newspaper open in front of him. Laurie thought she saw his head nod slightly. She waved and followed her best friend up the steps.

"Got something," Joanne said as soon as she closed the door behind her.

"I heard. Who would sell the Storches' house to Negroes?" She was echoing what she'd overheard at the diner. "Don't they know there'll just be more of them, then more, until we're crowded out and it's Harlem on Long Island?"

Joanne shrugged. "Oh, that. Yeah, I heard. Dunno." She waved the thought away. "I don't care about that."

"Well, maybe you should," Laurie insisted.

"Uh-huh," Joanne said. She had turned and was digging in her closet, rummaging through a pile of her clothes—dungarees, bell bottoms, blouses, halter tops, bras.

Laurie heard a faint, barely audible cry as Joanne turned to her and stood up, her palms together, cradling a tiny gray-and-black striped kitten.

"Oh my God! Where'd you get him?"

"Her. I found her by the curb up the street, in front of the Storches' house. They had a cat that looked kind of like this. Maybe this one's mom?"

"Or dad," Laurie added.

Joanne gently stroked the top of the kitten's head. "Poor baby. She was shivering and hungry." She reached inside her blouse and came out with a crumpled napkin, which she spread out on the floor next to the closet, shoving several blouses off to one side, ready to be thrown atop their guest if needed. On the napkin was a small piece of pot roast. The kitten looked about, mewled several times, and took two tentative steps toward the food, then stopped and mewled again. She finally began to eat, stopping now and then to look around.

"I've got something too." Laurie opened her pocketbook and took out a small mayonnaise jar that was a little more than half filled with a grayish liquid.

"What is it?" asked Joanne, glancing from the jar to the kitten.

"I'm not sure," Laurie answered. "Definitely blackberry brandy, and there's some gin in there, and some vodka, and some other stuff. Triple threat, maybe?"

"Here, gimme." Joanne held out her hands, "but keep your eye on the kitten."

"What're you going to call her?"

"Dunno." Joanne opened the jar, took a deep breath, lifted the container to her mouth, and took two deep gulps. "Wuh!" She breathed heavily for a moment; her eyes watered.

"Gimmee," said Laurie as she tried to do the same, but she could not drink the way Joanne could, and she sputtered, spilling some of the concoction on the faded gray carpet.

"Don't waste it!" Joanne complained.

"Sorry." Laurie was embarrassed by her struggle to drink what she had brought, as though ownership implied some kind of drinking expertise. She tried to look regretful.

"That's it!" Joanne cried.

"What?" Laurie was confused.

"Her name! We'll call her Sorry."

• • •

The next morning, Lou Derico opened the front door of his diner and waited a moment before he brought the hero bread and kaiser rolls inside. It was four-thirty, and a faint pink of dawn brightened the eastern sky, turning the blue-black above it to softly glowing violets and blues. He waited, listening; there it was. The first bird of the morning—a robin, looking down at him from the telephone wire across the street, tipping its head first to one side and then the other. Talking to him. Lou smiled.

He went inside, put the coffee on, and quietly set about preparing the day's soups. Anna was already at work, buttering the grill and boiling eggs, after which she would mix the tuna, egg, and chicken salads. He briefly watched her—a petite, sallow presence with black Sicilian hair and once-pretty features sunken with age and stress—now hard at work at the grill and then moving quickly between the long wooden countertop and the shining steel doors of the refrigerators opposite.

"Last night, Debbie told me Mike Storch sold their house to Negroes."

He didn't answer, but waited, knowing she had more to say.

"Who do you think was the realtor?"

He shook his head. He didn't want to have this conversation. If that's what Mike Storch did, it was none of his business—though he wasn't thrilled with the idea. His concern was the personality of the neighborhood, his customers, and the value of his home.

From the register the previous evening he'd overheard the Kowalskis talking about this over their minestrone, his cheeseburger deluxe, and her broiled salmon. To the Kowalskis, a Negro family meant more Negro families; they were frightened. While he was concerned for the diner, he knew that Anna felt more strongly than he did. Negro customers would pay with the same green as did everybody else. But he kept his thoughts to himself. The Dericos' marriage worked because they did not discuss business-related issues. The business side of the diner was his domain alone.

"You coming?" he asked.

While Anna worked at the counter, Lou laid ten strips of bacon out on the grill and quickly slid them to one side, to be cooked then rewarmed and used as customers requested.

A half hour later the Quinns came in, as they did every day. Carl and Prissy were older than he and Anna, but they seemed younger because they were still so in love. They sat at the counter, their heads bent together, their voices low, their laughter frequent and musical as they shared a newspaper before returning it to the rack. Sometimes their hands would drift together and briefly clasp. Lou tried not to notice, but how could he not? Theirs was a forty-year marriage, going strong, their love still burning, and probably still in the bedroom, whereas he had never burned for Anna. His was a marriage fashioned out of common sense and convenience and the fact that neither of them had better prospects. Time had passed them by as the '50s wore on toward the '60s. They had married, enjoyed their honeymoon in a sensible way at the Jersey Shore, then set out to raise a family and keep his father's— now his—restaurant running.

Lou had no illusions about romance with Anna. Yes, they loved each other, and they were faithful and loyal to one another; they were good friends, perhaps even best friends to the degree that either of them had time for friends. But there *was* no time. The diner ran their lives, and what the diner didn't take, the kids took. For the most part, their relationship was one of passive presence.

Their oldest, Debbie, was well on her way to becoming a working musician with teaching music as her sensible backup and future. She played flute wonderfully, and Lou and Anna cherished their evenings of listening to their daughter's sweet sonatas drifting from the room she shared with Laurie. They knew the neighbors appreciated Debbie too. If they had the time, they would worry about Laurie, who was a hand-ful, but the Dericos were too busy with the diner and with wringing their hands over Ernie, who was so often in and out of trouble. He had the attitude and he had the mouth, and at any given time he might be out with friends—if that's what you could call them—vandalizing someone's property or saying whatever came into his head to anyone who got in his way, including the police.

But none of this bothered Lou very much. He forced his eyes away from the Quinns as he left the counter area and focused on stirring in-gredients into one of the big soup pots, which would feature today's soup of the day: cauliflower and cheese.

• • •

The bells on the front door jangled, but Lou didn't look up from his soup preparation. Anna was out front and would handle any customers. But then her head appeared in the kitchen doorway, her expression pointed. Lou washed and dried his hands and strode into the restaurant proper, his walk echoing his wife's expression.

Officer Tom Kelly had just sat down and was looking through the day's newspaper.

"Tom," said Lou.

Tom nodded. "Lou."

Lou filled a mug with coffee and slid it, the sweeteners, and a container of half-and-half to a spot in front of Tom. "How's the family?" He didn't really want to know, and he knew the answer would not reflect any real truth. This was their conversation every day.

"Great," said Tom, which is what he always said. He didn't look at Lou, but stared straight ahead, at another place and time. "I haven't seen them in two days." He barked a bitter laugh. "I get up at three, and Jimmy, Julie, and Erin are asleep, and maybe Lady will get up and whine for a snack, maybe not. Happy family. Living the dream. I go to work, and I still don't see them. Julie and Jimmy're at school or out with friends; Lady hopefully peed and crapped out back, Erin's shopping or doing the wash or cooking. Happy family. I get home and I see them all. Maybe not so happy. Julie has some knucklehead calling, Jimmy hasn't done his homework, Erin gives me a hard time about meaningless shit, and Lady's just fine. But really, even then—happy family, since they leave me alone and I get to knock back a couple and watch a ball game or some crap. So overall I'd say we're pretty happy, even when we're not. A grand life I have." He sipped his coffee.

Lou rested his hands on a cutting board behind the counter. "Same shit, different day."

Tom didn't look at Lou but continued staring straight ahead, acknowledging with a bare flicker of the corner of one eyebrow upward. "Of course, there's work itself, but let's not get into that. Coffee's strong today." He nodded approvingly.

Rachel Arnsbarger came in and ordered three coffees, an Earl Grey tea, a coffee cake, and a blueberry muffin to go. Tom watched her, not bothering to hide his interest. Rachel appeared to feel him watching and shifted away from him at the counter.

Lou also watched Rachel Arnsbarger, but less obtrusively—his desire hidden as he sliced tomatoes and onions, and occasionally wiped the tears from his eyes.

Chapter 4

Elly Thomas plucked a raisin out of her cereal, and when her mother wasn't looking, tossed it at Dwayne, who was busy separating the raisins from the bran in his bowl. The raisin hit him on the cheek.

"Ma! Elly's throwing food at me!"

Their mother, Shirley, frowned in her daughter's direction. "Eleanor," she said a warning in her tone.

"I'm not goin', Ma. My stomach hurts."

"That's probably just anxiety. You'll feel better once you get there. It's the anticipation that's causing it."

"Why do I have to go to school here?"

Shirley, who had been packing lunches for her daughter, son, and husband, stopped and turned, her hands on her hips. "Because this is where we live now, Eleanor."

"But why do we gotta live here?"

"We've been over this a dozen times, young lady. You know why, and it's a good thing for all of us."

Elly got up from the table and walked to the window overlooking their front yard and, beyond it, the street. "All I see when I look out there is white, white, white. They hate us. I can tell."

Dwayne, who had finally separated his cereal the way he wanted it, filled his spoon with equal parts cereal, raisins, and milk. "But you haven't even met anyone yet."

"I saw how those people watched us moving in. They hate us, and they've got plans to prove it."

Shirley exhaled, lifted an eyebrow, and clenched her jaw. "Nobody's going to hurt you. Nobody hurts my children or anyone else in my family. Eat your cornflakes. I have to get your father to his school, then you to yours."

"And a word to the wise," said Elvin as he arrived at the bottom of the stairs and knotted his tie. "You will have catching up to do. The kids here will be ahead of you, so get your books and your assignments, and get to work. And remember what Papa Elvin says: you can overcome just about everything with reading and writing."

"It's a blessing," said Makayla, who was in her favorite cushioned crimson chair in the living room. Elly finished her cereal, then came into the living room and sat on the edge of her grandmother's chair. Makayla took her granddaughter's hand. "Catching up at school will give you something to do, so you won't be so focused on what all's going on here." She tapped the side of her head.

Elly shook her head. "But if I'm doing schoolwork, I'll have to be focused on what's up here." She tapped her head, then stuck out her tongue. "Silly!"

Makayla smiled, her eyes twinkling with the joy of being with her granddaughter. She reached out and pressed her palm gently to the side of Elly's face.

• • •

When Connie Wilson met John Welles in the early 1950s, she was looking for a strong, stable man with whom to make a home and have children. She had been taught by her parents, who had struggled through the Depression, that this was the American way, and so she charmed the taciturn veteran with the rugged good looks. They went to restaurants and bars, and John, who'd been traumatized by his wartime experiences in Europe, allowed himself to be charmed without immersing himself in the relationship. It was easier to go along with Connie's wooing of him than to resist, especially given the looks of revulsion he saw on the faces of most of the women to whom he'd been attracted since the war. With Connie, he did not have to do anything except go where she arranged for them to go, have a few drinks, dinner, and perhaps dance a little bit, ignoring everyone they met or with whom they came in contact, except perhaps the waiter, waitress, or bartender. They did not have sex right away because, despite Connie's flirtatiousness, neither Connie nor John had any experience. Connie had done a little of what was then called petting after her prom with a boy named Kevin Scowfin, a boy whose lack of experience left him literally unable to find the parts of his date he had been so conditioned to seek out.

While John Welles was not a virgin, his experience with sex had been quick and entirely directed by a woman more than ten years his senior, whom he had met in a bar the night before going off to war. He came away from the encounter minus his virginity and with a vague sense of accomplishment, but without the knowledge he needed to facilitate his next sexual experience.

John Welles recoiled from a post-war world that was too bright, too loud, and moved too fast for his frazzled sensibilities. He was unable to hold the sales jobs that were available to him soon after his return. He knew that his eye patch and the crevice that extended from beneath it to below his cheek frightened others, so he became what was known as an inside salesman, one who used the telephone to connect with his clientele. But he grew impatient too quickly with reluctant customers, exactly the opposite of what was required for success. The interactions exhausted him, so he opted for driving a cab out of a little shack at the village train station. He could interact with these customers if he wanted to, which was rare, or he could simply drive them to their destinations and ignore their efforts at small talk.

Connie was satisfied that her handsome war hero boyfriend was hers to do with as she wished. John told her nothing of his wartime experiences, except to say, "You don't want to know," before changing the subject. She imagined he had performed heroic acts during his brief stint in Europe, a notion she encouraged with her friends, without saying so directly. She assumed that, once they were married, he would get over the effects his wartime memories seemed to have had on his job prospects and personality, and they would go on to have a reasonably comfortable and happy life.

Connie nourished and fed this impression among her relatives and friends until it became clear that John was not going to change. He would not seek out another sales job, and he would not warm to her, despite her occasional attempts at deepening their relationship. He remained a cardboard cutout of a man—a disfigured war hero whose personality was buried beneath his wounds.

Instead of her husband, Connie developed a relationship with the bottle. She drank at home because she did not want to let the neighbors, her friends, or her family know about what she suspected was her failure as a woman. Connie was determined to have a family. Perhaps her husband's failures in the job world would be overshadowed by her success at childbearing and motherhood. She reduced her drinking a bit during her pregnancies but was stunned to learn that her husband's apathy extended even to the birth of their children. John's refusal to participate in any but the most cursory demonstrations of fatherhood left Connie breathless and emotionally staggered, and so when she nursed her babies, she did so with detachment. There was little oxytocin and little bonding between the Welles mother and children. Nursing was a chore.

J. J. never learned that the world was a safe place, an environment where anything was possible. He did not learn to believe in himself. He lacked the nurturing of a healthy relationship with his parents, especially his mother. He lacked the biologically transmitted guarantee that he was safe and loved.

So J. J. lived believing that life was dangerous and people were threats. He expected to be hurt and was in a constant state of anxiety. He was always on guard. Worst of all, he was deeply afraid of his father's rage while being accustomed to his mother's detachment. She, too, was capable of violent rage, but when she was drinking, J. J.'s mother tended toward dreamy sadness, which was the most tolerable emotional experience available in J. J.'s home life—one reason that he was rarely at home.

Somehow, the gulf between mother and daughter was not the chasm it was between mother and son—perhaps because Connie saw in Joanne the possibilities that had passed her by, and she made an effort to give to her daughter what was missing in her own life. Connie's attempts to live vicariously through her daughter enabled Joanne to have a less isolated existence than her brother, who received nothing from his father and very little from his mother.

J. J. was afraid of anyone who was potentially violent, which seemed to be about a third of the student body at school. He employed several strategies to keep himself safe; distraction and disguise were two of his favorites. He had learned that he would be safe among scary people if he looked like one of them, so when he was sixteen, he cut school with a couple of the other boys and went to Mount Vernon for tattoos. He'd worn long sleeves for a week afterward, and from that point on he cultivated a tough, confident outward appearance, shunning vulnerability.

He thought a lot about Debbie Derico. Just thinking about her calmed him down. He had once walked past her house and overheard her practicing flute, and was drawn to the long, sweet tones with their gentle waves of vibrato. Her music seemed to speak directly to his heart. He'd quietly gone around to the back of the Dericos' house and pressed his back against the wall of the room in which she was practicing, picturing her playing, imagining her eyes on his, and feeling the music vibrate through his body.

Chapter 5

There was a palpable tension in the south Valley Stream air. From Sunrise Highway to Rockaway Avenue, to Munroe Boulevard, to Peninsula Boulevard. Something had changed. From some, there was indignant racism, a "How dare you move here" aimed at the Thomas family. From others there was more of a "Hmm, we'll see how this works out." From many, there was no reaction at all. Some new folks had moved in. So what?

• • •

J. J. Welles was aware of the tension set off by the Thomas family's arrival. He was aware of a vibration in the air; if it were a sound, it would have been a plucked violin string—a pizzicato chime that he felt in his throat and his skin rather than heard with his ears.

The hum went up in pitch in algebra class, but because of the stress of attempting and failing to learn this basic math skill more than any change in social tension, and when the teacher called on J. J. to answer one of the previous night's homework problems, the hum took on a sharp edge that caught in his throat, and he began to cough and then to retch. As the teacher, Mr. Murray—a slight man with short gray hair and pale-gray, owlish eyes half hidden behind wire-rimmed glasses—began to berate J. J. for being unprepared, J. J. heard a soft sound just before he retched again and was thrown forward by the force of his lunch—a liverwurst sandwich on rye bread with mustard—hurling up his gullet and spewing from his mouth and onto the surface of the desk and floor. He didn't wait to hear whatever Mr. Murray would say next, nor what his classmates would do in reaction to this humiliation. But as he left the classroom, he recalled that soft sound of which he had not been aware at the time. It was a whispered word—*seventeen*—and was the answer to the homework problem. The word had been spoken by Elly Thomas, who had been sitting behind him and one desk to his left.

J. J. wiped his mouth on the sleeve of his flannel shirt as he rushed from the classroom and down the hall, ignoring the hall monitor's request for a hall pass. He hurried out the doors of the Jedwood Place side of the building and broke into a run. So much of being a teenager revolved around fear of humiliation, and throwing up in class was very nearly as humiliating as it got.

He ran for a few blocks, then slowed to a fast walk. He had been heading toward the Dericos' house, unaware of his subconscious plan to stand against the back of the house and listen to Debbie practice flute. Once his plan crystalized in his mind, he slowed to a walk, realizing that Debbie would still be in school.

He stopped walking, trying to decide which way to go. He felt in his pocket for money, pulled out a few coins, and saw that he had two dimes, a quarter, and three pennies. Ted's had two pinball machines— an older one that still took dimes and a new one that took quarters—so he knew he could play for a while to kill time before Debbie got home. He started in that direction, shuffling through curbside piles of crisp multicolored leaves. It was late September, and most of the leaves were still on the maple and oak trees that lined the streets. He stopped again, thinking how much more fun pinball was with Ernie or Jimmy Kelly.

He thought about heading back to school and waiting at the gate, just off school grounds, where certain cliques collected to smoke and hang out. Seventh period would soon end, and quite a few students were sure to leave the building. He might catch someone who would come with him to Ted's, but there was also the possibility that someone who saw him throw up would be there, and word might have spread. The potential benefit of having someone to hang out with outweighed the risk of ridicule so he headed back toward school, where he found a small crowd of kids, already congregated at the gate, including Ernie Derico, who was smoking a Marlboro.

"Hey," J. J. said.

"Hey," said Ernie.

J. J. waited, but neither Ernie nor anyone else spoke.

"Want to go to Ted's?" J. J. asked.

Ernie shook his head. "Got something to do here." He explained what he and the other guys, older fraternity boys around whom J. J. was intimidated, were planning, and J. J. listened but didn't comment. He would wait and watch the spectacle, but this was not something he wanted to be a part of, despite the very real pull of peer pressure.

They waited another fifty minutes—smoking, gossiping, speculating about which girls would or wouldn't put out—passing time.

Just before the final bell rang, students began pouring from the building, some stopping and joining the boys at the gate, others walking by in pairs, small groups, or alone. The guys at the gate were Kenny "Kick Ass" Jones, Ricky Taylor, Donnie Richardson, Billy "Big Mac" McCarthy, Willie "Po Boy" Potter, Tall Tom Langston, Ernie Derico, Jimmy Kelly, and Benny Boone. All except Jimmy Kelly were tough kids with dangerous reputations. Three girls—SueAnn Barlowe, Debbie Derico, and Marcy Madden—walked over together, listened to the plan, and stayed. When J. J. saw Debbie Derico, he brightened and tried to summon up the courage to talk to her. She saw him, and he thought he saw a smile flicker across her face, but then Marcy Madden caught his eye, opened her mouth wide, and pretended to stick her finger down her throat and retch. He wanted to run, but there was nowhere to go; he looked away, cringing inside, waiting for the inevitable onslaught of taunting, but it didn't come.

What came instead was something else. Ricky Taylor, probably the most dangerous boy in the school, coughed and muttered something unintelligible. Big Mac, who was enormous and red-faced, with ham hands and heavy fists, gave a nasty laugh.

Several boys were suddenly talking at once, their voices low and menacing, their words alternately sharp and cutting, blunt and battering. The nastiest of epithets were made worse because they were repeatedly thrown from one boy to the other as the crowd of angry boys, now a single mob, homed in on their targets.

Two teens had exited the school building; one was the girl J. J. recognized from algebra class—the girl who had given him the answer when Mr. Murray had called on him, immediately before his being sick —the Negro girl. With her was a boy who was obviously her brother; he was slightly bigger than she was but younger—perhaps fifteen. He had that awkward look boys often have in their early teens, and he wore black horn-rimmed glasses.

Though the words thrown at them were low and half-muttered, the two obviously heard. J. J. could see the anxiety in the girl's eyes—her fearful glances from the crowd of boys to her brother and back again. He was more vulnerable than she was; whatever the gang at the gate was going to do would probably be done to her brother. She would be the target of words only unless some of the girls got involved, which J. J. doubted; the three girls who were present were not street fighters. He knew only two girls who had street-fighting experience, and they were older and wilder than any of these girls, who were there as spectators and to support the boys. The girls were there for the action—whatever happened, they could say they'd been there.

To J. J.'s surprise, the girl's brother suddenly began walking toward the gang at the gate—directly at Ricky Taylor.

"Why would you say that?" the boy asked, his tone reasonable, as though he were asking the time of day—a simple question. The boys at the gate were so surprised that at first, no one said anything. And in that brief silence, the girl took her brother's hand and pulled him away.

"Dwayne!" was all she said.

"Dwaaayyyne!" came several mocking cries, along with more name-calling—the nastiest, dirtiest words, about color, about the girl, about their plight as the only people of their kind in a sea of hostility.

As they hurried away, the girl caught J. J.'s eye, and he felt himself blush. He was embarrassed and turned away, toward the bright-white first house off school grounds. A monarch butterfly flickered past, its wings outlined in black, bordered by pink and white spots and orange rectangles. Along with hundreds, probably thousands, of its kind, it was fleeing its northern home for warmer winter locales as monarchs did every year as late summer gave way to the chilly fall.

• • •

Dwayne opened the front door and held it open, and Elly walked inside and laid her books on the oak table just inside the front door, then went to the kitchen to see if any lemonade was left. There had been a half bottle—about a pint—that morning, but her grandfather had a taste for lemonade and had grown forgetful enough that he might not have remembered to save any for his only granddaughter.

Papa Elvin didn't mind very much that he was losing his memory, but he did mind anyone who was less than courteous and conscientious to him or his family. He demanded courtesy from his son, daughter-in-law, and their children. His wife, Makayla, was very nearly perfection itself.

Perhaps today was a good memory day, or maybe it was not as hot as the last days of summer had been, or perhaps she'd just been lucky, as Elly found plenty of lemonade left. She poured herself a glass and drank it in front of the open refrigerator. The sound of jazz was drifting through the screen door to the back porch, where Papa Elvin was sitting in his rocker, his eyes closed, snoring gently.

"'Scuse me," Dwayne said, so suddenly that Elly jumped.

"Why are you sneaking up on me like that?"

Her brother frowned. "Why're you drinking your drink in front of the fridge?"

"Smart ass." She couldn't meet her brother's eye. She felt as though she'd been kicked in the gut by the kids at the gate, that she had not properly defended her brother, who, she feared, had come close to a beating from those white boys on the very first day of school. She didn't want to talk about it; she didn't want to think about it, and looking at her brother, who was looking past her for a carton of milk, just made her more aware that she had let him down. She turned away, went to the back door, and watched Papa Elvin for a moment, then came back in and went to the foot of the stairs.

"Nana Makayla?" She looked up at the darkened stairway and paused, listening, but heard nothing. She supposed Nana Makayla was napping. Elly was glad that her grandmother had not changed much with age, except that she occasionally grew tired in the afternoon, especially in the warm weather, and often took a nap before helping Mama with dinner. Elly listened for a moment more, then walked quietly up to her room and softly closed the door, just as the downstairs front door opened and she heard her mother's voice.

"Elly! Dwayne! Come on and tell Mama 'bout school while you set the table!"

Elly sat for a moment, steeling herself, determined not to talk about the incident at the gate; then she walked purposefully downstairs and found Dwayne already at the kitchen table, calmly sipping from a glass of milk and picking strawberries out of a bowl, examining them for bruises, and eating those he chose. Mama and Nana Makayla were unpacking grocery bags. Nana Makayla turned, saw Elly, and held her arms wide.

"How was your first day? Tell Nana Makayla all about it."

"I thought you were upstairs napping! You went with Mama?"

Nana Makayla gave her a look that said, "Don't ask silly questions," and, faced with Nana Makayla's love, Elly's resolve to keep silent about the bullying crumbled. "Dwayne didn't tell you that a gang of kids …?" Her lower lip trembled.

Nana Makayla pulled Elly into her arms, where they swayed together in one of Nana Makayla's power hugs. "Oh, *mtoto*."

Elly could feel the vibrations of her mother's rage from across the room. She had been taking tomatoes from a bag and placing them into a drawer in the refrigerator. Now she turned, a tomato in her fist, and as she spoke, the tomato's juice began to run out from between her fingers. "What did they say?" she demanded to know. Elly told her, and her mother was silent for a moment. "Did you tell anyone at the school? Did you tell the principal?" She noticed the mess in her hand and laid what remained of the tomato on the counter, took a napkin from the table, and rubbed it against her palm. "I'm taking you both to school tomorrow, and we're going to see about this. Papa Elvin did not go through what he did for his grandbabies to be treated this way!" She took a few steps until she was standing next to Dwayne, who was reading one of his textbooks.

"Is this true?"

Dwayne looked up, and Elly was amazed that his face remained so placid; she peered at the book he was reading—*Advanced High School Trigonometry*. Dwayne nodded. "Yes, Mama."

"And what did you do about it? I didn't teach you to take such things lying down."

"I wasn't lying down, Mama. I went over and tried to ask why they would say such things, but—"

Mama glared at her son, and her head drew back several inches in disbelief. "Oh, I can tell you why they say such things. Tomorrow we goin' see what the parents of—"

"Shirley!" It was Nana Makayla, who was looking hard at her daughter-in-law. Elly was startled. Nana Makayla rarely raised her voice, and never at Mama; no one raised their voice to Mama.

Shirley turned to her mother-in-law, looking as surprised as Elly felt.

"He doesn't understand," Nana Makayla said, softly.

"I do understand," Dwayne protested.

"I know you do, honey." Nana Makayla cupped the back of her grandson's head while holding her daughter-in-law's gaze.

"We have to deal with this ourselves," Nana Makayla continued. "If we go to the principal or the police, you know what people will think?"

Shirley raised an angry eyebrow. "If we *don't* go, people will think they can harass our family."

"Shirley, we're going to deal with this ourselves." There was steel in Nana Makayla's voice. Do you know what Papa Elvin had to deal with?"

"Somebody call me?" came a groggy voice from the other side of the screen door. The music from that direction grew fainter and, when no one answered, grew louder again.

Dwayne went back to his studying while Elly went upstairs, turned the radio on, and tried to make sense of her social studies homework. Soon, the house was permeated with the sweet smells of that night's dinner. After an hour, the front door opened.

"I knew it!" came Elvin Jr.'s excited voice. "Pork roast and hoppin' john." Both children ran downstairs, into the living room, and hugged their father, who looked tired but happy, a sheen of sweat glistening on his forehead.

"How was your first day of school?" He looked at each of them.

They answered practically in unison. "Fine, Papa."

Mama had appeared in the doorway to the kitchen and nodded at her children's answers, then gave them each a gentle push as they walked past her into the dinette. "How was your first day?"

Elvin's lips tightened. He did not look at her. "Fine, baby."

"What?" Shirley Thomas knew her husband. "What happened? I got three fine first days. I know something happened."

Her husband pushed past her. "Nothing happened. It was fine. Let's eat. Then I want to hear from the children what really happened."

Chapter 6

J. J. just wanted to make it through the school day. He knew he'd have to go back to algebra and face the class that last saw him throw up all over his desk and run away without cleaning it up. But the class didn't go as badly as he'd expected. He ignored the few grins and half-hidden grimaces and pretended to be absorbed by an algebra problem that was as impenetrable as Debbie's friendship.

Debbie. He watched for her at the gate after school and didn't see her—which didn't mean she wasn't at school; she could have left the building through a different exit. He also watched for the new sister and brother—Elly and Dwayne. He knew their names because everyone knew their names.

At the gate, he ran into Ernie, who invited him to meet at the corner near their house after dinner. Jimmy Kelly would be there, as would just about everyone else. It was understood that they would be there to vandalize and frighten the Negro family that now lived in the Storch house. Afterward, they would go to Shakes Bar, where they would probably have to hang out in the parking lot. Shakes was a bar on Rockaway Avenue south of Sunrise Highway that was frequented by dangerous young men and the women they attracted. Girls were rarely carded because their presence encouraged young men to come and drink and to buy drinks for the girls. Boys under the age of eighteen were rarely allowed inside the bar, though that would depend upon who was working the door.

J. J. set off in the direction of home, but, as he did on many afternoons, he went first to the Derico house to see if he might run into Debbie, listen to her play, and maybe say hello to her. Maybe she would notice him.

• • •

Joanne and Laurie were sitting on Laurie's bed beneath an enormous poster of the singer Bobby Sherman; they were sharing a mixture of vodka and blackberry brandy from a jar while playing a game of hide-and-seek with Sorry, the kitten. They took turns hiding their hands behind pillows or the side of the bed and then, when the kitten was distracted, launching them suddenly into view, like giant spiders. The startled kitten would leap into the air or rear up on her hind legs, and the girls would laugh, drink from the jar, and pass it back and forth.

"Everyone's going to Shakes later," Laurie said. "Wanna go?"

Joanne shrugged. "Maybe, after homework. I heard people are going to the Storches' old house."

"Homework?"

"Won't take long."

"Why are they going there? To throw stuff at the house?"

Joanne nodded. "I guess. Want to watch? Something to do."

"To watch Ernie, you mean."

Joanne pretended to glare at her friend. "I was thinking of inviting that girl to hang out."

"*That* girl?"

"Her name is Elly. She looks okay."

"Why would you hang out with her?" Laurie lunged toward the edge of the bed, where Sorry had been backing away from Joanne's hand. "Ooh, catch her, she's gonna fall."

Joanne reached for the kitten, who teetered then fell off the side of the bed, landed on her feet, and instantly spun around, as though ready for whatever next came her way. "She could probably use a friend."

Laurie picked up the kitten, which fit in the palm of her hand; she used the fingers of her other hand to gently pet her.

Joanne sipped from the jar, which was nearly empty, then passed it to Laurie. "You can finish it."

"Thanks." Laurie took the jar and finished its contents. "How 'bout we meet at the corner by the Storches' at nine, and see what's happening, then go to Shakes, and see which guys show?"

Joanne nodded, took a yellow pack of Juicy Fruit gum from her pocketbook, and held it out to Laurie, who took two pieces, unwrapped them, and put them in her mouth. Laurie did the same. "Sounds like a plan," Joanne said.

• • •

J. J. leaned against the back of the Dericos' house for a few minutes, but there was no sign of Debbie. He was about to leave when he heard a tiny, high-pitched squeak. There it was again. He looked around but didn't see the source of the sound; then he felt something on his foot and looked down.

"Hi there!" He knelt and scooped the kitten up and pressed it against his belly, then brought it close to his face. "Hello! And who are you?"

"Sorry."

J. J. lifted his gaze and found himself looking into the eyes of Laurie Derico, who was standing uncomfortably close to him.

"Sorry?" he answered.

"Sorry," she repeated.

He didn't understand, or perhaps he hadn't heard right? "Sorry?" he said again, feeling foolish.

She laughed, cupped her hands around his, and took the kitten. "Her name is Sorry."

She looked at him with her eyes full of some kind of meaning he didn't understand. It was a look meant to keep him where he was while she disappeared around the corner of the house with the kitten. He stayed where he was.

She came back and again stood too close to him. "I've been watching you."

"Really?"

She nodded and brought her face to within a few inches of his. She smelled like fruity alcohol.

"Why don't you kiss me?"

He didn't answer; he didn't quite understand.

She smiled. "I think you'd like to kiss me. I'd like to kiss you." She brought a hand up to his shoulder, leaned closer, and kissed him gently on the lips, then again, harder, pushing her tongue into his mouth.

J. J. pulled back. He had never been kissed this way; he had never been kissed at all, except by relatives, and this was an overwhelming experience—but nice. He allowed it to continue. And continue. Her hand slid down his shoulder to his arm, to his waist, and below.

He shuddered, leaned forward, and kissed her again, while her other hand took him and guided it inside the elastic of her gym shorts and then her panties, which were soaking wet.

• • •

An hour before his shift ended, Lieutenant Tom Kelly had gone to Dericos' and had been sipping his second free coffee refill for twenty minutes, when he'd grown restless and vaguely aware that he didn't want to go home when his shift ended. Without really being aware of what he was doing, he went to Steve's Liquors and bought a bottle of Connemara, brought it back to his car, and drove to his favorite spot at the far end of the parking lot at Grant Park, where he took the bottle from the bag, twisted the top off, and took a swig. Then another. He came to the park now and then to drink and relax, sometimes smiling to himself when he did because the Fourth Precinct—his precinct—was barely one hundred yards behind him. He liked the feeling that he could do this. He was a good cop, and his shift—a busy, stressful one—was over; he deserved this.

He thought of his father, Shamus, who was gone three years now. He'd been called James on the force—the NYPD, not what his father had referred to as this "training wheels force" on Long Island. Shamus had been a good, tough cop who took no shit and was well respected because he earned and demanded it.

Tom held the bottle up in an imaginary toast, but not so high that it might be seen. "Hell of a day, Da. You'd think you get pulled over for speeding, you'd take care to keep the open beer out of the car, or at least out of sight, and to keep your trap shut." He looked around and took a pull from the bottle.

"Oh, I know you've had worse. You don't have to tell me. I know what the city was like, but you also had good cops by your side—the best."

He took another swig and blinked, feeling better. "And, truth be told, so do I." Maybe tonight would be okay. Maybe Erin and the kids wouldn't get on his nerves. He sighed and raised the bottle again, vigilant of his peripheral vision. "That calls for another." He took a drink and watched a gaggle of geese waddle en masse across the far end of the lot and disappear over the crest of the hill and out of view toward the lake. He thought of Erin, who, since the children were born, walked a little like one of those geese, come to think of it. He started to laugh, and the laugh took him over until he coughed up a bit of phlegm and then, with a snort, inhaled the phlegm and started coughing again. He took another drink and finally stopped coughing.

"I know, Da. I do appreciate her—you know I do. It's just that she gets on my nerves. She knows what I'm asking of her, but she has to question me, doesn't she? Oh, but she does walk like a goose sometimes now." He started laughing again. "Alright, alright. But Da." He took another drink. "If you take a hard look at her expression when I try to get her to pay attention to whatever thing it is I'm saying, you'll see that she has a blank look, and you can see she knows what I'm asking her. She does! And she pulls that face just to get me angry. I know it, and it does." He smiled suddenly. "You're right, Da! That blank look of hers does indeed look," he sputtered with laughter, "rather like a goose. It's not just the walk, it's the face too!"

He hooted and slapped his knee.

"Well, but Da, if I tell her how much we all depend on her, she'll think …" He frowned and shook his head unhappily. "She'll know we all depend on her, and she'll get complacent. I can't have that, just like you couldn't. Next thing, she'll be wanting her own checking account." He took a deep breath and blew it out in a sigh. "Oh, but I know she has her hands full, with her hippie radio music and, oh, the cleaning and the washing and the shopping! How can one person stand it? She's worked to the bone, she is." He laughed bitterly. "Worked to the bone. Thinks she has so much more to do than Ma, who did every bit of what she does, and with less money and gallstones. But Erin, you're right, Da. Erin's a saint who thinks she deserves better than the likes of me, a nineteen-year veteran police lieutenant with a good salary and a pension on the horizon, a house of our own, a generous allowance, all the cake she can eat—which is maybe a little too much."

He took a drink.

"And with a son who has yet to have his head on straight, and a daughter who wants to sing in the church."

He drank again.

"Sing in the church. She does sing like a bird, Julie does. You'd think my girl would have some real ambition—at least to find a boy and get married. Maybe she'll be a nun." He giggled. "Too late for Erin, but maybe Julie. Though what's good for the goose …" He sputtered with laughter and looked down at the front of his uniform, which was stained with whiskey.

Eleven teens milled about in front of the house next door to what had been the Storch house and was now owned by the Thomas family. Several had cans of Schaefer Beer, a few had quart bottles. A half dozen empty cans and bottles were piled at the curb. The atmosphere was festive with a layer of tension as everyone waited to see who would be the first. J. J. and Jimmy Kelly were at the edges of the group, farthest from the Thomas house; Ernie Derico was in the middle of the pack. Now and then he glanced back at his friends and edged closer to the front to make a good impression.

"Po Boy" Potter started it. He took a few steps up the path toward the Thomases' front door.

"Go back to Africa!" he yelled.

Benny Boone joined him. "We don't want you here!"

With a glance toward J. J. and Jimmy Kelly, Ernie Derico stepped onto the Thomases' lawn. "We don't want you here!" He walked back to the curb, picked up a bottle, and hurled it through the front window.

A few teens laughed; several, including Ernie, ran. Not wanting to miss anything, J. J. and Jimmy Kelly backed a few steps up the street but remained within watching distance.

• • •

Elly had been behind the curtain next to the front window, one knee on a wide oak bench her Grandpa Henry, her mother's father, had built many years before. When the bottle came through the window, she screamed and ran into the dinette, where the rest of her family had been trying to ignore the commotion and eat dinner—except Dwayne, who was already upstairs, doing his homework.

"Mama, people here are crazy. They don't want us here. They hate us."

Shirley took a breath to answer, but her daughter wasn't finished. "I don't want to live here, Mama! I hate it. Why do we have to live here?"

While Elly was speaking, Shirley had gotten up from the table and walked to a spot between Elly and the broken window.

"Because your father has a new and better teaching position, and we can afford to live in a better neighborhood."

"But why can't we live in a different better neighborhood?"

"Get me the police." Elvin Jr. had picked up the telephone receiver and stretched the coiled cord into the living room, where he stood next to his wife and between the window and his daughter.

Shirley had fetched a broom and dustpan and was doing her best to sweep the broken glass from the carpet; she plucked stray bits with her fingers.

Dwayne had come downstairs and was standing on the bottom step, holding on to the banister. "To survive in this world," Shirley said, "you need to grow a thicker skin, hold your head high, and go out there and be the Thomas you can be."

"Maybe," Elly ventured, "we need to stay out of places we don't belong."

Shirley stopped what she was doing and rose to her full height. "There's no place my family doesn't belong!" she roared. "No place!"

Papa Elvin was slowly pushing himself to his feet with two hands pressing down on the dining room table. Nana Makayla slid her chair back, stood up, pressed Elvin Sr. back down into his chair with a hand on his shoulder, then swiveled toward Elly and held her arms out. "Come here, *mtoto*." Elly went to her, and Nana Makayla sat down, pulled her granddaughter to her, and hugged her to her breast. Elly knelt beside her and laid her head in her grandmother's lap the way she had as a very young child and sometimes still did when she was particularly anxious or hurt.

"There are good people here," her grandmother said softly. "There are good people everywhere. You just need to find them."

Elly nodded. She was remembering a face she thought she had seen at the far end of the crowd as she peeked out the living room window.

• • •

Tom Kelly had taken the call since he was closest to the scene. He drove home first and parked there, then walked the short distance toward the group of kids but stopped when he saw Jimmy with them. He had hoped to defuse the situation from a distance, but that would take some creativity.

He moved under a streetlight and stood, hands on his hips. "Hey!" he called, in his deep, sharp cop voice, which was several tones below his off-duty voice. "That's enough. You go on home now!"

About half the kids wandered away, and he began walking slowly toward the remainder. "You want a ride to the precinct?" It was a bluff, but the bluff worked. He kept walking directly at them, and the group of teens dispersed.

Mr. Thomas was standing in his doorway, so Tom did not have to approach beyond the sidewalk. Tom shrugged, his palms up in a "What can you do?" gesture. "Kids being kids."

"Kids being trouble," said Elvin Thomas evenly.

"They're not really dangerous," Tom said.

"Gotta buy a new window." They looked at one another. "Would you call this a 'welcome to the neighborhood gift'?" Elvin asked.

"Did you see which one did this?"

Elvin shook his head.

"They bother you again, give us a call right away."

They looked at one another for a moment, then Elvin turned and went inside, closing the door behind him. Inside he found his mother with Elly's head in her lap, brushing the tears from her granddaughter's cheeks.

· · ·

The Connemara had worn off by the time Tom got home, which annoyed him; he had spent time and money toward reaching a goal, and the goal had been undermined by a bunch of kids, including his own son! When he walked in, there was Jimmy, lying on the couch with his sneakers up on one of the faux leather pillows, reading some superhero comic book.

"Hey, Dad," he said, smiling.

"Get your sneakers off the pillows." Then he saw the comic book. "What the hell are you looking at that crap for?" Tom demanded, and when Jimmy looked crestfallen, he couldn't bear to look at his son. "Go on to your room until dinner."

"But we ate an hour—"

"Go on!"

"Yes, sir!"

He was satisfied to see Jimmy leap to his feet and all but run up the stairs.

Erin was at the stove, ladling something from a pot into several Tupperware containers. She stopped when she saw him. "Could you be a little nicer to him?"

"Could you maybe look presentable when I come home? Wear a dress, maybe, and do something with your hair."

"If I'm feeding everyone and wearing a dress, it won't do the dress any good, and if I do my hair and then cook—"

He exhaled noisily, lips fluttering. "Alright. I get it. What have you got there?"

She stopped ladling and paused just long enough to let him know she was annoyed with him. "Leftovers from dinner. Beef and vegetable stew."

He raised his eyebrows and gave her a hard look, indicating that he wanted some and she should have known that. She went slowly to the cupboard and took out a plate, then to the silverware drawer and took out a fork, spoon, and knife, then moved to the counter and folded two napkins in half.

"Come on! Ain't got all day. Does it have enough salt?" he asked.

"Enough salt? For what, a heart attack?" She stood looking at him, expressionless, which to Tom was an expression—and not a very nice one.

He pointed to his place at the table and sat down there. Eventually, his stew appeared before him.

"Beer."

Slowly, Erin opened a bottle of beer and poured a glass. Tom rolled his eyes and sighed.

Finally, when all was in order, he began to eat while glancing at his wife, who had returned to stirring the stew.

"I know what people are thinking," he said while chewing. "Why would they want to live here? But I have nothing against them. I serve with Ray Ashby and Carl Nivens. They're fine, but they know to stick with their own. Not saying we're better, but we stick with our own too."

"We got neighbors who ain't Irish," said Erin.

"They're white. And honestly, I'd just as soon we were in County Kerry, wouldn't you?"

Now she turned to him and waved her spoon. "Starving. Is that what you want? For the kids? For me? For yourself? The sick man of Europe, that's what Ireland is."

"You want to talk like that, you can go upstairs with the boy."

From somewhere nearby came Julie's voice singing "Be Thou My Vision." Erin smiled and closed her eyes.

Tom shook his head. "That's right. I would. With our own."

• • •

Debbie waited at the corner for her sister Laurie, who was with the group who were hazing the Thomas house. She saw the Welles boy looking at her and smiled at him. He seemed harmless and maybe a little sweet, but she wanted to get home to practice. She had begun before dinner, done her homework, and then come out to see whatever fireworks there would be at the Thomas house. Before drifting to the corner, she surveyed the crowd, hoping to see Bonni Bird, but she knew she wouldn't be there. Bonni Bird was easy to spot—she wore spray-on leather pants, a matching vest, and very little else besides a silver heart pendant around her neck.

Debbie spent twenty minutes every day practicing long tones on her flute, followed by chromatic scales with increasing speed and exercises in a book a teacher had given her the year before. She then worked out flute parts to songs that Bonni Bird's band did at some of the nearby bars. Bonni was the only working musician Debbie knew. She had natural talent, which everyone said Debbie had as well. She also admired Bonni Bird's attitude. She was aloof, rarely seeming to notice anyone. Debbie had cultivated a similar quality for herself; she knew people thought of her as talented and did not associate her with much else, and that was fine. She wanted to be known for her music—as a musician—perhaps as a musician with an attitude.

Debbie had stalked Bonni for several months the previous year, hoping to audition for her band. Her stalking paid off when Bonni stopped to talk to her one day, and Debbie breathlessly explained that she loved Bonni's music, then heard herself start to go on about Bonni's clothes, hair, and attitude.

Bonni had looked at her and given Debbie an address—that of her drummer, a woman named Veronica, or Ronni. Bonni played guitar, and the bass player was another woman, named Randi. No one in the band, Debbie observed, seemed to believe in the silent letter *e* at the end of their name. The band was called The Leatherettes, and the women all dressed like Bonni. Soon Debbie began dressing like Bonni, though she was not yet in the band. She was mulling changing her name to Debbi, but was concerned about her father's reaction, though it occurred to her that he might not notice since he was working at the diner most of the time.

Debbie somehow managed to continue her practice routine while adding some of The Leatherettes' tunes, which included both originals and covers—they loved Lesley Gore and Rosemary Clooney. Her audition was a week away.

• • •

J. J. knew that Debbie practiced flute in the afternoons, then had dinner, then sometimes went out to meet the crowd at the trestle—often but not always with her sister Laurie. J. J. was still mortified about the sexual incident between himself and Laurie, though he was not quite sure what he had done; he only knew he could not face her. He had not done whatever it was he was supposed to do. He had done very nearly nothing at all, which couldn't have been the right thing to do.

So J. J. was in a quandary. He wanted to see Debbie and to try to make sure she saw him, but he did not want to run into Laurie, who had waved to him twice and called to him once in the hallways at school.

Fear vs. desire. Fear won. He did not go to Debbie's home to listen to her practice, nor did he try to run into her as she went out for the evening, though he was sure she had seen him and even smiled at him once. He told himself that she did not always go out, so didn't it make more sense to try to run into her at school?

It happened on a crisp fall afternoon in late October, under a sky so blue as to be unreal. The usual crowd was at the gate, many of whom had cut eighth period. Gym and study hall were popular eighth-period classes for exactly this reason; get out early, get to the gate, have a smoke, and don't miss a thing.

J. J. found Ernie and Jimmy Kelly at the gate; the three had arrived several minutes after the eighth-period late bell and begun taking turns picking up stones to see who could throw the farthest over the big brick dormered house that was diagonally across the street from the school gate. The goal was to clear the roof of the house without stepping into the street.

Tall Tom Langston and Benny Boone were already outside smoking, along with Debbie Derico, who carried her flute, and Marcy Madden. From what J. J. could hear, they were talking about a used GTO Langston had been looking at and was considering buying.

When it was J. J.'s turn to throw, he found a round quartz stone and hurled it sidearm toward the space above the roof of the big brick house.

"Bounced off the shutter," Ernie said, shaking his head. "Jimmy, you're up."

Jimmy kicked at the dirt next to the curb until he dislodged a sharp-edged rock that appeared too big for someone so small to be able to throw very far. But Jimmy was deceptively strong; he was small and he was shy, which made him seem even smaller. But he could throw; he was often alone or with Lucy, his dog. He spent hours throwing rocks or Pensie Pinkies or Spaldings at the side of the school or at just about anything. Jimmy's rock cleared the roof. He turned to J. J. and Ernie, triumph on his face.

"Alright, boys, watch how a man—" Ernie started to say.

"Look who it is," a voice behind them said, and the three boys turned.

A grin spread slowly across Ernie's face. "Hey, boys, it's the math whiz!"

Dwayne and Elly Thomas were coming toward them.

Ernie leaned toward J. J. and Jimmy Kelly. "Whatdya say we knock the whiz's books down, maybe take a few?"

J. J. felt Debbie's eyes on him. He shook his head. "Ernie—"

But Ernie had stepped to the curb and was bouncing on his toes. Elly and Dwayne had been deep in conversation, but Dwayne's eyes had swung toward Ernie. Elly said something, and Dwayne looked back at his sister.

"Hey, whiz!" Ernie yelled as they passed a few steps into the street. A car driving in the other direction honked, and the brother and sister swerved out of its way and toward Ernie, who stepped forward and slapped Dwayne's books out of his hands. The books clattered into the street, and Dwayne stooped to pick them up as another car drove past, veering close to the brother and sister, who were now in the middle of the street.

Elly pulled her brother's sleeve away from the car. Ernie took another step until he was standing on Dwayne's hand. Dwayne cried out, and J. J. watched the sister take a step toward Ernie, who was still on Dwayne's hand but leaning back now, away from the sister. The pain was plain on both siblings' faces—pain that went beyond a stepped-on hand.

"Ernie," J. J. said. "Let him go." He stepped into the street and took hold of Ernie's forearm. Ernie looked surprised, then angry, but he stepped off Dwayne's hand.

"What the fuck?" Ernie said as Dwayne and his sister hurried away. The sister cast a backward glance at J. J.

"What's wrong with you, man?" J. J. asked Ernie.

"Me?" Ernie pushed J. J.'s chest. He was nearly a head taller than J. J. and broader.

J. J. had no interest in fighting. "Whad'ya want to do that for?"

"Something's not right with that kid," Jimmy Kelly observed.

"Just having some fun," Ernie protested.

While they were talking, J. J. risked a glance at the others, most of whom had turned away. Debbie was still watching. She caught J. J.'s eye, and again he thought he saw a hint of a smile.

Chapter 7

Lou and Anna Derico were busy cleaning up the diner—putting away food, washing dishes, and getting ready to close—when Laurie burst through the back door. She had been at Joanne's house and had let slip to her friend that she'd gone to third base with Joanne's brother. Joanne had promptly stopped speaking to her. But while Laurie was embarrassed and angry, she could neither name those emotions nor explain their source. She only knew that she had to say or do something to feel better.

"Ma, Ernie's been picking on that Negro boy." Telling on her brother did not exactly make her feel better, but it did give Laurie a vague sense of satisfaction; for the moment, that would have to do.

Anna had been at the sandwich counter, putting away the chicken, tuna, and egg salad and washing down the wooden surface, when she heard her daughter and came into the kitchen to tell her to keep her voice down, lest someone in the diner hear her.

"Did he hurt him?" Anna asked.

Laurie shook her head.

"Then I'm sure he didn't mean any harm. Boys being boys."

"Ugh," Laurie huffed, turned, and headed back out.

"Where are you going, young lady?"

"Home. Tuesday night. *The Magician*." Laurie had a crush on its star, Bill Bixby.

"Lou?" Anna wanted to know what her husband had to say about Ernie bullying this new boy. "Lou?" She heard voices, left the kitchen, went into the dining room, and found Lou talking to Rachel Arnsbarger, who had come in for a strawberry muffin; she had wanted coffee, but the urn was off and washed.

Goodness, that girl eats a lot of muffins, Anna thought. She also thought something ought to be done about Ernie, who had been in more trouble than usual of late. He was turning into a bit of a bully, and she did not want people thinking that she and Lou could not control their son.

She would trust Lou's opinion on this as she did on just about everything. She idolized her husband, who was the hardest-working man she knew. He had built the business into a local success, was up seven days a week before dawn, and was home and snoring by eleven thirty. That was his life, and he never complained about what she spent on clothes—especially shoes. Anna loved shoes.

She opened her mouth to say something but stopped when she saw the look on Lou's face as he watched Rachel walk toward the door and out of the diner.

• • •

"Mama, I don't care about Daddy's job. We can't stay here with the way Dwayne's being treated by those boys!"

Elly and her mother both looked at Dwayne, who was in the big red living room chair, an open notebook in his lap, and a textbook open between the pages of the notebook. He was looking in the direction of the window, and his lips were moving, but since the broken window incident, the drapes had been kept shut.

"Dwayne, what are you doing?" Shirley asked. Dwayne didn't answer. He was speaking softly, but his words were inaudible.

"Dwayne!"

"Counting prime numbers, Mama. Shhh. Seven fifty-one. Seven fifty-seven …"

Shirley smiled.

Elly stamped her foot. "It's not funny, Mama. It's dangerous!"

"What's that, sweet girl?" Papa Elvin was making his way slowly down the stairs. "Have you done all your reading and writing?"

"The white boys are picking on Dwayne again."

Papa Elvin looked hard at his granddaughter, then at Shirley, then at Dwayne. "What boys?"

Elly stamped her foot again. "I told you, Papa Elvin! Don't nobody care about Dwayne?"

Papa Elvin arrived at the bottom of the stairs and enveloped his granddaughter in a hug. He did not recall hearing about any boys pick-

63

ing on Dwayne, but that would not keep him from comforting his favorite granddaughter. "Oh, sweet girl. Let's all sit down and call a family meeting." He sat at the head of the dinette table. Elly took a seat to his left, her mother to his right.

"Dwayyyne!" Elly called, and Dwayne wandered in, still counting under his breath.

"Ten thirteen, ten nineteen …"

"We'll fill your father in later," Shirley explained to Elly, who nodded.

"Mama!" Shirley called, in the direction of the stairs.

"Coming!" Nana Makayla was descending the stairs in a dark satin blouse that set off her blue eyes, a color she must have inherited from one of her few European ancestors. She wore just a hint of makeup.

"Family meeting," Papa Elvin said.

"We can't be living here!" Elly exclaimed as her grandmother lowered herself into a chair. "Rocks coming through the windows! White boy gangs waiting for us after school …"

"Maybe this was an isolated incident," Nana Makayla suggested.

"It's not! Every day they're out there. Every day they're waiting for us."

"Are you okay, Dwayne?" Papa Elvin asked.

Still counting, Dwayne nodded.

"He doesn't know if he's okay!" Elly protested.

"Eleanor," her mother warned, "tone of voice."

"It's not an isolated incident. These boys got it in for us. Every day they call us—well, you know what they call us—and now it's physical. There's more of them out there every day, and if we wait …"

There was a long silence at the table.

Papa Elvin was looking at his daughter-in-law. "She's right," he said.

Shirley pressed her lips together. "You want us to sell the house? You want to give up and give in? We just closed six weeks ago! That's not what you taught us."

"Not what I said," Papa Elvin responded. "Makayla?" His eyes drifted to his wife, the wisest woman he knew.

"It's time," Nana Makayla said, her voice calm, "to put our best food forward."

Everyone looked at her, confused.

"You mean best foot forward, Nana Makayla." Dwayne had finally stopped counting.

"No," Nana Makayla said. "I said what I meant, and I mean our best food forward." Everyone listened as she outlined her plan.

• • •

Lou Derico had come out to the cash register when he heard Rachel Arnsbarger's voice. Anna gave him a look that said, "Go back to the kitchen. I've got this," but Lou stayed a moment, his eyes on Rachel. She wore a clinging orange satin blouse and a short brown skirt, and Lou was drawn to the way her blouse was stretched tight at the sides of her breasts and the way her skirt clung to her bottom. He watched her until he could feel his wife's eyes on him, then retreated to the kitchen and began scraping the dried soup from the sides of the tureens and the images of Rachel from his mind's eye.

His mind wandered, as it often did, to the Quinns, regular customers who were so obviously still in love after forty years. Why did he and Anna not have that kind of adoration for each other? They were devoted and committed to their marriage and one another—there was no question of that—but the passion the lucky few seemed to retain even after decades had apparently eluded the Dericos. Lou grieved that gap in their marriage; he wondered why Anna did not.

He shook more powdered soap into the tureen, removed a new scouring pad from its box, and began scrubbing vigorously.

• • •

The rhythms of Debbie Derico's life were all connected to music. When she was overwhelmed, frightened, or hurt, she expressed her feelings in songs that were colored by those emotions; when she felt joy, she inhabited joyful music. Practicing was not work for Debbie; it was a building block of life. Love was a beautiful, caressing melody, pregnant with meaning; excitement and hope had their own musical colors and shades, as did pain and terror.

Debbie was practicing and learning The Leatherettes' music—two originals called "I Saw a Guy" and "Memory Man," along with the Willie Nelson tune "Crazy," as recorded by Patsy Cline, whose death in a plane crash had occurred almost exactly ten years earlier. She made sure to learn at least a few other Leatherettes' tunes but focused more on the feeling behind her playing than on the songs themselves. Debbie believed that her performance would be best if her love for the songs was also at its best.

She listened to the albums of some of her favorite flute players: James Galway, Jean-Pierre Rampal, Hubert Laws, Bobbi Humphrey— even Herbie Mann, whose technique was more stylized and perhaps less pure than that of the others. She thought of Rampal as a machine, perfect but perhaps lacking some of the feeling the others expressed. Laws was brilliant, but she did not yet understand jazz as well as she hoped she might one day. Only Galway embodied all of the qualities she aspired to in her playing.

She knew The Leatherettes were a rock band in the eyes of many, but to Debbie, Bonni Bird was the first of perhaps many doorways to the universe she planned to inhabit for the rest of her life, and she knew that the way to get there and to prove herself in Bonni's eyes was to practice hard and to believe in herself.

• • •

Connie Welles sat at the kitchen table, thumbing through an issue of *Better Homes and Gardens* while sipping cranberry juice and vodka over ice. She was looking at a spread featuring a blue-and-white Victorian home whose yard was a riot of perennial and annual flowers, ground cover, and blooming bushes with fruit trees dotting the multi-acre landscape. She sipped her drink, imagining she lived in a similar home and was sitting in a rocker on her terrace drinking a julep of whatever people who lived in such homes drank.

"John," she said, still looking at the magazine. When there was no answer she looked up. "John?"

He was in the living room with his eyes closed against the noise of a group of small boys who were playing a game of Giant Steps in the street several houses away. Or was it Red Light, Green Light?

"John, why don't we have a garden?"

John opened his eyes and blinked. "Hmm? A what?"

"Wouldn't a garden be nice?"

"What?"

"Wouldn't it be nice to have a garden?"

Now he looked at her, incredulous. "Where are we going to get a garden?"

She was taken aback by the question. Where did anyone get a garden? "We could hire a gardener."

"Hire? What are we, the Rockefellers?" He shook his head, stood up, and went to the front door, intending to ask the boys to quiet down. He returned with the mail, having forgotten about the boys and their game. He was turning a light-brown envelope over in his hand.

"What's that?"

He looked at his wife, then back at the envelope, which he opened, read, then sat down and read a second time. "It's an invitation."

Chapter 8

The evening air was just cool enough for Ernie Derico to begin wearing his denim jacket. Jimmy Kelly was waiting at the corner of Lyncrest and Horton Avenue, and together they walked up to Sunrise Highway, turned left, and headed west toward Rockaway. They found Ricky Taylor and Benny Boone sitting on the stippled gray-blue iron beams that held up the Long Island Railroad trestle where the Rockaway Line branched off from the Babylon Line, east of the Valley Stream Station.

"Hey," said Ernie, nodding to the older boys. Jimmy Kelly smiled shyly, unsure of whether he was expected to speak.

"Nice shoes," said Benny, and when Ernie looked down at his shoes, Benny slapped a palm upward from his waist, swiping Ernie's face, then immediately shook out his hand and wiped it on the back of his jeans. "Ugh, snot!"

Ricky laughed and pointed at Benny. "Nice, Ben—way to make total."

Ernie shrugged and shook his head as though he regretted Benny having to wipe his hand, which he did, since he was afraid of both Ricky and Benny.

Ricky glared at him, as though aware of Ernie's fear. "Do that to me and I'll crack you one."

"Come on," said Benny. "Let's go to Steve's and wait for someone to buy, then come back here."

It had begun to drizzle. Hanging out under the shelter of the train trestle, drinking beer, whiskey, or vodka, and doing recreational drugs was especially popular when it rained.

As the four set off for Steve's Liquors, which was around the corner and two blocks southwest, Ricky pointed to Jimmy Kelly. "Not him. We don't allow children."

Ernie took a moment to consider what to do. He liked Jimmy Kelly, who was like a loyal puppy dog, his biggest fan, but he coveted the respect of Ricky and Benny, older boys who had pledged with the streetwise fraternities and gone through reputedly brutal hell night beatings.

"He won't be a problem," Ernie began.

"It's all right," Jimmy Kelly volunteered. "I'll catch up with you later." He began walking north, then turned east on Sunrise Highway.

As they set off for the liquor store, J. J. showed up and started to follow Ernie and the older boys toward Steve's.

"Not tonight," said Ernie in J. J.'s direction.

"Let him come," said Ricky. "He can be the lookout."

Ernie was pretty sure Ricky said this only to put him in his place. Being contradicted knocked you down a peg and gave the impression of lifting the status of the person doing the contradicting.

They continued walking with J. J. hurrying to catch up. Ernie gave him a little nod; the other two ignored him. They had to wait about fifteen minutes a few doors from Steve's, pressing against the row of stores to keep out of the rain, which was now steady and more than a drizzle. In that time a woman of about forty went into Steve's. They never asked women to buy because they were not comfortable interacting with women who were not their age or younger. Two men, one in his thirties and the other perhaps sixty, went in and ignored Benny, who nearly always did the asking because he was the most comfortable speaking with adults. Speaking, asking, and lying all came easily to Benny Boone, who was also a natural joker.

The third man, who was big and burly with brown hair, long sideburns, and brown-rimmed glasses, appeared to be in his mid-twenties, close enough to their age to remember having to ask others to buy his liquor. He agreed to buy three six-packs of Schaefer, two quarts of Colt 45, and a fifth of blackberry brandy. He went in while they waited and soon came out, walked around the corner, which showed he knew what he was doing, and the boys followed. He handed Ricky the larger of two packages, then walked back around to his car, which was parked beyond Steve's in the other direction.

Moments later, as the boys began going through the bag and handing out the Schaefers, they heard a voice.

"I thought so." They looked up, and there was Steve, standing on the corner nodding, his arms folded. He was a small, coiled, fearless man with small black eyes, jet-black hair, and a perpetual five-o'clock shadow. He pointed at each of them. "I see any of you anywhere near my store again, I'm calling the cops." He stared at them, and they stared back; he then turned and disappeared around the corner.

"Cops won't care," Benny said. "They've got shit to do."

"The cops'll care." Steve had returned. "My brother-in-law's a cop." He widened his eyes, lifted his chin, and waited, defying anyone to disagree.

After he left, Benny waited a few moments to be sure Steve was gone before speaking.

"I told you to be the lookout," Ricky said in J. J.'s direction.

J. J. had heard him but had not known what he was supposed to look out for.

"Go on and see if he's still there," Rick continued.

They waited until J. J. walked to the corner, turned around, and shook his head. "He went back in."

"He's full of shit," Benny said. "His brother-in-law *was* a cop. Now he's a Marine in 'Nam getting ready to ship back."

"Come on." Ricky handed the package to Ernie, who handed it to J. J., then started back toward the trestle. Once there, Ricky and Benny sat on the trestle, while Ernie and J. J. stood facing them. Benny and Ernie lit cigarettes. Ricky finished handing out the beers—they were each given four cans, while the malt liquor was for Ricky and Benny. They would pass the brandy bottle around.

"Cops!" Benny said, and Ernie and J. J. put down their cans and stepped in front of them, hiding them from view. Neither Benny nor Ricky moved, then Ricky laughed and Benny pointed at Ernie and J. J.

"Fell for it," Benny said.

They each contributed money to pay for the alcohol, then settled back as a group watching cars, musing about girls and fights.

"I'll tell you what we've gotta do," said Ricky, after a while. "We gotta rob that asshole's store."

"Steve's?" Ernie said.

Benny laughed. "No, Ernie's."

J. J. didn't say anything. He hoped they might forget he was there; he wanted no part of robbing anyone.

"Teach him a lesson," Ricky continued.

Benny giggled. "Let's do it."

Ernie nodded eagerly. "I'm in." He looked at J. J., who said nothing. "We can't have a kid along. This is for men."

• • •

J. J. kept spare change in a small red-painted ceramic bowl in the desk drawer in his room. He had made the bowl in fourth grade, and his mother had liked it and kept it on a shelf for a time until, in a fit of rage, J. J.'s father had one day been yelling while grabbing items off that shelf and hurling them through the living room window, throwing items to punctuate each syllable, and smashing the window in the process. During the tirade, Connie surreptitiously removed the bowl from the shelf, brought it into J. J.'s room, and left it on his desk. He knew that the bowl had sentimental value to his mother because he had made it—and its value to his mother increased its value to him.

As he headed home from the trestle, he reached into his right pants pocket to see how much change he had, change he would drop into the bowl when he returned home. He pulled out one quarter, three dimes, one nickel, four pennies, a joint, and a book of matches with one remaining match.

A slow smile spread across his face. He liked smoking pot, though it inhibited him socially and made focusing on schoolwork nearly impossible. Marijuana also increased his already overwhelming anxieties. He had a vague sense that smoking this joint might not be the best idea, given that he was on his way home and would soon have to face his parents, but that notion was outweighed by the attraction of feeling good, right now. He reached into his left pants pocket and was satisfied when he pulled out the green packet of Wrigley's Spearmint gum with two sticks remaining.

He turned his back to the wind, lit the last match, and cupped it while lighting the joint. He held each inhale for as long as he could, to maximize the high and minimize the smell of smoke to anyone else in the vicinity. He crossed the street each of the few times he saw passersby coming his way, and by the time he arrived home, he had a nice buzz on and, he hoped, had chewed enough of the gum to hide the smell.

His father was sitting at the kitchen table, staring into space, his head swiveling to follow J. J. as he turned to walk up the stairs.

"Finish your homework?" his father wanted to know.

"Don't have any," J. J. lied. He had played pinball rather than attend most of his classes today. He hurried up the stairs. After a few moments, he heard his father follow. He had closed his bedroom door, but now his father opened it without knocking.

"Do I smell what I think I smell?" He closed the door after stepping into the room.

J. J. shrugged, his response churlish. "I don't know what you smell."

It was a mistake, and his father was on him before he could say or do anything. He grabbed J. J. by the shoulder and spun him around, then slapped him hard, twice, across the face. The slaps had the force of punches but were open-handed. Then he spun J. J. again, pushed him face-first to the bed, and began slamming him across the backside with a powerful open hand, bellowing, his mouth close to J. J.'s ear.

"No son of mine speaks to me that way! Do you hear me? DO YOU HEAR ME? No! Son! Of! Mine!" He hit and hit, then let go of J. J., his anger spent, and J. J. curled into fetal position as his father stormed from the room, slamming the door behind him.

Connie was in the kitchen sipping a vodka tonic that was more vodka than tonic. She too had smelled the pot, which was flavored rather than covered by the smell of the spearmint gum. She did not have to see John follow J. J. upstairs or hear his heavy footfalls; she could hear him. She knew. The very air vibrated with his rage.

She went to the bottom of the stairway, grasped the spindle atop the bottom rail at the base of the stairs, and looked up into the darkness, then hurried back to the kitchen, where she topped off her drink and went into the living room to sit by the window. She knew John was too enraged to do anything but return to the kitchen and sit with his shame; he would want to be alone, in the kitchen, staring inward with his missing eye, into his private trauma.

Connie sat at the window and noticed the uneven hedges that bordered the lawn of the house across the street, and shook her head. Why couldn't the Grangers properly trim their hedges? The Fleischers lived diagonally across the street. Their home was well kept, the lawn and bushes nicely trimmed. But their children—oh, but their children, with their shrill voices and filthy mouths. How could Murray and Estelle Fleischer hold their heads up at the supermarket or PTA? Connie shook her head, feeling sorry for her neighbors, and soon went back to the kitchen for a few more ice cubes. When she came back into the living room, she noticed the pretty brown envelope on the coffee table, peeking out from the bottom of the small stack of the day's mail.

Chapter 9

The next day, Laurie Derico and Joanne Welles were walking along Jedwood Place to the high school; Laurie carried an English notebook. Her homework had been to write an essay in the first person about her experiences with someone she knew. Joanne did not carry books; she rarely brought books home because she didn't need them. She was a naturally gifted student for whom schoolwork came easily. Her brother, on the other hand, rarely brought books home because he rarely did any schoolwork.

"Maybe you could do your essay on someone you wish you had experiences with," Joanne suggested. "How would Mrs. Heinlene know if it's true?"

Laurie thought about this. "Like who?"

"Hmm. Let me think about it."

Laurie leaned her head close to her friend's. "I still have the hots for someone. But I don't need to imagine. We already—"

"Yeah, I know!" Joanne had stopped walking and was staring at her best friend. "But you could have told me before you did something about it!"

Laurie shrugged. "I didn't know how you would take it."

"I'm your best friend. So you can share things with me. But tell me something. Why would you do it with my brother? My stupid, shit-ass brother? Are you kidding me?" As Joanne said this, she had begun thinking about Laurie's brother, Ernie, in a new light. He was not bad looking, and while he was a bit of a loudmouth, there was something to be said for a guy with confidence. Leadership qualities.

Laurie shrugged. "We didn't do it. We did some things."

Joanne rushed to a spot in front of Laurie and blocked her way. "Yeah," she said. "Third base." She began to hyperventilate. She forgot that she had begun thinking similar thoughts about Laurie's brother. J. J. was still a boy, as far as she was concerned.

"Do you girls live over on the other side of Brooklyn Avenue?"

The girls turned. Behind them, hurrying to catch up, was Elly Thomas. "I'm new to the area, and—"

"Like we couldn't tell," Laurie said and turned back to Joanne, but Joanne had hurried on ahead, shaking her head and muttering to herself.

"My own brother. My brother! Holy shit!"

"Why's she upset?" Elly asked.

"You don't want to know."

"Would you mind if I walked with you?"

Laurie shrugged. "Free country." She thought for a moment, then stopped walking and put out her hand. "Laurie Derico."

Elly shook Laurie's hand, which was warm against her own cool, dry skin.

• • •

J. J. slowly uncurled from his fetal position. His breath was coming fast and shallow, and there was a warmth on the insides of his upper thighs. He had wet himself a little bit. He sat up and swallowed, trying to clear his father's rage from his consciousness. For a while his mind was blank. He saw the walls of his room, the dresser, and desk, the blankets on his bed, and the air conditioner, but he did not hear any sounds from outside his room and had no thoughts about what had just happened or what might happen next.

He could only sit and breathe. After perhaps five minutes, he stood up slowly, rubbing his behind and the left side of his face. He changed his underpants and put on the same pair of jeans he had been wearing. He thought he might vomit, but the feeling passed.

He looked around and saw two notebooks and two textbooks on his desk. They were for English and science and included tomorrow's assignments. He had been reading a book by John Steinbeck for English class called *East of Eden* and was surprised by how much he was enjoying the book. Something was calming about the way Steinbeck wrote, particularly about Cathy, who was described as an evil phenomenon—inexplicable and dangerous. J. J. also loved the way Steinbeck wrote his own family into the story and in particular, the joy with which he wrote about Samuel, his grandfather. The book was like a gentle hand, caressing J. J.'s back, enveloping him in a bubble of safety.

J. J. was not consciously aware of any of this. He only knew that this book presented him with a world he wanted to be a part of, and all that was required of him was to take it from the small stack of books on his bed and begin to read.

Now J. J. reached for the book and began thumbing through its pages to reach the point at which he had left off, but his thumb caught and stopped at a different spot—a place held by a bit of folded lined white notebook paper. He took the paper out, unfolded it, and read its only sentence.

I saw you today in English class :)

His mind was still reeling from his father's beating, and he frowned, confused. A note in his English book? He tried to imagine how it had gotten there since he had always been either carrying his books or had set them on his desk in each of his classrooms.

Who was in his English class?

And then he knew, and a tingling joy spread from the center of his chest outward to his shoulders, arms, and legs. Yesterday Debbie had been in his English class, and she had caught his eye, and he was pretty sure that she had smiled.

Debbie Derico!

He did not quite know how the note had come to be in his book, but he no longer cared.

• • •

Lou Derico went to the kitchen and looked out over the customers at the counter, the tables, and booths. They were filled to about seventy percent, which wasn't too bad for two o'clock on a Thursday. Of course, things could be better; the meatloaf special could be moving faster. There was more meatloaf than potatoes and green beans. And why didn't anyone want the chicken noodle soup today? He went back into the kitchen, washed the jelly off two chickens, sprinkled them with spices, cut up the carrots and potatoes, and slid them into the oven to broil for the dinner rush. He knew he would need at least two more before the night was through. He was counting on it.

Anna had come into the kitchen and was watching him.

"Well?" he said.

"The invitation."

He didn't know what she was talking about. "The what?"

"The invitation."

"What invitation?"

She looked impatient. Did she think he could read her mind?

"The one that came to the house. For the party Saturday?"

Now he remembered. "Do we have to discuss this now?"

Anna nodded. "In an hour you'll be on the pot roast and steak and won't hear a word I say."

He shut the oven and wiped his forehead with his sleeve. "Okay. What do you want to do?"

She had apparently thought about this. "I'd like to go. We don't go anywhere."

"You really think we'll have a good time? Think about it. Who's going to work at the diner? It's a Saturday night."

"I could ask Laurie." She curled out her lower lip, the way she did when she had her heart set on something.

Lou sighed and took the small towel that had been draped over the oven's handle. "Laurie asked for the night off."

"This Saturday?" Laurie and Ernie alternated every other Saturday evening to allow their parents the evening off.

Lou shrugged and cocked an eyebrow. "I'll talk to Ernie."

"Maybe Marshall could handle the kitchen for one night." Marshall's job fell somewhere between line cook and *sous-chef*. The diner was too small and had too little equipment for him to be the latter, and he ranked higher and was respected more than a line cook would ordinarily be. He ran the kitchen when Lou was not present, but even then he answered to anyone in the Derico family.

Lou didn't want to deal with this now. "I'll think about it."

Anna put a hand on her left hip, which she jutted to the side. "It would be nice, for a change."

He gave his wife a hard look. "I said I'll think about it."

• • •

Erin was listening to FM radio, and it was driving Tom Kelly crazy. One stupid, hippie song after another. "Ramblin' Man," "Long Train Runnin'," "Shambala," and "Give Me Love" by that minor Beatle, George Whatshisname. And "Bad, Bad Leroy Brown"—a bad, bad song if he ever heard one. Why write songs about criminals? Why not songs about the guys doing the defending? "Fortunate Son"—finally, a halfway decent song. He toasted John Fogerty with another few fingers of the Connemara.

He could hear Julie singing "All Creatures of Our God and King," followed by "Blessed Assurance," and he tried to tune out the radio, which was not easy, given that Julie was upstairs and the radio was on the kitchen counter only twelve feet away. And here came The Goose herself, waving an envelope. Tom knew about the invitation. He made it his business to know about everything that went on under his roof, even those things Jimmy and Julie didn't think he knew. He knew about Jimmy's titty magazines and the occasional joint, pipe, and rolling papers the boy had hidden in a false compartment under his desk. Tom didn't do anything about them because he did not want Jimmy to be alerted to the fact that he knew his son's secrets. Better to let the boy have his harmless vices than to come down on him and have him seek out more serious crimes and learn to better hide his activity.

Julie, as far as he knew, had no vices. How could she, with her voice of an angel? Tom was certain his grandmother, Eileen, could hear the girl. At least it made him happy to think so.

"No!" he said before The Goose could utter a word, and he took joy that he had given her a start. She blinked, and her head jerked backward an inch or two.

"I haven't even asked anything yet."

He waved his glass in her direction. "We are not going to a party at that house. Why did they invite us, anyway? Now we have to call and tell them no!"

Erin shook her head. "There's no RSVP."

"Good!" He nodded and smiled. The Goose had gotten something right. And yet here she was, still standing in front of him, with the envelope in her right hand, tapping it softly on the breakfront.

"And?"

"Well." She was using that shy voice, pretending to be respectful when he knew she secretly vilified him. "Maybe they invited us because they're new and we're neighbors."

"Huh," he grunted. "Well, we're not going."

Chapter 10

The day was almost here!

After the final bell, Elly went out the door on the north side of the school and stood off to one side. Dwayne would know to find her there. They would go home, and Aunt Wanda—who was not technically an aunt, but was her favorite family friend—would be there and everything would be fun and joy!

She began to walk in small circles after ten minutes and to worry after fifteen. She tried to remember what Dwayne's last class was on Fridays, but she wasn't sure. She thought it might be that crazy trigonometry class or maybe chemistry—she just didn't know, and even if she did, she would not know his teacher or in which room to look for him. So she waited.

Though the party was tomorrow, Dwayne had insisted on wearing his "party suit," as he'd called it today. In his own way, he was more excited than she was. She smiled to herself, thinking of her brother in his brown-and-green striped corduroy bell bottoms, his hot-pink dress shirt, and his black-and-white two-tone platform shoes with their three-inch heels. He had paid for the outfit and shoes with his own money, earned from the paper route he'd had in Queens. Her brother sure had style!

She scanned the skies, which were clear, with only a few distant, hazy clouds. She hoped the weather held for the party. The streets were still puddled and muddy from yesterday's downpour; she wondered what tomorrow's forecast was but knew the weather would not matter to her mother, who was herself a force of nature. When Shirley Thomas planned a party, or anything else for that matter, little besides an act of God could stand in her way.

She heard the faint shouts from the other side of the building and realized she had been hearing them for several minutes, but they had not penetrated her awareness. She stopped thinking and listened.

Then started running.

When she arrived at the south side of the building, she saw the crowd around the flagpole, and when she got closer, her lungs, which were bursting from running, seemed to expand upward into her throat.

A crowd of boys and a few girls were moving around what looked like a brightly colored animal that was on the ground between them. Only she knew that was no animal. As she rushed into their midst, she heard the taunting.

"Pretty clothes don't make you a man."

He was on the ground, and she could tell from the way he was holding his side that he had been beaten. Several boys were splashing him with mud from the puddles around the flagpole and occasionally kicking him in the back.

"You'll never be a man."

"You'll always be a boy."

"Bark for me, boy!"

Elly shouldered into their midst and knelt beside her brother, who was quiet but did not look upset; he had the same placid expression he nearly always had, though he also had a cut on his forehead and mud all over his favorite outfit.

She helped him to his feet and looked around. "What the hell is wrong with you all?" She knew some of these boys and a few of the girls. She glared at their faces.

"With you all," someone echoed.

"Where you get them clothes, boy?" someone sneered.

"Think money grows on trees?" someone else taunted.

"Boy knows about trees," came another taunt.

Elly had her brother by the shoulders and was leading him away when he stopped and turned.

"Yes," he said, in the same tone he might have used in class. "Money does grow on trees. It's made from paper, which grows on trees."

• • •

Debbie practiced her long tones for an hour every day after school, followed by different kinds of scales—chromatic, major, relative and harmonic minor, pentatonic, and blues. To increase her stamina, she took fifteen-minute breaks every hour or so to listen to records by her favorite flutists. She liked to practice with the tone and style of musicians she admired fresh in her mind so that she could perfect her tone and technique.

Debbie related to the world via music. Her mood translated into music that reflected her feelings in her mind, and she had a collection of music—most of it classical but a growing number of jazz albums as well. She played the records on an inexpensive little phonograph in her bedroom. At any given moment, she would think of her feelings in terms of well-known flute pieces by composers that included Mozart, Ravel, Bach, Debussy, and Vivaldi.

Her musical studies had followed the typical school orchestra and private lesson trajectory, and her love for music, and flute in particular, led to what had become an immersive joy. She returned to her favorite pieces as long-lost friends, renewing her love of melody, harmony, tone, and what for her was an emotional experience as close to her heart as any friend or family member could be.

She had only recently been introduced to jazz by a crossover record by Rampal, who had recorded a series of duets written by and performed with the French pianist Claude Bolling. The melodies were evocative and wonderful, and Debbie worked some of them out and played them herself.

In preparation for her audition, she looked at Bonni Bird's set lists and transcribed four of her songs, writing flute interpretations. She had never written music, and certainly not for performance. That she was doing so for a musical idol of hers was more than a little frightening. Her identity was very tied to her musical expression—not so much her renditions of famous pieces, but her proficiency and creativity.

She tried not to think about how she would feel or what she would do if Bonni did not like her technique or her musical interpretations of Bonni's songs.

• • •

Bonni had told her to let herself in and to find her downstairs. The audition was in Bonni's basement—down a narrow stone staircase, above which a dog was frantically barking. Debbie wondered how Bonni was able to play with that dog making so much noise. She understood once the door at the top of the stairs was closed; the basement was soundproof.

Along one wall of the darkened two-room area was a professional mixing board with more than a dozen inputs. Beneath the board were columns of control dials. Bonni was dressed in a black blouse that was open at the neck, black jeans, and a black vest. Silver hoop earrings glinted against her tanned skin. She was all business, flipping switches and adjusting dials on the board. Eventually, she nodded toward a microphone and extended a hand as if to say, "It's all yours."

• • •

"Elly!" Shirley called, from the top of the stairs. "Set the ribs at four fifty! Broil!"

Papa Elvin's voice answered, "Bibs're sore nifty in the soil!"

Elly had begun walking toward the bottom of the stairs when she heard her mother's voice. "Yes, Mama," she answered, and went into the kitchen, removed the tray of smoked and rubbed ribs from the refrigerator, and, balancing them on her left hand, opened the oven with her right and slid the tray onto the top rack. She then set the oven to broil at four hundred and fifty degrees.

Papa Elvin was in the living room in his cushioned walnut rocker, rocking and repeating, "Bibs are nifty—soil! Bibs are nifty—soil!"

Dwayne was at the kitchen table working on extra-credit math problems and humming to himself. He bore no visible physical or emotional scars from the abuse he had so recently suffered, but Elly knew that her brother held his wounds close. Elvin Jr. was upstairs, having showered, and was now getting dressed. To Elly, her mother seemed to be everywhere at once, making lists of what to cook and when, anxiously checking the status of the food, and wringing her hands at a growing list of all that could go wrong as the hour of the party grew closer.

A half hour before the party was to begin, the doorbell rang just as Elvin Jr. came downstairs, paused at the landing, turned toward the kitchen, and smiled. "I smell my daughter's cornbread!"

Elly smiled and headed for the front door, but her father stepped in front of her. "I'll get it." He did not mention that he was answering the door to spare his daughter the anguish of any new racist surprise that might be waiting outside. He opened the door a crack, then all the way, and threw his arms wide.

Chapter 11

Debbie closed her eyes and began to play, instantly losing her sense of time and place and both transporting and being transported by the music. She played all of the songs she'd prepared and made few errors besides a moment or two of weak tone and two missed grace notes. When she opened her eyes, she watched Bonni's face for a reaction.

At first, Bonni only looked at her, but she looked deeply and as though she were not quite present—still immersed in the music. Then she smiled.

"That was wonderful," she said, extending her hand. "Welcome to the band."

• • •

"Elviiiinn!" cried the overjoyed voice Elly knew and adored. She watched from behind her father as Wanda, her mother's best friend, hugged and held him. The pair swayed from side to side for a long moment, then disengaged. Wanda was in her mid-forties and wore a matching black blouse-and-pants outfit with thin, twinkling gold lamé stripes that was draped loosely over her stocky frame. Her hair was braided in long red-brown dreadlocks, and her shiny black shoes twinkled with gold spangles. Wanda's eyes and smile sparkled nearly as much as her clothes. She saw Elly and stepped back.

"My girl. Look at the lady you are!"

"Hi, hi." Elly waved and smiled shyly.

Wanda, who was holding a wine-shaped gift-wrapped box that matched her dress, strode past Elvin Jr., took Elly by the arm, and led her into the living room, where she bent and kissed Papa Elvin on the side of his forehead.

"Hi, handsome." She lightly touched his forearm.

Papa Elvin looked at her and said, "Fibs spread swiftly. Oil!"

Wanda frowned and turned to Elly, who shrugged. "Papa Elvin has these spells, but they don't usually last."

Wanda nodded. "Old timer's?"

Elly shrugged, and Wanda patted her on the arm. "Okay then, how can I help?"

Elly took the wine from Wanda and led her toward the kitchen.

"Oooh, it smells good in here!" Wanda marveled.

"That my Wanda?" Shirley fairly flew down the stairs and into her best friend's arms in the hallway, where she and Wanda hugged and rocked, emitting "Oohs" and "Ohs."

As soon as the women were out of the living room, Elvin Jr. went to the front door, opened it, took a step outside, and looked around before coming back in and closing the door.

Elly was focused on the serving dishes, trays, and pans that were lined up on the countertops. Her mother had taped a list to the countertop of what to cook and when and whether each dish went into the oven or a pot on top of the stove.

Elly heard her mother say, "I'll be back down in a minute," and her footsteps faded up the stairs. Wanda appeared in the kitchen; her wide smile made her cheeks look like twin ripe red apples. She gave off the scent of Charlie, the perfume that was Elly's favorite, though she did not yet have the courage to wear the scent herself.

Wanda walked over to Dwayne, who was still writing at the dinette table, and put a hand on his shoulder. "Anyone tell you that you don't have to do homework today?"

The tip of his tongue showed at one corner of his mouth. "This isn't work. I like trig," he said, without looking up.

"Well then, you and trig have a fine time." Wanda surveyed the bounty on the countertops. "What are we having?" she asked Elly. "Give me a menu rundown."

Elly grinned. "What *aren't* we having?" She pointed to each dish. "There's sweet potatoes, my corn bread, okra, rice, collards that Dwayne made, Daddy's honeydew, and potato salad—that's from the store. For dessert, we're having cherry pie, blueberry pie, and chocolate layer cake."

Wanda drew back and pretended to be dubious. "That all? Folks'll go home hungry!"

"No, that's not all," Elly quipped. "We barbecued the chicken and ribs this morning, and we're broiling them now." She opened the oven so Wanda could see.

Wanda bent toward the oven and dutifully inhaled. "Mmm, mmm, mm!"

"Oiling the cow!" Papa Elvin called, from the living room. Wanda cocked an eyebrow.

Elly gave her a long look. "He does this more when he's stressed— 'cause of the party. Repeats what sounds like the last thing he heard."

Wanda concentrated, digesting that. "So it's not all the time."

Elly shook her head, and, as if on cue, Papa Elvin appeared in the kitchen doorway and made for Wanda with a grin nearly as wide as hers.

"Come here, little girl! You're prettier 'n ever!"

"Oh, Elvin." She gave a poo-poo wave with one hand while reaching the other around his ample waist. After a moment, Papa Elvin's eyes grew distant, and he wandered out of the kitchen, toward the living room. Wanda followed as far as the doorway, watching, then turned, her eyes moist.

"He sit in that rocker a lot?"

Elly nodded. "Between that and the one out back, nearly all day."

"Long as he don't get himself in trouble and wander off."

Elly shook her head. "They say they do that, but not yet."

"Okaaay!" Shirley sang as she clumped down the stairs in her emerald platform sandals. She arrived in the kitchen and primped her hair.

"How's my hair? How's my makeup? How's my dress? I smell okay?"

Wanda laughed. "Fine, fine, gorgeous, and how would I know with this feast in here?"

Elly had opened the oven to show her mother. "Ribs and chicken are at four fifty, and I'm putting the okra in this pot, sweet potatoes in that one, and the rice will go in here." She indicated the nearest of the three pots on the stove. "I'll just warm up the rice and okra for ten minutes."

Shirley paused. "Make it twenty for the okra on low heat, and remember to put a third of a cup of water in with the rice. Not a half, not a quarter—a third of a cup."

Elly nodded. "Yes, Mama."

"So, Shirley," Wanda said, her smile on full force. "You serving colored folks food at a white folks party?" It was obvious to Elly that she was joking, but her mother did not appear to be amused.

"This is not colored folks food, and this is not a white folks party. 'Sides—we don't speak like that. We say 'Afro American' or 'Black.'"

"Really?" Wanda folded her arms. "I don't see as how you'd know. Seeing as how you're white."

Shirley's eyebrows went up. "'Scuse me?"

Wanda shook her head. "Ain't no colored—Black—folks living in this neighborhood."

Shirley paused, then took a breath and turned to Elly. "Why don't you tell Wanda about school."

Elly shrugged. "School's okay. I can handle it."

Wanda's smile vanished. "Handle it? How many other girls like you in your school?"

"None."

"And you can handle it?"

Elly pressed her lips together. "I can."

"How the girls treat you? Girls can be mee-eaann."

Elly shrugged.

"That bad."

She shrugged again.

"What about Dwayne? Girls are mean, but boys can be physically nasty. White boys beatin' on your brother?"

Elly looked down, then briefly at her mother.

"Shirley." Wanda was concerned. "Seriously?"

"Stop that, Wanda!" Papa Elvin called from the living room. "They will be fine. They love to read and write, and they love their figures. That's all they need—that and a good family. They will be fine!"

Shirley closed her eyes, and when she opened them, she glanced at the kitchen clock with a worried look.

"What if nobody comes? Aren't guests usually early to parties?"

Wanda shook her head. "Not me. I like to be fashionably late." She twirled. "So I can make my entrance and let the men see what's what." She laughed, and Shirley had to laugh with her. Wanda pointed as though to say, "See? I made you laugh."

"Seriously," Wanda said. "How many colored folks you invite to this party?"

"Don't start," Shirley warned.

• • •

Ernie Derico was angry. He was often angry, but today his anger had a focus. He had decided to take Ricky up on his idea—burglarize Steve's Liquors, and teach that bastard a lesson.

He had never done a burglary and wanted to practice before hitting Steve's, so he approached Ricky Taylor, and since the original idea had been Ricky's, he was all for it. Like the rest of the guys Ernie hung around with, Ricky rarely admitted to being impressed by much of anything, other than the body of some girl on the street or someone's fighting prowess. Expressing interest implied vulnerability; it was much easier and cooler to casually despise just about everything.

Ricky agreed that a practice burglary wasn't a bad idea, and he brought Donnie Richardson in on the plan. Donnie was respected because he was a great hater; he hated anyone and everyone who was different in any way. He particularly hated Jews. His father had worked in a clothing factory on the lower west side of Manhattan that had been owned by Jews. Donnie suggested they burglarize a synagogue.

"Synagogue?" Ernie looked from Ricky to Donnie and back again. Donnie had that half smile and look in his eye that said trouble was coming.

"Yeah," Ricky said. "One of them Jew temples." Ricky widened his eyes with a smirk.

"We could take some of them scroll things," Donnie said, beaming now; he looked at Ricky, who nodded.

"Jew scrolls," Ricky agreed.

"And this would be for practice?" Ernie was trying to understand. "And you guys would come?"

"Right. Right!" Ricky exclaimed. "Then we'd do Steve's."

"And we'd do Steve's together?" Ernie was looking for confirmation.

"Yep," Ricky said, with a secret smile at Donnie, who looked sideways at Ricky and waggled his eyebrows.

"Yeah," Donnie said. "Together."

• • •

"Oh, I think I hear her coming!" Elvin Jr. exclaimed, and everyone quieted down and turned toward the stairs.

"That's riiight!" came a musical alto from the top of the stairs. "The queen is descending!"

Nana Makayla sauntered slowly down the stairs, pausing once she came down far enough to be seen, angling so everyone could see her, resplendent in a floor-length cobalt-blue dashiki dress printed with multicolored geometric patterns and a turquoise central keyhole shape on both front and back. The dress was bordered with handwoven, silk kente cloth of brilliant colors around the neck and waist.

"Whoa," Dwayne breathed. "Nana!"

"Now that," Wanda exclaimed, "is an entrance!"

Papa Elvin had appeared at the edge of the family cluster, and now he stepped to Makayla, took her right hand lightly in his, and kissed it, turning so his bride could float down the rest of the steps into the room and the loving embrace of her family. Makayla swept into the kitchen, where her granddaughter was just finishing setting up the warming pots.

"Oooh, Nana Makayla. You're beautiful!"

"I am, and so are you. In fact, you get it from me, if you don't mind my saying." She lifted the lids from the pots and opened the oven, nodding with satisfaction.

"I don't mind, Grandma. But Mama's worried people won't come."

"I forgot to put RSVP on the invitations," Shirley said. She stood in the doorway, leaning against the doorjamb with one shoulder, arms folded across her chest, fingers drumming on her upper arms.

Makayla shrugged. "Well, if people don't come, we'll have an even bigger feast, won't we!" Her smile remained resplendent as she tapped the tip of Elly's nose and Elly giggled.

"Yes, we will, Nana!"

Wanda's smiling face appeared over Shirley's shoulder. "Givin' these white folks a taste of soul food?"

Makayla smiled and nodded. "Mm-hmm. Yes, we are!"

"I'm going back to my rocking chair for a nap," said Papa Elvin. "Let me know when the company arrives."

Shirley huffed an exhale. "If they arrive." She shook her head. "It's not neighborly to not show up and not call, even if I did forget the RSVP."

"Maybe you left off the RSVP," came Elvin Jr.'s voice, "so no one could hurt your feelings."

"What? I did not!" Shirley replied. "If no one comes, we are going to represent our people as fools."

"Shirley, honey, you're tying yourself up in knots!" He looked with concern at his wife. "And we're not here to represent anyone but our-selves!"

"*Nots*!" Elly said, giggling. "That's funny, Wanda."

"It is *not* funny," Shirley insisted.

"Another *not*!" Elly laughed and pointed at her mother.

"Stop it, young lady! I will not—"

Now both Elly and Wanda were exploding with laughter, and Shirley couldn't help but smile.

Two tones of a chime rang out.

Shirley gasped. "They're here!" She patted her hair with both hands. "I knew it!"

"You did *not*!" cried Elly, still laughing.

Dwayne appeared in the doorway. "There's a white lady, a girl, and a boy outside. And the lady brought food!"

Shirley nodded and followed her son toward the front door.

"How many neighbors did she invite?" Wanda asked, in Makayla's direction.

"I have no idea," Makayla said, making her way in the small steps her dress allowed out of the kitchen and into the living room. "All I know is we invited people who live within three or four blocks of us and who have kids the same ages as ours. Wake up now, Papa Elvin. Company's here!"

Papa Elvin's eyes flew open and his chair rocked suddenly forward as he shifted his weight. "Timpani's cheer!" His eyes were wide and radiated anxiety.

Makayla put her arms around her husband and pressed his frightened face to her bosom. "Shhh. It's okay. It's just a few neighbors come to visit. Why don't we get you washed up, so you can meet them? Doesn't that sound nice?"

He gave a tentative smile and let his wife lead him from the room.

Chapter 12

J. J. had all but exhausted himself after school, running from one exit to the next. He was pretty sure that Debbie was involved in a music program before school—band or orchestra or the new chamber music group; he could not tell them apart, so he had given up trying to find her before the start of the school day. He wondered if she would seek him out. She certainly had gone to some trouble sneaking the note in with his books, so didn't it stand to reason that she was motivated to connect with him—that she wanted to be with him? And if she was busy before school and they had this one thing in common—the school they both attended—didn't it stand to reason that she would seek him out and build on the fantastic impression she had instigated with her note?

He had no understanding of how girls thought. His sister, her friends—what had happened with Laurie. Girls were beyond his understanding. He did not understand their bodies and had no clue about their minds.

He wondered if she wanted him to make the next move. She had no way of knowing that he liked her as much as she seemed to like him. So maybe the next move was his; perhaps he could signal to her that he liked her too!

He had set about trying to run into her by making sure he was at whichever exit she used at the end of the day. Unfortunately, he couldn't be in two places at once, and somehow he seemed to have missed her. What happened was obvious; when he was at one exit, she had come out the other, and now he had the sudden fear that his run of bad luck might continue. So he went to her family's diner, and when she wasn't there, he went to her house, looked around to make sure no one spotted him, and skulked around to the back. Sure enough, she was practicing flute, only these were songs he knew. Popular songs. "Kodachrome," "Crocodile Rock," "Ramblin' Man," and "Right Place Wrong Time."

She was playing along with albums, putting on the records, playing them once, then playing along the second time. He stood there smiling until it occurred to him to signal to her. Perhaps that was what she was waiting for. It was his move, and he had found her, so what was he going to do? He thought about it while she played several more songs —"Bad, Bad Leroy Brown" followed by "Shambala."

Then it came to him. He didn't play an instrument, and she probably knew that. But he could whistle; in fact, he could make a pretty sound by clasping his hands together with his thumbs lined up next to one another and blowing between his thumbs, then varying the tone by flapping the outer of his two hands. He did this now but was drowned out by her music.

Next, she played "Angie" by the Rolling Stones. This time he waited until the moment she finished the song, and whistled again. He paused, waiting, but she did not begin to play again, so he whistled once more, and tried to put the love he was feeling into the whistle.

He heard the scrape of the window lock above his head opening, and then there she was, looking down at him, a confused expression on her face.

He waited, expecting her to recognize him and welcome him with her eyes. Instead, her eyes narrowed, and she shaded them with her palm.

"Who is that? Hello?"

"J. J.," he said, and when her expression didn't change, he added, "Your neighbor, John Welles Jr."

She smiled, but it wasn't a smile of recognition; it was a smile of kindness.

"Right. You're one of Ernie's friends. And you know Laurie, I think, right? Listen, I've got a ton of practicing to do, and neither of them is here, so maybe come back another time?"

He nodded, and it was all he could do to say, "Sure. Of course."

She smiled again and closed the window.

• • •

Elvin Jr.'s reel-to-reel was playing Elly's favorite music: Marvin Gaye, Gladys Night and the Pips, and the O'Jays. The food was arrayed, buffet style, on the dining room table. The guests were seated side by side on the sofa. One woman had a pale-pink complexion, and her eyes darted from one person to the next, widening at the bounty of food, and hurrying on when someone met her gaze. She had a plate of something wrapped in aluminum foil in her lap. To Elly, she appeared to be looking inward, at a memory perhaps or imagining she was someplace else. She shifted her weight from side to side, and repeatedly clasped and unclasped her hands.

"I'm Erin Kelly," she said, finally. "And these are my children, Julie and Jimmy." The two teens smiled at the mention of their names and settled back into whatever worlds their minds had retreated to.

The Thomas family were arrayed opposite the Kellys on the two armchairs and the four folding pine chairs Elvin Jr. had brought in from the garage. He stood and went to each of the guests, hand outstretched.

"I'm Elvin Jr.—just plain Junior around here, because that gentleman over there is my father, Elvin Sr., or Papa Elvin, as we call him."

Papa Elvin was clutching Makayla's hand and, at the mention of his name, looked over the guests. "We fall in."

Erin cocked her head. "I'm sorry?"

No one answered right away. Elvin Jr. stepped back, making space for his mother, who stepped forward.

"I'm Makayla Thomas. Welcome to our home." She offered her hand to Erin, who took it and smiled slightly.

"What a beautiful dress," Erin managed to say, after a short silence.

"It's a dashiki," Dwayne said.

"That's my grandson, Dwayne, and this is my granddaughter, Elly."

Elly stepped forward and offered her hand to each guest.

"And this," Makayla said, her left arm extended, palm out, in a flourish, "is our hostess, who was responsible for this evening's dinner. My daughter-in-law, Shirley."

Shirley smiled and waved. Elly could see that her mother was as nervous as she had ever seen her, and that included Shanice Carter's wedding, where she'd had to give the maid of honor speech.

"Shirley?" Wanda looked at Shirley, tipping her head to one side and waiting.

"Ohhhh, and this is my very best friend, Wanda Richardson."

Wanda smiled and stepped forward. "Welcome!"

Shirley went to the dining room table, then turned back to the guests. "Please make yourselves at home, take some plates and napkins. There are forks, spoons, and knives on the right side of the table, and you can work your way through the food from right to left."

Erin stood, still holding the food she had brought.

"Why don't you put that on the table with the rest of the food?" Shirley gently took the plate from her and set it on a corner of the table, bunching up a few items to make room.

"I made a batch of chocolate chip cookies," Erin said.

"I like chocolate chip," Dwayne said.

"Rocket ship!" Papa Elvin exclaimed.

Makayla ran her right hand in circles on her husband's upper back. "Papa Elvin likes chocolate chip too."

The doorbell rang.

"More *company,*" Shirley sang out and rushed to answer the door.

• • •

Joanne and Laurie turned from the sidewalk toward the stone steps to the Thomases' house. They had been walking without speaking, each carrying the items they brought, along with the hidden burdens of their thoughts and feelings. Joanne found it hard to believe that Laurie was willing to have sex with J. J., which to her was a disgusting betrayal that trampled on their friendship. If Laurie couldn't see that loyalty to friends was more important than boys, and brothers of friends no less, she would—well, she didn't know what, but she would do something!

But in the end, she did nothing. The friends came to an unspoken agreement to let the subject of J. J. and Laurie's sexual experience, which to Joanne's relief didn't go all the way, fade into memory—a bizarre bump in the road of their friendship and, Joanne hoped, nothing more. She looked at her friend, who looked back and gave a tentative smile, which Joanne returned just as tentatively. She raised her eyebrows, took a deep breath, and let it out in a sigh. Laurie was carrying a tray of prepared sandwiches from the diner. Joanne had both hands clasped over her belly, which hid a different sort of package.

The sound of a man clearing his throat behind them made them both jump.

"Daddy!" Joanne exclaimed. John Welles wordlessly stepped past them and rang the bell.

• • •

"Elly!" Shirley called as she motioned for Wanda to follow her up the stairs and join her in the bathroom. "Please let our guests in and get everyone seated. I'll be right down."

Without waiting for an answer, she stepped into the half bath at the top of the stairs and beckoned to Wanda. As soon as Wanda closed the door, Shirley spun around and grabbed her friend by the shoulders.

"Help! I cannot do this!"

"You cannot do what?"

"I don't know how to throw a white people party!"

"Honey," Wanda said, holding up a palm and waving it from side to side. "You are throwing a party—an integrated party, not a white people party, and you are doing just fine. Think of it as a color-free party. Now, let's get back to it before anything can go wrong—like the hostess hiding in the upstairs bathroom." Wanda turned and walked halfway down the stairs, then looked back at her best friend, who was breathing heavily, with a stricken expression.

"Look," Wanda said, "just go down there and tell them they were invited so they could get to know the Negroes before we start dating their children."

Shirley was horrified. "What?"

Wanda laughed. "Oh, come on! Relax!"

"You think that's funny?" Shirley put her hands to her hips. "You can go on home." She looked deadly serious.

"Okay." Wanda shrugged and continued down the stairs.

"No! Don't leave me!" Shirley whimpered.

Wanda turned again. "Here's another idea."

"Okay."

"Pray."

"Seriously?"

Wanda nodded; this time she was serious. "It's my go-to. Never lets me down. Silently—to yourself."

Shirley followed Wanda down the stairs, her lips moving, as she stepped into the living room. "Welcome, everyone. I'm so glad you could make it." She saw that all of her family except Makayla were present and seated.

John Welles and his daughter, Joanne, were standing in the living room with Laurie Derico, who was holding a Saran Wrap-covered tray, which Shirley took from her. "Oh, what's this? You shouldn't have!" She brought the tray into the kitchen. Before Laurie could answer, Shirley called toward the living room.

"Dwayne, please put out three more chairs for our guests." She returned with the tray, now uncovered, and found a place for it at the buffet.

"Those are roast beef, turkey, and salami sandwiches from our diner," Laurie said.

Shirley gave a grateful smile. "Oh, you didn't have to do that! We have plenty of food."

Laurie shrugged. "Well, I wanted to, and my father and mother have to work, so he sent these as sort of an apology."

"That's okay," Wanda answered for Shirley. "Tell him he can come next time."

Shirley glared at Wanda and mouthed, "Next time?" Then she said, "Well, please be sure and thank them for me." She turned toward the kitchen.

"That man has one eye!" Dwayne pointed at John Welles.

For a moment, everyone was silent.

"I was in the war," John Welles said, his voice barely more than a whisper. "Europe. Infantry." He looked around the room. "I was a child."

Shirley glared at her son. "Dwayne, that wasn't very polite."

Dwayne looked at his shoes. "Sorry."

Joanne and Laurie exchanged looks as they sat down. Shirley introduced her family; Erin introduced hers, and Laurie introduced herself.

"Aren't you the musician?" Erin asked once the introductions were complete. "My Julie loves to sing."

Julie blushed. "Ma."

"She's a standout at church. Really!"

Laurie shook her head. "You're thinking of my sister, Debbie."

Erin blushed, in much the same way her daughter had. "Oh, my mistake." There was a brief silence. She turned to Elvin Jr. "My daughter tells me you're a teacher. What do you teach?"

"High school English. In Queens."

"And how are you finding it?"

"Well, it's a new position for me, and kids like to figure out a teacher's boundaries, so it has its challenging moments, but I can see I'm going to love it."

"What aspects do you like most?" Erin asked.

"Literature. Hands down. I am a proponent of reading as a foundation of one's education."

"Isn't that wonderful!" Erin said, a little too enthusiastically.

Makayla fluttered the fingers of one hand toward her grandchildren, who had taken seats on the floor to make room for the newest guests.

"My grandson, Dwayne, excels in math, don't you, Dwayne?" said Makayla.

"Yes, Nana Makayla."

"And Elly—"

Papa Elvin was looking at Joanne; he cleared his throat. "Young lady, I believe your blouse is moving."

"Papa." Shirley was shaking her head and looking apologetically at the guests, then she put a hand to her mouth. "My goodness, her blouse *is* moving."

Joanne had both hands cupped in her lap. Her shirt rippled, and a kitten dropped into her hands, looked around, saw everyone looking at it, leaped into the air, and tried desperately to wriggle back inside Joanne's shirt.

Everyone in the room roared with laughter, which went on for a long moment. Shirley wiped the tears from the corners of her eyes, looked at Wanda, and mouthed, "The answer to my prayers," and Wanda gave her a "Didn't I tell you?" smile in return.

"Who is this feline guest, and was he invited?" Papa Elvin asked.

"Sorry," Laurie answered.

"I said, who is this feline guest—"

"His name is Sorry."

"Ohhh." Papa Elvin looked at Shirley for confirmation.

"Why doesn't everybody help themselves to some food," she said as she rose to her feet. "There are plates, forks, and spoons on the right."

"And knives, Mama. You forgot knives," said Dwayne.

"Yes, honey. And knives. And—"

"And napkins too, Mama."

"Thank you, Dwayne," said Shirley. "You are such a gentleman. The perfect host."

"Thank you, Mama."

"He is!" Erin agreed.

Everyone stood up and formed themselves into a ragged semblance of a line, with the adults encouraging the children to go first and John Welles motioning Erin to a spot in front of him. The Thomas family hung back, waiting for their guests to serve themselves.

"Julie, do you know any of the girls here from school?" Erin asked her daughter.

"I've seen them," Julie answered.

"Did I mention that Julie is quite the singer?" Erin said.

"Yes, Ma, you did," Julie moaned.

"Is that so?" Shirley and Elvin Jr. said at once.

"She's in the choir at church," Erin continued. "She's very good."

"Maaa," Julie complained.

"What church do you attend?" Elly asked.

"Holy Name of Mary," Julie answered for her mother.

"Where you do folks attend?" Erin asked.

"We worship at Valbrook Baptist," Makayla answered. "It's small —thirty members or so at present, but growing."

"Mr. Welles," Erin said, determined to keep the conversation flowing, "don't you have a son who is friends with our Jimmy?" She reached for her son, who had been silent and now smiled.

Joanne answered for her father. "J. J. is sixteen, and I believe he is friends with Jimmy."

"You're friends with J. J.?" Erin asked Jimmy. He nodded, still smiling.

"And also with Laurie's brother, Ernie," Joanne continued.

The conversation continued, but Elly didn't hear the words; she was watching her brother. Dwayne was frowning in Laurie's direction, his lips pressed tightly together, his body clenched and swiveling from side to side.

"Tell me, girls," Erin said to Joanne and Laurie. "What are the names of your hairstyles?"

The girls looked at one another. Joanne was the first to answer. "Mine was supposed to be a pageboy, but—I dunno. It isn't a pageboy, exactly."

Erin looked at Laurie, who thought for a moment. "Mine's called a flick, because of the way it flicks up at the bottom. I had it done today, so it's still flicking. Tomorrow it might not be."

"How 'bout you?" Laurie had been drawn by Dwayne's attention and was frowning back, her eyes narrowed, but now she smiled toward Julie.

Julie shrugged. "I don't know."

"Sure you do," her mother said. "It's—"

"Maaa!" Julie spoke with such vehemence that her mother blinked and sat back. "Okaaay."

At that moment, the kitten made a mad dash out of the bottom of Joanne's shirt and leaped from her lap to the coffee table, where she had rested a small plate with a roast beef sandwich. The kitten tore off a hanging bit of meat, turned, and leaped back onto Joanne's lap and back into her shirt.

"Whoa!" Joanne exclaimed. "Did you see that?"

Laurie, Wanda, and all three Kellys were laughing, their hands to their mouths so as not to spit out food. The Thomases were focused on Dwayne, who had relaxed but was still staring at Laurie while taking a tentative bite of a spare rib.

Chapter 13

Debbie sat on the wooden stool, conscious of her body position—her left heel resting on the bottom rung, her right on the floor, her body leaning slightly to the right, her hair just over her shoulders in a Jane Fonda shag. Her flute was loose in her right hand and lay across her left thigh. No one said a word to her, and she wondered if she had somehow misunderstood until Bonni came in and everyone settled into their positions.

"Hey everyone, this is Debbie." She flashed a smile her way. "With an e. She'll be sitting in on flute today, as you can tell. Debbie, this is everyone." Her eyes returned to Debbie's for confirmation. "You have parts for all the songs?"

Debbie nodded and wondered if everyone could hear her heart, which was pounding so hard it all but drove her forward with each beat.

Bonni flashed another smile, a smile that welcomed Debbie into a private, oh-so-special world—a smile that left her breathless, but only for a moment, as the drummer tapped her sticks together, counting the band in. And then they were playing.

The songs were all recent hits by female vocalists with one exception—a song called "Can't You See," from a brand-new album by the Marshall Tucker Band. The song had obviously been chosen for its flute part, which was easy enough. The others required her to create her own flute parts, something Debbie had never done, since she had never before played with a band. She spent hour after hour practicing long tones and scales at home and played whatever she thought sounded good along with her records on her record player. But that rarely left her enough time to come in with the bands on the recordings because of the time it took to place the needle on the record. She assumed that Bonni would change the parts she'd come up with, and that was fine— to be expected. She was prepared for it and told herself that rejections of that sort were no reflection on her playing.

But what happened was not at all what she expected. What happened was a miracle of sorts. The rest of the songs were "You're So Vain," "The Night They Drove Old Dixie Down," and "I Feel the Earth

Move," and after every song, Bonni said exactly the same thing: "That was great!"

Was she dreaming? She was living! She was in the flow of life; she was life—a part of it anyway. There she was, expressing the joy of it—the creation, the exuberance, the harmonies with the other instruments, the riding on the beat of the drums, carried along by the mobile foundation laid down by the bass. She caught herself several times starting to laugh for the joy of it, which, of course, would never do since she needed her breath, her embouchure and the strength and position of her lips, her fingers not as disparate parts, but all as one. And she was doing it. She was doing it! She was flying!

Afterward, she didn't know what to say. How did one express the gratitude one couldn't help but feel for being allowed entrée into this indescribable shared yet private experience? She looked from one musician to the other as they packed up. All were women; none paid her any attention, except for the rhythm guitarist—who was tall and lanky, all bones and angles. She nodded. "Next time," was all she said.

• • •

The next afternoon, J. J. was waiting under the streetlight at the corner near the Dericos' house, only this time he wasn't waiting for Debbie. Each night, between seven and eight in the evening, most everyone he knew made their way over to the trestle on Sunrise Highway near Rockaway Avenue. Tonight though, it was just a few days before Halloween. Laurie was dressed in a tight black leotard top and blue dungarees tucked into high, tight black leather boots. She wore gold hoop earrings, black mascara and eyeliner, and dark-blue eyeshadow. She was chewing gum, snapping it every so often.

She saw him and nodded, continuing to walk. No one made the assumption they were included unless specifically invited; vulnerability and potential ridicule were avoided, but J. J. had more important things on his mind. He fell into step beside her.

"Trestle?" he asked.

She nodded. "You?"

He nodded back. They walked west on Forest Avenue, past the firehouse to Brooklyn Avenue, then continued west, past the school, to Sunrise Highway. He was too distracted thinking of what he was going to say to pay any attention to Laurie's attitude toward him. Finally, Laurie veered into the parking lot of Wetson's fast-food hamburger restaurant and toward the nearby railroad trestle.

J. J. stopped, breathing hard—the moment of truth.

"Ain'tcha coming?" Laurie asked.

He took a deep breath, and when he spoke, his voice sounded as though it were coming from someone else. "C'mon up to the tracks spot and hang with me."

She knew what he meant and paused, considering; then he was rewarded with a broad, toothy smile and her cheerful answer.

"Okay!"

The tracks spot was an area below the village train station and behind a thick hedge of bushes that their crowd had claimed for drinking, smoking weed, hanging out, and sex.

Given the nature of the note he'd received—which he now understood had been sent by Laurie rather than her sister—and their recent experience, J. J. was pretty sure she would understand and agree. He was right.

He had thought hard about whether to say what he was thinking of saying next, and as they walked, their arms swinging and Laurie's hand brushing his fingers, he went over his decision. A guy never admitted weakness, indecision, or inexperience around a girl, but he had also seen that with some girls, in some situations, admitting to needing some help brought out a degree of kindness, and this was what he was hoping for now.

As they passed the accountant's office and the bar below the station, he reached into his pocket for the condom and tried to keep the anxiety out of his voice.

"It's my first time," he said softly.

Laurie slowed and broke into a broad smile. He slowed beside her, and she took his arm in hers and resumed walking.

"Don't you worry 'bout a thing."

The tracks spot had a hidden area where the bushes and many of the leaves had been cleared away, and old boards discarded from a nearby lumber yard had been laid on the ground beneath a couple of old sleeping bags. Several long boards had been stood on end, their tops leaned together teepee style, with one side left open, for shelter and cover.

Laurie sat down, took J. J.'s hand, and pulled him down next to her. "I gotchu, baby," she murmured, as she lay back.

He fumbled for the condom. "I brought, I brought—"

"Don't worry 'bout it. I got a diaphragm." She cupped his face in her hands and kissed him, then let her hands wander down his body, still kissing. Before he knew it, she had wriggled out of her jeans and pressed a firm hand to the front of his, then unzipped him and pulled off his pants, giggling when they caught at his knees. Then she tugged at his underwear.

He had been worried about not knowing what to do, or worse, about doing things wrong, but he need not have worried. Laurie knew exactly what to do, and before he knew it, they were rocking and she was moaning.

"Wait, wait, wait!" she said suddenly, and he stopped as she frowned and reached behind her back, bringing it back with a small stone. "Fuckin' rock." She threw it away and smiled the most welcoming of smiles. "You're doing great." And he was.

Voices and footfalls approached, and J. J. stopped and held her to him, but she moaned a few times and the footfalls stopped. "Someone's getting some," a voice said and snickered. The footfalls began again and faded.

After a while she flipped him onto his back and sat up, threw her head back, and wailed into the wind, her cries rising and falling with the rhythm of their bodies.

When they were finished, they lay together, breathing hard, the sweat evaporating in the cool fall darkness.

She smiled and looked into his eyes with what he could only describe as love. "So, I'm your first?" Her hand was rubbing wide, light circles on his chest.

He nodded. "I'm so glad I got your note."
Her hand stopped moving. "What note?"

David E. Feldman

The Neighborhood

Chapter 14

The Valley Stream of my childhood looked more homogenous than it was. While everyone was what is commonly referred to as "white," we had as neighbors Italian Americans, Irish Americans, German Americans, Mexican Americans, Chinese Americans, and a few Korean Americans. There were also Pakistani Americans and Indian Americans. We had many people of color, but no one who was of obvious African ancestry.

• • •

While Judaism is not a nationality, being Jewish American was and is a heritage of sorts—a cultural heritage, complete with its own history, several languages, and its own cuisine. Since 1948, we had another country that was not exactly one of origin, but one to which many of us felt allegiance, especially in the shadow of WWII and despite Israeli policies vis a vis the Palestinians and people of Arab ancestry.

Once I entered the seventh grade at Valley Stream South High, my childhood friendships were rarely with kids from other Jewish families. Many of those students achieved high marks, were well behaved at home and in class, and made their *B'nei Mitzvot* at a local temple. None of these applied to me, and I found most of these students to exist behind a wall of social behaviors and values that were foreign to me. Our little enclave north of William L. Buck School had its share of Jewish American families, but my friends and girlfriends tended to be from Italian American, Irish American, or German American families. I remember anti-Semitism to be common. I was accepted, not because of my Jewishness, but in spite of it.

When I was about six or seven years of age, some teenage boys playing stickball at Buck School called me over, asked me if I was Jewish, and, when I said I was, told me that was bad and to go back home and stay there until I wasn't Jewish anymore.

I heard a lot about how bad Jews were, and heard casual comments that were said by those who used them to be figures of speech rather than anti-Semitism.

"He Jewed me down."

"Don't bother asking him for money. He's a Jew." This could have been said whether or not the person in question was, in fact, a Jew.

"He's a cheap Jew."

"He won't fight. He's a Jew."

And so on.

While these are certainly anti-Semitic phrases and epithets, and when used were damaging in ways that went beyond what could have been observed, I also believe that as teens, many of those who spoke in these ways in the days before the phrase "political correctness" was in fashion were doing little more than boosting their egos or repeating phrases heard from parents or older siblings. Does this excuse such words? No, but it explains their use.

I hope that at least some of those who used such speech eventually learned about and saw images from the Holocaust and came to better understand the role of bigotry in human affairs.

That hope is faint at best.

• • •

The Thomas party was held on a Saturday; by Tuesday, the Kelly, Welles, and Derico homes had been pelted with eggs and spray-painted in red with an epithet that described their friendship with their new neighbors in the least friendly terms possible.

All three families immediately painted over the words, though only the Kellys could afford to paint their entire house; both Lou Derico and John Welles bought primer and paint at Brown's Hardware on Rockaway Avenue that was as close a match to the color of their houses as they could find. Then they painted large rectangles in multiple layers, which were necessary given the brightness of the offending red paint.

John Welles had fought in France during the Second World War. He and Connie had spoken to their children about bigotry years earlier.

Without speaking with his wife, who had grown more and more distant during the last year, John decided to talk to his son about how hard it can be to be one of the few and to be subjected to bigoted words and acts. He planned to tell his children about Jonathan Weiss, who had been his best friend in the service and who had told him all about being a Jew among gentiles, and about Willie Montgomery, who had worked at the Friendly Orange supermarket at the intersection of Peninsula Boulevard and East Rockaway Road. As a teen, John had gone there occasionally to help his mother carry packages and had seen Willie. Because they were the same age, John had nodded in greeting to him, and Willie had nodded back. That was all there was to it until John decided one day for no reason at all to ask Willie to walk over to Jack's candy store, which was west on Rockaway Avenue, to maybe have an egg cream and play a few games of pinball. Willie hadn't met his eye but shrugged and said he didn't think he could and besides, they didn't serve Coloreds there. John had never thought of that.

He had not seen Willie at the supermarket after that day, but one day he was buying spark plugs for his father in south Hempstead, at the other end of Peninsula Boulevard, and he came upon Willie, who was walking along the sidewalk just as a car full of bullies had yelled at him. Willie hadn't answered, but nor had he run, so the car had come around again. And when the boys ordered him to run, John could see in Willie's expression and posture that he wasn't going to—that though outnumbered, he preferred to fight if he had to, but he wasn't going to run.

John had jogged over and stood next to Willie, not saying anything. He didn't even know if Willie remembered who he was. He'd just stood there, and when the car came around, the boys had called him the same words he had just now painted over, and their car had slowed but hadn't stopped.

Willie had looked at him then but didn't say anything, and then he'd continued walking, so John had continued on his way in the opposite direction.

A few years after that, his mother had told him that Willie had served in the 92nd Infantry Division, the only Black infantry division that saw combat in World War II Europe. Known as The Buffalo Soldiers, their members wore a patch depicting a black buffalo on an olive background and kept a live buffalo as their mascot. Legend has it that the name was a term of respect derived from Native Americans' description of Black soldiers as black white men who resembled buffaloes because of their skin color and hair texture.

Willie Montgomery fought in Italy with the 370th Regimental Combat Team and died defending America, as did many Black American soldiers—like Lieutenant John Fox, an artillery observer for the 366th Regiment, who, when surrounded by enemy troops, ordered artillery fire on his own position, sacrificing his life but saving the day.

John had planned on telling his children these and other stories to give them some perspective to offset the cruel things they heard at school and in the neighborhood, and which had now been painted on their own house.

• • •

J. J. came home from school that Tuesday in late October of 1973 with those same words ringing in his ears—words he had heard from several kids, including some girls, and including his own friend, Ernie Derico, whose sister attended the very party that caused all the trouble, and whose house was graced with accusatory red words.

He noticed the bits of red paint on Ernie's hands.

J. J. didn't know how he could return to school; he didn't know how he could face his friends. He only knew he had been rejected by the only people he thought worthy of being a part of. He had to get back to the status he'd had before, even though it wasn't much. He had to somehow show them those awful words did not apply to him.

Twenty minutes after J. J. came home, John called both his children down to the living room.

"Your mother and I know it's been a bad couple of days." John glanced toward the kitchen, where his wife was looking down into a glass of what he knew was probably vodka and a little bit of ice and perhaps some lime juice.

"I want to tell you about an old friend of mine, a Jewish friend, and another—someone I didn't have the chance to get to know, but a man who died for our country."

Joanne was listening, expressionless. J. J. was aghast, his mouth open. He looked around wildly. "So it's true!"

"Johnny, listen to me."

"It's true what they said at school, what they're saying on the street."

"Just listen!" John barked, and breathed out against the pain in his chest.

"You really are one of—one of those! Well, I'm not, and I never will be," J. J. said.

There was a pause, and then John was charging at his son, bellowing, "Don't you be disrespectful to me—ever!" He grabbed J. J. by the arm, yanking him close, and with his other hand slammed his son repeatedly on the back, shoulders, rear end, and backs of his thighs. The muscles of John's face were drawn and clenched, as though he were focused on an athletic event or a feat of strength.

J. J. whimpered, terrified, and cringed away from his father, sobbing out a reaction. "But you went to their party! What they're saying is true!" All he could think of was what they were saying at school and at the trestle—the accusations against his and a few other families, including Laurie's. How would he ever live this down? How could he show his face anywhere in the neighborhood again?

His thoughts were interrupted by a renewed burst of violence and more yelling. "I taught you better than that! I taught you better than that!" John's eyes were bright with rage, but now the rage retreated as he became aware of where he was, what he was doing, and to whom. He was not in France; it was twenty-nine years later. Ashamed but still angry, he stormed from the room, and J. J. heard glasses breaking in the kitchen and his mother's voice.

"John. Stop. Just stop! You're only making it all worse."

And then his father was back, pointing at J. J. and jabbing that finger into his collarbone. "I'll tell you what else. That family had the courage to invite everyone back again next Saturday. And you're coming with me."

Despite the physical pain and the hurt of his father's words, J. J. was adamant. "No, I'm not."

His father thrust his face close to J. J.'s and nodded emphatically, his expression an ugly mask of mottled rage. "Yes! You! ARE!" John stormed from the room, leaving J. J. shaking and cowering. Out of the corner of his eye, he saw his sister, who was staring from the doorway.

Without thinking, he reached out and grabbed her by the hair. "What are you looking at? Huh? HUH!" He yanked her hair, and she screamed and tried to pry his hands away. Disgusted, he let go and turned to leave.

"You did it," she said.

He realized he had snot spilling from his nose over the bottom half of his face. "I did what? I didn't do anything."

"Yes, you did." She was starting to cry, from both shock and pain. "You did it with my best friend. Why? What's wrong with you? She was my best friend." She started to shake with sobs.

"So? I'm supposed to care?"

Her mouth clenched closed, and she flailed at him with her fists. "I hate you! I hate you!"

"Yeah, well—fuck off." He walked to the stairs, paused, and glanced toward his mother, who had a freshly filled glass and was looking in the direction of the front window and the street, refusing to look at him.

He shook his head, went upstairs, and turned on the TV.

• • •

The three boys agreed that burglarizing Steve's Liquors right away was preferable to first stealing Torahs from the synagogue. There was no money in the Torahs; it was as simple as that.

Benny Boone was to be the lookout, and Ricky Taylor the driver. Ernie was to do the burglarizing. They had been assured by Scotty Findell, who worked part-time at Steve's, that the alarm would be off.

On Monday and Friday mornings, Steve took the store's receipts to the bank, so it was agreed that a Sunday night, after a busy Friday and Saturday, would be the best time to do the job.

Ernie had only to break a window in the back door to get in and make sure to set the alarm as he was leaving; the broken window would trigger the alarm as they left, yet leave the trio time to get away while keeping Scotty, who would leave the alarm off, in the clear.

At first, the job went according to plan. The alarm was off; Ernie broke the window, fumbled a moment with the register, but managed to open it and exhaled his surprise and delight at the thick stacks of twenties, tens, and fives inside.

He stuffed the money into his pants pocket and was hurrying toward the street, where Ricky Taylor was idling in his chartreuse 1971 Plymouth Barracuda, with its flat-black rear quarter panels. As Ernie neared the Plymouth, he heard Benny Boone's frantic voice.

"Fuckin' cop car!"

Ernie stopped and turned back toward Steve's just as the alarm went off. He turned and sprinted away from the street, to the fence behind the store, jumped up, and grasped the top railing and a handful of fence as he flung his legs over the top and dropped to the ground in the yard of a bar that fronted Rockaway Avenue.

He knew not to run. The cops would be all over him if he ran. He could hear the sirens of police cars as they converged on the scene behind him. He exhaled, the sweat on his forehead evaporating in the cool night air.

"Hey! Yeah, you!"

He slowed and turned. Nassau police car #518 had slowed and was creeping along beside him.

"Yes, sir." He stopped, his arms at his sides.

"What's that you got in your pocket?"

Ernie tried to remember if police were allowed to search someone walking along the street and what constituted probable cause—a frequent topic of conversation at the trestle and the creek behind the high school. He didn't know the answer, but he was pretty sure the police could do whatever they wanted and say whatever they wanted about it later. His only option was to run.

He was caught three blocks, two fences, and four yards later, and hauled down to the police station, followed shortly thereafter by his parents, who had taken his one phone call, then closed the diner early to bail out their son.

• • •

John Welles sat in his living room chair listening to the Yankees game on his transistor radio. The broadcast transported him out of his head for a time; it gave him something to focus on that was outside himself, and that was a blessing. He deeply regretted losing his temper with his son, but at the same time, he wished the boy were better behaved. He understood that his temper, which was out of control now and then, was probably connected to the traumas of his military service. He had no real friends; he seemed to have lost the ability to develop and maintain friendships. His neighbors were okay, but he had little in common with them. When he had seen the party invitation and Connie told him who it was from, he had been intrigued. He had overheard J. J. and Joanne talking about the controversies surrounding the Thomas family's arrival in the neighborhood, and he felt sorry for them. He lived much of the time in a purposeful, mindless haze that blurred his memories, but this invitation brought to the here and now some of the reasons he had fought in the war, and he had decided to support the family who had sent the invitation, though he did not think there was very much he could do besides show up. Socializing was beyond him, and he did not expect his family to understand or to attend the party, but now there was to be another party, and he was going to make sure J. J. attended. He had lost control of the boy and now grasped at the dim hope that being around some people who had different life experiences might be good for his son.

• • •

When John launched into his rages, Connie retreated further into her alcohol-fueled cocoon. Like her husband, Connie lived in her head, but it was a head full of memories of a happy childhood, of playing tag, of happy neighbors hanging around outside on their stoops, and of selling lemonade on street corners. She had loved to dance; she had loved Frank Sinatra and Mel Tormé; later, she had developed a wild streak, and, for a few years that coincided with her engagement and marriage, she learned to love Little Richard and Chuck Berry. John Welles was a mysterious bad boy, a strong, quiet war hero who had chosen her, and Connie had shown him off to the girls around the neighborhood at the VFW dances and when they were out at restaurants. Though he never spoke about the war, she had read in magazines that many men had been through terrible times and had seen awful things. She had made up her mind to leave John alone and never to be that wife who tried to pull him out of a morass of troubles she could never understand. She would wait.

But the morass was emotional quicksand, and with time it only deepened and pulled him down. So she did the only thing that had served her over time: she drank. She also gardened. Seeing the roses, irises, lilies, and hostas thrive around their property gave her satisfaction that her children rarely did. She did not understand her children. Life in the 1960s and 1970s was so much more complicated than it had been when she was a child.

She wished John would work. He looked healthy enough to her; he could mow the lawn and paint the house, so why couldn't he find some kind of work so they might have a newer car, or a steak now and then? Their dirty white Dodge Dart with its push-button transmission was ten years old. The GI Bill had enabled the Welles family to buy a home in the suburbs, and had gotten John some counseling for what was referred to as "shell shock." He had also started college, but quickly decided that a secondary education was not for him. He had never explained to Connie that he could not focus for more than a moment or two on schoolwork. Instead, he told her he would rather do "real work," and took a class on fixing cars, worked part-time at a gas station on

Rockaway Avenue, and did odd jobs for contractors and neighbors in the area.

He remained as silent with Connie as he'd been when they first met. She longed for the day that he would open up to her about his troubles and she could hold his head to her breast and comfort him. She didn't need to know the details and had never asked; she had assumed he would come to her, with or without explanation, seeking love and comfort from his wife. But he never did, and Connie was left with the fading image of the home and family she had longed for, and her disapproval of the homes and families of neighbors made plain to her through the living room window.

She was surprised and confused that John wanted to go to the Thomases' party, particularly because he had never even asked her to go.

• • •

Though it was only a week later, the second rehearsal found Debbie in the same swooning frame of mind as the first. She knew her parts and had worked out structured semi-improvisations that built on the music she had developed for the first rehearsal, parts that had delighted Bonni. She had also worked out parts for what she knew would be two new songs—"Me and Bobby McGee" and "Stoney End"—songs sung by female artists that would show off Bonni's unique timbre and impressive vocal range.

So the change in Bonni's reaction came as a shock to Debbie, who had begun to think of herself as "Bonni Bird's flutist"; she had even daydreamed of dropping the *e* from the end of her name. When they finished, Bonni turned to Debbie and stared at her, then cocked her head slightly as though trying to understand what she had just heard.

"What the hell do you think you're doing?"

Debbie looked at everyone there, casting about for an answer she had thought was not only obvious but appreciated. "I'm playing flute."

"Riiight." Bonni smiled and turned to each of the other band members, holding the gaze of each for a brief moment before turning back to Debbie. She blew a raspberry, bubbling her lips. "And I just sang a new song! Did you like it?"

Debbie's face grew hot, and she knew she was blushing. "I— I— I don't understand."

"Well, I can see that."

"B- b- but you liked what I played last time."

Bonni looked surprised. "Did I? I don't remember that." She turned to the other members of the band. "Did I ever say that I liked this girl's playing?"

The band members all looked at one another and shrugged or shook their heads.

Debbie managed to fight through the rest of the rehearsal, but was mindful of Bonni shaking her head and sighing after each song and emphasizing that, "This is exactly how you will play this song." Her instructions were so specific and arcane that it was all Debbie could do to follow them. By the end of the rehearsal, her blouse was stuck to her back and she was sure she smelled of sweat and trauma. She couldn't wait to get out of there.

After the last note of the last song, she pulled her flute apart, laid the pieces in the fitted velour cushions of her case, threw her coat over her arm, and ran out to her car. Then, as she was driving up the street, she stopped and sat still for a long moment. She had left her handkerchief on the table; it was her grandmother's handkerchief, which Debbie used to clean her flute. She would have to go back.

As she turned the car around and drove slowly back to Bonni's house, she saw the other band members filing out the door and down the brick steps. She waited until they had driven away; none gave her so much as a glance.

Debbie went up the walk, climbed the steps, holding on to the cold, black wrought iron railing, and knocked on the door, but there was no answer. She knocked again and then opened the door and went inside.

"Hello?" She stood still and listened. "Hello?" she called again. The stairway down to the basement where the rehearsals were held was to her left, and she took a few tentative steps down and listened again, then decided she would head downstairs, grab the handkerchief, and get out of there. Wherever Bonni was—in the upstairs living area, probably—she couldn't possibly mind, but Debbie didn't dwell on the question, given what the last two hours had been like.

But when she got to the bottom of the stairs, all she could do was stand, rooted to the spot, her mouth slightly open.

Bonni was slumped sideways in a plush, leather armchair, her head thrown back, her right arm—the arm closest to Debbie—extended along the chair's armrest, a piece of rubber tubing tied around her forearm, the other arm resting, half open, across her chest, on which lay an empty syringe. She was snoring softly. Debbie stood for another moment, tiptoed into the rehearsal room, grabbed her handkerchief, and rushed up the stairs and out to her car.

• • •

J. J. made sure to keep his head down and his mouth shut, and to walk straight home from school across the field rather than pass by either of the gates or the path to the creek. He wanted to be as invisible as possible—offering as little chance as he could for anyone to say anything about his father and sister going to that party. He was particularly concerned about Ernie, who had a habit of saying exactly what you didn't want him to say and at the worst possible moment. But a rumor was going around about Ernie, and by lunchtime on Monday, J. J. had learned that the rumor was true.

The week crept by and mercifully no one said anything to J. J. about the party or his father or sister having attended it. By Wednesday, he was focused on the next party, which his father had told him he would have to attend.

• • •

On Thursday evening, Tom Kelly was sitting in his squad car listening to Game Five of the World Series. Game Four had been a wild celebration of the great Rusty Staub, who seemed to have cemented his place in all-time Mets lore. Game Five was a pitcher's duel, with both

Jerry Koosman and Vida Blue pitching well. By the time Tug McGraw entered the game, Tom decided that the Mets would probably win, and he left his car and went into Dericos' Diner for a cup of coffee, a muffin, and what he knew would be an unpleasant conversation.

Lou had the game on a transistor radio behind the counter. He looked up at the tinkle of the bells hung on the door, saw it was Tom, and nodded a little too quickly. He was pouring the mug as he asked, without looking up, "Coffee?"

Tom didn't answer. A moment later, a blueberry muffin appeared on a plate, next to the coffee.

"Not toasting the muffins tonight, Lou?"

Lou looked apologetic. "Sorry, Tom. I'll take care of it." He came over and reached to pick up the plate that held the muffin, but Tom had a firm hold of the plate, his lips pressed together in a little grin, shaking his head.

"I'm kidding, Lou. I don't take my muffin toasted."

"Oh, right."

Tom felt for the man and understood his stress. He saw stress just like it nearly every day. They listened to the rest of the game together and breathed twin sighs of relief when the Mets won, with McGraw getting the save.

"Looks like they might do it," Lou began.

"Why would you say that?" Tom slammed the counter with his palm, rattling his coffee cup and making the crumbs on his plate jump. The muffin itself didn't move. Dericos' muffins were known for their density and weight.

"What?" Lou wanted to know.

Tom glared back. "You can't say a thing like that. Now they'll never win. Hold on." He closed his eyes. "Oakland will win the Series. Oakland will win the Series. Oakland will win the Series." He exhaled and looked relieved.

Lou looked baffled. "What was that all about?"

"Undoing your evil eye with a bit of my own. Learned it from my Aunt Molly, but I won't tell you a thing about it, so don't ask."

Lou leaned forward and spoke softly. "There's something I did want to ask."

Tom nodded. "I know. Was waiting for it. Can't say for sure. A judge has leeway, but—" He shook his head. "How old is your boy?"

Lou studied the countertop. "Sixteen."

"He's a man before the law."

Lou stared at the Formica for a long moment. "What will they give him?"

Tom shrugged. "Depends. If the judge's wife wore the right nighty the night before, he might go easy on him. On the other hand, technically, you're looking at third-degree burglary—a class D felony and, since he had over a grand on him, fourth-degree larceny."

"*Madon*'! Both?"

Tom nodded and raised his eyebrows, then he thought of something. "Say, you didn't go to that party at those new people's house last week, did you?"

Lou paused as though he did not understand, though he did. Then he shook his head. "Nope."

Tom nodded as though this were the answer he expected. "Understand they're having another this week."

"That so?" Lou said, sounding disinterested, though, with the news he had been given about his son and Tom Kelly's lack of even a speck of compassion, he had just made his mind up to go to the party in question.

• • •

Debbie gave up trying to sleep. Her mind was too full of images, questions, ideas, musical phrases, lyrics, and feelings. She accepted what she had seen in Bonni Bird's basement at face value, but there was also shock value. She had heard of kids, especially older, legendary kids, who did hard drugs, but she had yet to wrap her mind around someone shooting up all but right there in front of her. The impact to her psyche was beyond her comprehension. She did not understand how Bonni could have done what she did, so she gave up trying and

121

went on with her life, steering clear of Bonni Bird and staying away from the phone—she let Laurie answer it or she let it ring. Her parents were always at the diner, so they never answered anyway. No one of any importance would complain if their calls went unanswered; she couldn't be blamed for not being around.

She had some ideas about what she had seen, but they seemed beyond her reach, and the little she understood was a bizarre combination of feelings and thoughts. She was accustomed to having feelings she did not understand; that was the soil in which her music flourished.

While she thought of heroin as a destructive power that had no connection to her, she also knew that many of the world's best musicians were attracted to the drug. So while she was repulsed by what she had seen and had decided to stay away from Bonni and her band, she was strangely attracted in a way that was all the more powerful because it was forbidden while being strangely chic.

She went back to practicing her scales, her arpeggios, and her Mozart, Bach, and Gluck, while her subconscious mind gnawed and chewed, presenting her with disturbing ideas and images.

Chapter 15

"Dad."

"Yeah, Jimmy. What's up?" Tom had opened the door and taken a step outside, but when he heard Jimmy call, he stepped back in and closed the door.

"I know you're heading to work. I can ask you later."

"No, no. What kind of father would I be if I didn't have a minute for my boy?"

"Um. Am I supposed to answer that?"

Tom laughed. "That's what we call a rhetorical question."

Jimmy looked confused. "Sooo, *am* I supposed to answer it?"

"A rhetorical question is when the question kind of implies the answer."

"I'm still not sure, but if you think I should answer, just let me know."

"I'll do that, son. Meantime, how 'bout we sit down on the couch."

"Sure, Dad."

Once they were seated, Tom waited. After a moment he cleared his throat. "What is it you wanted to know, Jimmy?"

"Oh, right. I almost forgot. So, um, if you have a friend, and he does something wrong, should he still be your friend?"

Tom nodded a few times. "That's not an easy question, and in different situations you might have different answers."

"Ohh." Jimmy sounded disappointed.

"It's something you have to decide for yourself."

Jimmy nodded and continued to look disappointed. "Okay. You can go to work now, Dad."

Tom gave a hearty laugh. "Well, thank you, Jim." He stood up and went to the door, then turned. "I'll tell you this, though."

"Yeah, Dad?"

"Loyalty between friends is really, really important."

Jimmy considered this. "So, even if a guy's friend does something wrong, it might make sense to be there for him?"

"That would be for you—or a guy—to decide. But maybe so."

• • •

"Come on, John. Let's go." John Welles stood in the doorway, tapping the aluminum frame with his key ring, one foot propping the screen door open. He looked at the ceiling and sighed. "Joanne! Come on."

"Is my brother going?" Joanne called from the top of the stairs.

"Yes, he is, and so are you."

"No, Daddy, I'm not—not if my brother's going."

"Your brother has a name."

"I know it."

John closed his eyes for a long moment; then he took a deep breath. "J. J.! Get down here!"

J. J. all but tumbled down the steps, in a hurry to forestall his father's wrath. He had hoped his father would have forgotten having told him he was coming to the party. Why did they have to throw so many parties? And why did they have to invite strangers? And couldn't the kids at school understand that his father was making him do this? Going to this party wasn't his choice; it was the last thing he wanted to do.

The car had been sitting in the afternoon sun, so J. J. opened the little triangular vent window on the passenger's side of the front seat. He looked out the window, hoping that looking away might keep his father's anger at bay. The strategy seemed to work, as his father started the car and began to drive, without saying another word.

J. J. had tried to explain to his father that he would never live down going to this party, but his father neither understood nor cared. So J. J. asked why his mother wasn't going.

"Your mother's a grown woman who makes her own decisions," his father told him.

"Well, what about Joanne?"

The look his father gave him told him that the conversation was over, which was just as well. He didn't want to be anywhere near his sister.

• • •

Since she was a child, Debbie Derico had thought of herself as apart from the rest of the world. Of course, many of us do exactly that as part of the development of our sense of self. We see what others allow us to see, and because we cannot see the interior worlds of others, we lump them together as being different from us and the same as one another. Eventually, we get to know some people well enough to understand that they have their own inner experience, and to them, that experience has as much depth as our own does to us. While this growth of understanding happened for Debbie, she had long since developed her own process for coping with the alienation she often experienced around other people. Debbie had her own process and her own language—music. Listening to music calmed her; playing music, chiefly the flute, engaged her on every level: physical, mental, emotional, and spiritual.

She badly wanted to be accepted by Bonni Bird and to be a part of Bonni's band, and her successful audition had been one of the happiest moments of her life. For Debbie, such moments were rare, not because they were happy, but because they depended upon others. So when Debbie had found Bonni in the immediate aftermath of her shooting dope, she had been deeply conflicted. She experienced a deep desire to be accepted by Bonni, along with an equally deep revulsion at what she had just seen, and the conflict was all the more difficult because she was unable to transcend it with music.

Debbie had gone home and, as always, set up to practice and began her long tones, followed by her chromatics, followed by blues and pentatonic sequences and progressions that were as deeply experienced and to which she was as powerfully drawn as to prayer.

But for the first time, her music didn't work. She kept trying; she kept playing. She played the parts she had composed for Bonni Bird's tunes. She played songs she had been playing since she was a child. She played ideas that were beyond her reach and at which she had been aiming with her practice for many months. She kept playing. She did not know what else to do. But for the first time in memory, the music, the magic, didn't work; she did not feel better.

• • •

J. J. decided that since he had to be at this party or risk his father's wrath, the best approach would be to be as quiet as he could be, and somehow get through what promised to be an extremely unpleasant Saturday night.

"Hey, J. J.!" He knew that voice. He looked, and sure enough, Laurie was there. He should have known she would be there, and there was no mistaking that look in her eye. She was thinking sex, remembering sex, and somehow wordlessly pulling him back into sex. She was reeling him in or trying to. What could he do about it? Maybe it was all in his mind—but he didn't think so. She gave off some kind of magnetic force he could feel just below the level of his skin. He wondered if he could deal with her by nodding, smiling, and ignoring her.

He was equally repulsed, but in a very different way, by his father. But repulsed wasn't quite right. Terrified. That was it—terrified.

He could feel Laurie looking at him, so he looked back and tried to smile. She licked her lips. Mortified, he looked away. Girls should not be allowed to treat boys this way; it was…it was … He didn't know what it was, but it wasn't good. So he looked at Dwayne, who also was looking at Laurie with fear, but a different kind of fear.

"Your brother," Dwayne began, pointing at Laurie. "Your brother is Ernie. Ernie is your brother. Your brother is Ernie."

Laurie had been looking at J. J., amusement plain on her face, but as she turned to Dwayne, she gave a baffled shrug. "Yup, Ernie is my brother."

Dwayne pressed his lips together and moaned, his body swiveling—turning halfway around in one direction, then the other. When he continued to moan, J. J. saw Mrs. Thomas give a pointed nod to her daughter, who went to Dwayne and pulled him to her in a hug. He continued to moan, his face against his sister's neck—but the timbre of his moan was different—less plaintive and more comforted. Elly stroked the side of his face and spoke softly to Dwayne, whose moans dwindled to coos and hums and then vanished altogether. Elly took Dwayne by the hand and led him to the stairs, where they sat together, holding hands, watching the party through the balusters—the decorative spindles that held up the banisters, which rose up from the bottom three steps on the staircase.

Only then did J. J. notice the other people in the room—Lou Derico, Erin and Julie Kelly, Shirley and Elvin Thomas Jr., and Makayla Thomas.

The long, uncomfortable moment was broken by Erin Kelly. "Lou, my son Jimmy tells me your boy's had a bit of trouble."

Lou Derico looked stricken. He was wearing a brown corduroy sport jacket over a crisp yellow shirt, brown pants, and a matching tie. Now he examined his tie and didn't answer.

"I only ask because I know how hard it is with kids nowadays. All sorts of trouble. I have two, so I know."

Lou looked up from his tie.

Erin continued. "And my husband. Tom. He might be a police officer, but he's like a kid who wanders into trouble." When no one said anything, she nodded emphatically. "Really!" She continued, speaking rapidly, perhaps chased by the silence in the room. "I believe my Jimmy is a friend to your son."

"Yes," said Lou Derico.

"Yes, he's a friend of your son's?"

"Yes, my boy's been in some trouble. It seems he'll be going to jail for a little while."

Erin Kelly put a hand to her mouth. Julie Kelly took her mother's other hand.

But it was Elvin Thomas Jr. who continued the conversation. "You're right, Erin," came his gravelly reply. "It's hard having kids these days. It's hard being a parent. It's hard being a child, a husband, a wife …"

"A neighbor," Shirley finished for her husband.

"Amen," Makayla said, vehemently shaking her head.

"What I mean," Elvin continued, "is that we're new in the neigh-borhood. That hasn't been easy for us, and from what I've been told, it hasn't been easy for you."

"Oh," Erin said, waving him away, "that isn't so!"

"It *is* so," Shirley answered. "There's plenty of trouble to go round."

"So," Elvin looked at his wife, "what I want to say is, thank you. We had no idea if anyone would respond to our invitations." He looked at his wife. "At least I didn't, and your being here has made a difference for us."

J. J. looked at Mr. Thomas, then toward the stairs, where he could feel the Thomas daughter, Elly, looking at him, but this was not the same feeling as Laurie's unspoken magnetism; this was a gentle smile of a feeling.

Julie Kelly cleared her throat. "How are you finding your new teaching job, Mr. Thomas?"

Erin turned and looked at her daughter with such surprise that J. J. couldn't help but laugh to himself. He had that smiling feeling again, looked toward the stairs, and saw Elly giggling and looking at him.

"I like it," Elvin said with a kind smile. "I love teaching. I love lit-erature. Truly, we would not have been able to make this move if it weren't for my job."

"And even then, for some of us," Shirley said, drawing a sharp look from her husband.

"I'm sure I'll like it even more," he continued, "once I get to know the kids a little better."

"You teach English?" Julie asked, as her mother looked at her in amazement.

"That I do."

"Who are your favorite authors?" she continued.

He smiled and shrugged. "There are so many. Who doesn't love Shakespeare?"

Lou and Erin put up their hands, looked at one another, and laughed.

"Fair enough," Elvin said with a chuckle. "I confess to having a strong social conscience. So, I would have to say James Baldwin and Lorraine Hansberry." He paused. "And you?"

Julie nodded, expecting the question. "I like John Steinbeck."

"A worthy choice, young lady," Elvin said.

"Really?" Erin breathed, staring at her daughter, then turned to Elvin. "Isn't Mr. Baldwin a Negro writer?"

"Well, he's a writer and he's a Black man, but I don't know that I would call him a Negro writer."

"He's friendly with Marlon Brando, isn't he?"

J. J. was surprised that the question had come from his own father. He had never imagined his father as having any connection to literature, or actors, for that matter. He thought of his father as a silent, wounded, rather terrifying force of nature.

"As a matter of fact, yes, he is." Elvin Jr. smiled.

"Is there anything Mr. Baldwin wrote," Erin asked, "that would shed light on life for all of us, not only for the Negro?"

Elvin Jr. appraised Erin Kelly for a moment, then said. "All good literature is for and about humans—and sheds light on our human experience. Except," he chuckled to himself, "for some works by E. B. White and Richard Bach, which shed light on human experience by anthropomorphizing animals." He looked around and tipped his head back. "When he was ten years old, Mr. Baldwin wrote a play that was directed by a teacher at his school. She saw how talented and special this student of hers was, and offered to take him to plays, which, because this teacher was white, led to a backlash from Baldwin's stepfather. Mr. Baldwin's mother gave permission, though Baldwin noticed his stepfather's disgust when the teacher came to pick him up. That was a frightening situation, and later, Baldwin realized it was frightening for his parents too—it was a risk in their eyes, because of the way they were accustomed to seeing Black families treated by white folks." He paused and looked each of them in the eyes. "That situation reminds me of this one. The one my family finds ourselves in. We are doing unexpected things. We did by moving here, and we've paid a price. My family, my children particularly, have paid a price." He looked with both sadness and kindness at his two children, who still sat on the stairs, their hands clasped together. "Baldwin later understood that his father went along with that situation against his own will, against his own experience. That must have been difficult." While Elvin Jr. was speaking, his father came down the stairs; Elly and Dwayne shifted to the side to allow their grandfather to pass.

"You've all met my father, Elvin Sr."

Everyone murmured a greeting, and Elvin Sr. looked at each of them, finally fixing his stare on John Welles, who stared right back at him.

"Were you in the war?" Elvin Sr. asked.

John Welles didn't answer but gave a barely perceptible nod. The Thomas patriarch continued. "I was in the Great War, the war to end all wars, and—"

"Combat?" John Welles asked, his lone eye unblinking.

Elvin Sr. shook his head. "I wasn't a soldier. Few of us were allowed to be. I saw combat—in the faces of men like you. I recognized it soon as I came downstairs. My son served too. So, yes, I saw combat. And I know about shell shock, and I learned that there are people who can help with that."

"Why are you telling me this?" John Welles asked.

Elvin Sr. shrugged. The intensity had gone out of his voice. "Just making conversation."

J. J. had the sudden sense he was being watched, looked around, and saw Elly, still seated with her brother on the stairs, watching him intently. She smiled.

J. J. smiled back, blushed, then looked away.

Chapter 16

Over the next several days, members of each family who had been guests at the Thomases' party had similar experiences in the community.

Laurie Derico stopped by one of the neighborhood delis for a sandwich and a soda and was told she was not welcome and would not be served.

Julie Kelly, who had auditioned for the school choir, was told she had failed her audition.

J. J. walked up the road that ended at the high school and, as he approached the main gate, was called over by Ricky Taylor and Benny Boone, who called him nasty names that referenced his friendship with the Thomas family and roughed him up—not hurting him physically, but frightening him and bruising his feelings.

He went to English class, where the work of the writer Lorraine Hansberry was discussed. Members of the class took turns reading from Hansberry's autobiographical play, *To Be Young, Gifted and Black*. J. J. was pleasantly surprised to find that he understood the play, which was written in easy-to-understand language he could absorb and follow without having to tease meaning from each word.

At the party, Elvin Thomas had talked about Hansberry, who died of pancreatic cancer only eight years earlier, when in her mid-thirties.

The Hansberry family had purchased a home in the south side of Chicago, where a covenant had been in force that barred Black families. The Hansberry family was represented in court by the civil rights attorney Earl B. Dickerson, who successfully fought the covenant, allowing the Hansberry family access to the neighborhood.

John Welles never mentioned to anyone that he had been told to buy his gas elsewhere when he'd driven in to fill up his tank the following Saturday; Lou Derico never mentioned the sudden drop-off in customers at his diner in the days following the Thomas parties, and Officer Tom Kelly barely noticed the sudden racist tinge to the near-constant ribbing and banter coming from some of his fellow officers.

At the same time, John Welles was still welcomed at the local hardware store; Lou and Anna Derico still served many of their neighbors at Dericos' Diner, and Tom and Erin Kelly remained well-respected among much of the community of police families.

J. J. began arriving at school as close to the late bell as possible, spending little time at the school gate; and he began leaving the building at the end of the day by little-used exit doors that opened onto the athletic fields or teachers' parking lots.

• • •

On the Tuesday before Thanksgiving, J. J. was hurrying home. He rarely saw Jimmy Kelly anymore, except from afar, walking Lucy. Jimmy seemed to no longer be around. J. J. did not know why. Ernie was now doing time at the county jail.

J. J. would leave the school building as soon as possible and hurry away from school grounds. The reaction of the older, tougher boys frightened him, and he wanted to stay clear of them in the hopes that they would forget about him. The strategy seemed to be working.

As he walked southwest on the north side of Forest Avenue, he saw out of the corner of his eye Elly Thomas and her brother, Dwayne, walking parallel to him and slightly behind on the south side of the street. He stopped, turned toward them, and smiled. He saw words pass between brother and sister, then Elly jogged across the street to where J. J. was standing, while Dwayne continued on. The two did not speak, but walked together until they arrived at a point where their paths diverged in the directions of their respective homes. Elly glanced at J. J. then, and he looked back at her and gave the same little nod he reserved for his friends—a lifting of his chin.

He looked for her the next day, but saw neither Elly nor Dwayne, and he found himself thinking of her as he ate his Thanksgiving dinner of turkey, stuffing, string beans with almonds, and cranberry sauce.

The weather turned chilly over the next few weeks, which saw cold rains and the first flurries of snow.

Several letters to the local newspaper protested unwanted changes to the neighborhood, ostensibly brought on by greedy, overzealous realtors showing local homes to "the wrong people."

J. J. began walking home from school with Elly every day, with Dwayne walking with them, albeit on the other side of the street as though affording the pair a level of privacy they didn't really need since neither J. J. nor Elly ever said a word. Elly would give him a shy smile as she and her brother broke away toward their home, and J. J. would nod back as he headed toward his own.

The last week of November, Shirley Thomas sent out invitations for a party that was to be held on December 23rd, so as not to conflict with her guests' holiday parties on Christmas Eve or Christmas Day.

• • •

In the middle of the afternoon a few days later, Debbie phoned Bonni Bird and asked to come by. Bonni's tone was brusque, even sharp; she said she didn't care one way or another—which was okay with Debbie, who had a plan.

When she arrived, she sat quietly while Bonni made herself a cheese sandwich on white bread with a little mustard, and was pleasantly surprised when Bonni offered her one. She gratefully accepted though she didn't much like mustard. She was careful not to be too demonstratively grateful; she intuitively knew that that would not go over well. She had brought her flute, but Bonni didn't seem much interested in music. She sat on the couch with her sandwich, reading the latest issue of *Rolling Stone.*

Debbie sat quietly; Bonni offered her a glass of iced tea, which Debbie politely declined. A few minutes later, Debbie asked for a glass of water, and Bonni pointed to a cabinet over the sink. Debbie poured herself some water and swished it around her mouth. If Bonni wanted to play music, Debbie wanted to be prepared and to be sure not to spray crumbs into her instrument.

Eventually, Bonni gave Debbie a long look and said, "Listen, I've got stuff to do downstairs, so—"

Debbie quickly said, "Let me come."

The two girls looked at one another for a long moment, then Bonni cocked her head and gave Debbie a questioning look.

"I saw you," Debbie said. "Last time."

Bonni was shocked. "Aw, shit!"

"It's okay," Debbie said quickly. "I mean, I want to try."

Bonni looked away then—at the floor, then at the clock on the far wall. Debbie waited. Finally, Bonni stood up. "Come on."

She led Debbie to the stairs to the basement and the plush armchair in which Debbie had found her on her previous visit. Bonni sat Debbie down in the chair and gently leaned her back. "You sure?" she asked.

Debbie nodded, frightened yet excited.

Bonni took a bag from behind the chair and removed the rubber cord, one of several syringes, a lighter, and a spoon. Then she opened a leather case that was affixed to her belt and took out a tiny clear vial with a black top. She unscrewed the vial and tapped some light-brown powder into the spoon. She tied the rubber around Debbie's forearm.

"Arm okay?"

Debbie shrugged. She didn't know. She was certain that her parents were so busy with the diner that they would never think to look at her arms. And it was just this one time.

A moment later, she was in another world. The basement and Bonni had disappeared, and she was in a world that abounded with senses that transcended sight, sound, smell, and touch. The world was one of gorgeous feeling. Magnificent feeling. Like flying with a glorious pressure on her brain.

She had a vague sense of sitting back—of being unable to hold her head up. Of vanishing into a tunnel of love. Of returning to the room and seeing Bonni beside her on the floor, her arms on Debbie's knees, a grin on her face. The two girls hugged, and then kissed, and then Debbie wanted her flute. She wanted to play, and for Bonni to play with her.

So that is what they did. For an hour. For two hours.

Then Debbie wanted to go outside. To see the outside this way. Through her new ideas, and with her new senses.

So she went outside, spun around on the lawn, stumbled onto the sidewalk, then back onto the lawn. She stepped into the street.

She never saw the school bus.

Chapter 17

Dericos' Diner remained closed for two weeks, and when they re-opened, Anna was no longer there. With Ernie in jail and Debbie gone, there were only Laurie—overwhelmed, grief-stricken, and bitter, who served—and her father—gaunt and haggard and resigned. Lou prepared the food, with assists from Marshall, the tall, lean assistant *cum sous-chef.* Laurie helped Maria serve during nonschool hours, with Marshall and her father staffing the kitchen.

Though her father did not know it, Laurie had stopped attending school and spent her days outdoors, along the creek near the high school with Ricky Taylor, whose long hair, bony body, and cigarette smell attracted her and papered over the frightened, grieving parts of her consciousness. He was what she needed. She'd been surprised to see him at the wake and made sure to catch his eye, and, when he saw her, to look brazenly at him, sending him a message of her intentions.

On some level, Laurie blamed the Thomas family for Ernie's incarceration and Debbie's death. She did not understand why, but she nurtured a hatred of that family, and now that she was with Ricky, she had no time for nor thought of J. J.

When she was with Ricky, her mind was shut to her ever-encroaching, ever-growing demons, which came for her when she was at the diner and when she was drifting off to sleep at night. She did her best to focus on her work, and it was all she could do to keep from hurling plates of spaghetti, meatloaf, or soup at her family or customers, or against a wall. One day, when Elvin Thomas Jr. came in, she stayed in the kitchen, hoping he would get the message and leave, but he remained, and she served him two roast beef sandwiches on kaiser rolls with ketchup to go.

Her other respite was Joanne, who for some reason had decided to begin visiting Ernie at the jail. Laurie could not for the life of her figure out why anyone would want anything to do with her brother. He was no good, and his having committed a burglary proved it!

After several months apart, which Laurie knew was because Joanne had been upset about her involvement with J. J., the girls cautiously circled one another, and, eventually, Joanne asked Laurie over, and they again pooled the alcohol they stole from their parents, as they had in the past. They didn't talk much; there was little for them to say to one another. So they drank, listened to music, danced a little bit, and were entertained by Sorry the cat, who was not really a kitten anymore and who had somehow found a way out of the Welles home and begun roaming the neighborhood, looking for a mate.

Laurie knew the feeling.

• • •

It was a chilly Sunday afternoon in the second week of December 1973. The Thomas family was seated at the dinner table, except for Dwayne, who was in the living room, doing schoolwork. He had finished the weekend's required homework and launched ahead into theoretical, yet very real, math problems that would be covered in the coming days. Dwayne had explained this desire and habit to his bewildered family as his "Christmas math"—not because of the time of year, but because of the joy he felt when he approached new problems, theories, and the wonderful mathematical structures he was learning in his advanced geometry and trigonometry classes.

Wanda had accompanied Shirley and the children to church—something she insisted on whenever she came to stay a weekend. They went to ten o'clock Mass together in their Sunday best, then came home and relaxed as a family for a few hours, until Sunday dinner, which was between two and three in the afternoon.

Between them, Wanda and Shirley carried a large white china bowl of vegetables that had been simmering in cider vinegar, a matching plate of baked ham, a platter of bread pudding, and another of rice pudding. A chocolate cake sat on the kitchen counter, waiting its turn. Elly's offer of help had been refused, so she sat quietly with her father and grandparents at the table.

Makayla and Papa Elvin didn't see much of their grandchildren during the week, since they retired early—usually soon after dinner—while the children were still doing their homework. Today, for the first time all week, the grandparents had Elly to themselves, with Dwayne in the living room, within earshot.

Elly had been talking about the books she was reading—*The Great Gatsby, The Catcher in the Rye, To Kill a Mockingbird, Lord of the Flies,* and *Of Mice and Men.* She admitted that she understood only the last three of these well enough to discuss them, particularly because she understood the hurtful behavior demonstrated by people in those stories. In Elly's experience, these were the more true-to-life of the class's assigned literature.

Shirley and Wanda had just sat down, Elvin Jr. was carving the ham, and the grandparents were listening to Elly wind down her explanation of English class and begin explaining about the essays she would be writing for that class over the weekend.

"This," Makayla said, after chewing and swallowing a forkful of ham, "is heaven."

"Mm-hmm," Elvin Sr. said. He was holding up his fork, on which thick, dripping, pungent strands of vegetables were wound. He was turning the fork every which way, examining its contents.

Shirley was serving bread pudding, and Wanda was looking at her plate, her head giving sharp jerks as though she was repeatedly trying to say something and could not. "I do not—cannot understand why you would want to antagonize your neighborhood by insisting on throwing this party in the aftermath of such a tragedy!"

Shirley pulled her head back and dropped her chin. "What? What are you saying? We are bringing people together!"

"White folks ain't gon' see it that way." Wanda's tone and the cadence of her speech changed as she grew angrier. "You just watch. They gon' put this, this, whatever it is—their problems—on you. They gon' think we're *celebrating* their problems!"

Shirley shook her head slowly. "Wanda! Come on!"

"No, they're not." Elvin Jr. was poised with his fork halfway to his mouth. "That hasn't been our experience with the folks we've met here." He looked at Wanda with curiosity more than agitation. "Not most of them, anyway."

Makayla's eyes were looking hard at Wanda, unblinking. "These parties are the right thing, for everyone concerned, whatever anyone thinks! They're about love. We've been putting our best food forward."

Elvin had begun making a small sound, deep in his throat. No one heard him, but if they had, they would have heard what sounded like, "Huh? Huh?"

Wanda's lips were pressed together, and she was vigorously shaking her head; her hair, which had been sprayed in place, was flying. Deep down she was terrified for her friends, but her fear came out as vehemence. "Why're you even living here? What're you trying to prove? That you're white? It's goin' to come down on you. You'll see!"

Elvin Sr. was frowning at his fork, turning it vigorously in front of his eyes. The sound he'd been making was louder now. A desperate croaking of the word *help*.

He looked wildly around and sank to the floor.

• • •

J. J. continued walking home with Elly, with Dwayne keeping pace on the other side of the street. No one spoke until one day Elly began telling J. J. about how her grandfather's stroke had affected everyone in the family. She began to speak, and the words tumbled out—about Papa Elvin who, when questioned by his doctor, had explained that he was losing feeling in his hands and feet and that his extremities frequently felt cold. He had never mentioned any of this to anyone else and, when prodded for a reason, claimed that no one had ever asked. All of this frightened Elly and, she was certain, her brother, Dwayne, as well, though he never mentioned it. He remained lost in his schoolwork. Elly also explained that her mother was having difficulty getting everything done. She was overwhelmed. She could carve out time to get dressed and make sure the children were dressed and fed and sent to school in the morning. She made time to shop for food and drug store items, but by the time she got home, she had a new to-do list plus another that Makayla had ready for her that involved lending a hand with Papa Elvin and a bunch of her in-laws' other needs. This meant that she could neither put away the groceries nor prepare dinner and clean up after.

The fact that these items were now required of her was fine with Elly, but J. J. could feel the fear emanating from her—the nameless, bottomless fear that comes from having one's family upended, and from having the foundational pillars of one's life shaken and nearly toppled.

He offered to help out at the Thomas home, and when Elly protested, he insisted. His mother did not miss his help, because he had never offered much at his own home. She did question his whereabouts when he didn't return home from school at the usual time, especially since Ernie Derico was now in jail. Jimmy Kelly hadn't been around either, except to walk Lucy.

"Where does this go?" J. J. held up a drinking glass in the Thomas kitchen.

"To the right of the plates," Elly told him.

He looked at the cabinets, which were in front of him, to his left and his right. "Where are the plates?"

Elly looked at him. "To the left of the glasses." She giggled, and he laughed with her, as she reached up and opened one of the cabinets, which held a stack of dark-blue plates.

They continued putting away the plates, glasses, and cutlery. Shirley came in and watched them with a look that was part concern, part amusement. A few minutes later, Makayla came in, followed by Dwayne.

Several plates and a few forks and knives remained when Elly looked up and saw her family watching. J. J. noticed and looked at each of them.

"Did I do something wrong?" he asked. "Did I put everything in the right place?"

"I'm sure you're doing just fine," Shirley said and gave her daughter an amused look.

Elly's father was still at work; her mother was at home but was helping Papa Elvin, who, Elly explained to J. J., needed help with bathroom issues and eating. Makayla helped him as best she could, but she needed help herself, and, more than that, she needed emotional support. Though Papa Elvin had been losing his sight, his being there and being whole had given Makayla strength. With him diminished as he was, she had lost some of her strength and needed someone to lean on.

All of this was less like work and more like a date or a visit with a friend for J. J., who, when he learned about the Thomas family's needs, offered to help more than he was. Elly turned him down, but he insisted on accompanying her, and she did not know how to respond, so he began spending more time with the Thomas family.

• • •

When he left the Thomas house, J. J. went home; he knew his father would be expecting him to do his math homework, but when he arrived, he found the house in an uproar. J. J.'s mother put a finger to her lips, encouraging J. J. to stay quiet and unobtrusive, so as not to rile his father.

J. J. tiptoed up the steps and sat on the landing at the top of the stairs, listening while his father raged—bellowing and yelling and throwing plates and glasses—and J. J.'s mother pleaded with her husband to calm down.

J. J. saw something small and furry dart across the space at the bottom of the stairs. A few minutes later, Joanne leaned over his shoulder. "Have you seen Sorry?"

"She ran by the bottom of the stairs just a minute ago, but I wouldn't go down there."

"I know."

"What happened?" J. J. asked.

"His disability check didn't come." Joanne sighed. "Long story. He was expecting it today and was planning on going to the hardware store to buy a snowblower. There's supposed to be a blizzard tomorrow. They've got a snow blower across the street, and the Dericos have one, so …" She rolled her eyes and shook her head.

J. J. understood. "His checks come on the ninth."

"Well, not this month," Joanne said.

141

"What?" His father's mottled face appeared at the bottom of the stairs, his neck twisted at a bizarre angle so he could glare up the stairs at his children. J. J. jumped to his feet and bounded into his room. Joanne did the same.

"Get back here!" their father ordered, and, after a pause, he could be heard stomping away from the bottom of the steps. Something crashed in the kitchen. Connie cried out, though J. J. knew she was in the living room, drinking—her way of coping with her husband's rages.

Chapter 18

Tom Kelly was still on duty, but he stopped in at Dericos' anyway. He no longer came in toward the end of the evening shift very much. He was more of an early-morning coffee guy, but he had sympathy for the Derico family, and he happened to be driving by, so he came in.

Lou didn't have to be asked; the coffee just appeared in front of Tom.

"How's it going, Lou?"

Lou was putting away salads and the day's soups. Tom could hear Marshall in the back, washing dishes. A radio played something unintelligible from the kitchen. Maria waited on customers, her apron bunched around her burgeoning belly.

"I say, how're you getting by?" Tom repeated.

Lou continued what he was doing. "Just prepping and cooking and cleaning."

"Maybe take some time off."

"If I wasn't doing this, I'd lose my mind."

Tom took a flask from his pants pocket and poured some of its contents into his coffee. He held it out. Lou shook his head.

"My boy Jim's been to see Ernie."

Lou looked at Tom and nodded. "Tell him thanks." He went back to work, then stopped again. "I can't see him, after—" He bit his lip and went back to work.

"How's your wife making out?" Tom asked.

Lou looked right through him. He shook his head. "No idea."

• • •

"I'm canceling the holiday party," Shirley announced.

Dwayne was bent over a science book in the living room and didn't seem to hear.

Makayla's voice could be heard murmuring to Papa Elvin one flight up. The only person present was Elly, who was wiping down the counters and kitchen table while her mother gathered her strength to help with Papa Elvin's evening routine.

"No, Mama!"

Shirley's head pulled back. "No, Mama? What do you mean, 'No, Mama?'"

"Please don't cancel the parties, Mama. They're the best thing about living here—the only good thing about living here. They're the reason we aren't dead at school. The kids from the parties look out for us.

"They defend you? From who?"

"Not the point, Mama."

"It certainly is the point."

"Some of the kids at school don't like us being there, but the kids from the parties—no one comes after us when they're around."

Shirley looked at her daughter for a long moment. "It's been hard for you and Dwayne, living here, I know. But in the long run, your father and I think it's best."

"But it's the parties that make it okay, Mama. Please don't take those away."

"J. J.'s been a big help, I admit."

"He's the only one."

"He's the only— Your only friend?"

Elly shrugged, and her mother laid a comforting palm on her daughter's shoulder.

Elly shrugged. "Now that he's my friend, his sister's been nice to me too."

• • •

Though his father was off duty, Jimmy Kelly asked if they could ride in the squad car to see Ernie, and to his surprise, his father agreed. So after dinner, Jimmy took Lucy for a walk and afterward climbed into the front seat next to his father, who had worked the early shift to-day—six to two—after which he had taken a short nap.

They drove into the complex that housed the county jail and parked in the lot across a small street from the main building, which, along with the lot and the street, was surrounded by fencing topped with a tall tier of barbed wire.

They waited along with a dozen or so others, mostly women—inmates' wives, mothers, or sisters—inside a small shed until they were led by two guards across the street and into the main building.

The outer room was divided in half—with one half consisting of lockers into which they placed all of their belongings, including their wallets, belts, and jewelry.

While his father waited in the outer room, Jimmy was beckoned to a doorway, then into a small vestibule, and then a waiting room—while the inmates who had visitors were rounded up. Eventually, he was led from the waiting room into a large room that was bisected by a three-foot-high wall that snaked around the room. Above the wall was four feet of plexiglass. Chairs were permanently affixed to the floor on both sides of the wall, behind a table that extended at waist level to both sides. Mesh-covered openings had been cut at mouth level so that conversations could be conducted. Guards armed with batons but not firearms were stationed every few feet on both sides of the wall.

A buzzer sounded, a metal gate at one end of the room on the prisoner side of the wall opened, and a long line of prisoners filed in, Ernie among them. Jimmy looked at his friend with curiosity; he looked older, more seasoned, and serious. He grinned the old Ernie grin when he saw Jimmy.

"Thanks for coming."

"Good to see you," said Jimmy.

"Good to be seen."

"How you doing?"

Ernie shrugged. "Well, you know. What you been up to?"

"Keeping busy."

"I can see you been up to something."

Jimmy smiled.

"A girl?"

Jimmy didn't answer; he shook his head. "But I hear a girl's been coming to see you."

"Where'd you hear that?"

"Little bird."

• • •

Connie Welles sat as close to the window as she could get without pressing her face against it. No one would have guessed her reason for this. It was the same reason she spent her days and nights in an alcoholic haze. She was terrified of her husband and was desperate to get as far away from him as she could. That the farthest she could get from John was the front window of her living room was pathetic, she knew.

And yet, she also knew she would never leave him. She needed him. As meager as his disability checks were, the family depended on them, just as they needed the few dollars he brought home from his cab-driving job.

Perhaps she could work. The thought drew her attention to the degree any thought beyond her own self-pity did. She turned the idea over in her mind, examining it, and when she found its defect, she discarded it. John would never stand for her working, just as he would not stand for her leaving. If she mustered the courage to leave, he would find her. She would feel his terrifying rage wherever she went.

Sitting at the front window was as far as she dared go. Through the dirty streaks, she could pretend for moments at a time that she was part of the activity she saw outside—the neighbors, the couples strolling up and down the sidewalk, the children playing in the street, the people driving by. And when she was tired of pretending she was one of them, she could judge them. She could hate them. She could tell herself how awful her neighbors were because they didn't mow their lawns the way she thought they should; they didn't have the right model cars; they didn't dress the way she thought they ought to. And their children. Why, look at their children! The Derico boy was a prime example. In jail for burglarizing a liquor store! And his sister—stepped off a curb into the path of an oncoming bus—and they say that had been her intention all along!

• • •

When J. J. emerged from his house that Saturday morning, the bitter air collided with his cheeks and covered his face in bone-deep chill. He hopped from one foot to the other, waiting next to the car for his father.

The drive to the VFW hall was just under twenty minutes, during which J. J. thought of little besides the Christmas cookies that waited inside; he gave no thought to what his father would be doing, despite knowing what that would be. Perhaps he buried the knowledge deep below his consciousness until his senses forced him to confront the truth.

The hall was festooned with Christmas decorations—crepe streamers, tiny Santas and elf figurines, and a tall, decorated tree that the veterans and their children were invited to help decorate. Loose decorations lay in piles at the center of each of the round tables, on top of red crepe paper tablecloths. Eggnog and mulled wine were served, along with turkey, stuffing, vegetables, cranberry sauce, and the cookies J. J. loved.

The men all wore their service uniforms, even J. J.'s father, although few were active military. Most were newly returned from Vietnam. There were eleven today, and some of their wives helped to serve the refreshments, while others greeted one another warmly and still others sat quietly, with anxious eyes on their husbands or boyfriends.

John Welles went from veteran to veteran, approaching each with quiet confidence, friendship, and understanding. He listened to whatever they had to say, whether war memories, struggles to cope with day-to-day life as a civilian, difficulty getting or keeping jobs, or the challenges of fatherhood. J. J.'s father listened more than he spoke, often while laying a large, comforting hand on the veteran's shoulder. When he spoke, J. J. could not hear much of what was said, except that the tone was encouraging and warm, and evoked memories from J. J.'s earliest childhood, when his father had spoken to him in similar loving tones.

J. J. was confused by the bitterness he felt. These men seemed special to his father in a way he was not, and he longed to be similarly special. His feelings toward his father lived in soil bereft, as far as J. J. could tell, of fatherly love and were grown from hurt and terror.

Several of the men were familiar to J. J. He watched them as he munched on sugar cookies, picked the chocolate chips from the tops of others, or opened sandwich cookies and licked the jelly from the insides. He had seen many of the men at holiday parties.

J. J. was overwhelmed with bitterness, and after a while the feelings became thoughts. *My father loves these guys more. Why'd he bring me here?* He blinked back tears.

One of the men stood out, as he was particularly familiar to J. J. His name was Mel, and he was one whom J. J.'s father had particularly taken under his wing, perhaps because their roles and experiences in the service had been similar. J. J. watched Mel with the same bitterness, the same envy for his father's love with which he watched all of the others, only with Mel, the feeling was stronger because his father's relationship with Mel was closer.

As he watched Mel and his father greet one another with smiles and warm handshakes, and saw his father listen and smile broadly while Mel talked about his life this past year, J. J. was overwhelmed with a sudden, powerful fear that enveloped his mind and froze his body in place. He managed to put the remains of his cookie on his plate, but could then only sit and shudder and try not to soil his underwear. He could not identify the source of his panic because, at the moment, he could not think.

But he could remember; in fact, he had no choice but to remember, and the memory exploded into his consciousness.

Mel had been part of the first wave of American soldiers in Vietnam, in 1965. He had been there a year, perhaps slightly longer, and had come home wounded in both body and mind. Like John Welles, he was scarred over one side of his face; unlike John Welles, he had not lost an eye.

Mel was also one of the first men John Welles had mentored, and the two had developed a bond—Mel because he was receiving aid and comfort from a fellow serviceman whose experience had been similar to his own; John Welles, because this young wounded veteran was giving him the opportunity to be of further service, to be of help—something John Welles badly needed. He had not bonded well with anyone after his own wartime experiences—not his wife, not his children, not his neighbors.

One night in 1967, when J. J. was about ten years of age, his parents had gone out to dinner and left him with Mel as babysitter. His parents had been grateful to Mel because they had never been fully comfortable with some of the neighbors' children who babysat for J. J. and Joanne. But they trusted Mel.

While J. J. was aware of the content of his memory, what he was most aware of was the smell. He had no way of describing the smell, except that it was pungent and disgusting—the smell of Mel's body.

Mel had set seven-year-old Joanne up in front of the family's TV in the living room watching *The Ed Sullivan Show*, which she loved. Mel had then explained to J. J. that he wanted to show him something upstairs, in J. J.'s bedroom, which confused ten-year-old J. J. because everything in his room was his, so how would Mel have anything to show him in his own room?

Once they sat down on Mel's bed, Mel lay down on his back and pulled down his pants and underwear, and asked J. J. to touch him. J. J. hadn't wanted to, but Mel had insisted and explained that his father had specifically instructed Mel to do this—to have J. J. touch him in this way.

Afterward, J. J. had been upset and confused, but was comforted in the knowledge that he was somehow pleasing his father. Over the years, he came to better understand what had occurred and to realize that his father had nothing to do with what happened, and while he felt shame and remorse over the incident, he buried it along with other painful memories—diluting and diminishing its power until the incident was no longer a part of his conscious memory at all.

Until today.

Chapter 19

After school the following Monday, J. J. walked home with Elly, paced by Dwayne across the street. Elly invited him to spend the afternoon at her house. From Elly's kitchen, he called his house and told his mother where he was, and then he and Elly started up the stairs.

"Leave that door open," Shirley warned after them.

"I will," Elly said.

Her room was pink and neat and tidy—a girl's bedroom if ever J. J. had seen one—more feminine than his sister's or Laurie's room. Elly's bed was covered with a violet blanket printed with cartoon images of animals. On the walls were posters of Gladys Knight and the Pips, Roberta Flack, and The Supremes, along with a more psychedelic poster of Sly and the Family Stone.

"Want to listen to records?" Elly asked, and J. J. nodded.

"What do you want to hear?" She pointed to a horizontal stack of 45s between bookends on her dresser.

J. J. shrugged. He really didn't care; he was happy just being there.

Elly set up several records to play in succession, stacking them up so that each was suspended above her turntable and would drop when the preceding record finished and the turntable's arm retracted.

They sat next to one another, cross-legged on the floor, their backs against Elly's bed. Elly's mother peeked in once and nodded her approval to see that they were not on the bed and that there was space between them.

The 45s were single songs currently on the charts, including "Keep On Truckin'" by Eddie Kendricks, "One of a Kind (Love Affair)" and "Could It Be I'm Falling in Love" by The Spinners, "Drift Away" by Dobie Gray, and "Let's Get It On" by Marvin Gaye. It never occurred to J. J. that many of these songs shared a common theme.

Without warning, his experiences of two days earlier spilled out of him; he told Elly about the visit with his father to the VFW and their meeting with the Vietnam veterans and Mel. He did not talk about his suspicions that his father preferred their company to his, nor his memory of Mel's abuse, but he did share that he did not like the veterans. Elly didn't answer, but her hand crept into his, and they sat that way for several minutes, holding hands, while the music played.

After the last song ended, Elly did not get up off the floor to add more music to her turntable. She remained seated next to J. J., holding his hand.

"My grandpa's really sick," she said. "He had a stroke and has something wrong with his spine, and he needs surgery."

"Oh," J. J. said. He didn't know what else to say.

"And they also found cancer."

He squeezed Elly's hand and she squeezed his in return.

"I think he's dying."

He could hear that she was starting to cry.

"He doesn't look like himself anymore. He's so thin and his skin is gray and he's … he's … he's hardly there at all." Tears spilled down her cheeks.

They continued sitting together—J. J. silent while Elly quietly cried. Eventually, she stopped and began to tell J. J. about Papa Elvin when he'd been healthy—how strong he'd been, how protective and supportive, always encouraging her and Dwayne to be creative and to find joy in their studies and life outside school. And about God. Papa Elvin was a big believer in God, and, while he went to church, his God was not so much a church God as an everyday God—his best friend. That was the way Elly put it because that was the way Papa Elvin put it.

J. J. nodded and said he understood as though he did.

• • •

Lou Derico was finding life unbearable. Debbie had been his and Anna's first child and had been welcomed with that special brand of unbridled joy first-time parents have for their firstborn. He had loved sitting in the living room with his eyes closed, listening to her practice—no matter the content of her playing. He could have listened to her practice simple scales all day.

He was in the back room at the diner, stirring soup ingredients and remembering a dream he'd had several days earlier. That morning, he had woken up with the bittersweet aftereffects of an especially vivid dream in which he had almost reunited with a girl he'd dated in his teens. The feelings in the dream had been as intense as any he'd had all those years ago, and as soon as he'd awakened he'd tried to fall back asleep to rekindle those feelings and reenter that lost universe.

He could no longer bear to look at his wife. His dissatisfaction with her as a woman and as his wife was now compounded by his overwhelming grief over the loss of their daughter. Looking at Anna made him think of Debbie and his failure as a man to attract and marry a woman for whom he felt the magnetism he thought was a man's birthright. It was not that he believed that only men were deserving of mates to whom they were irresistibly attracted; women had that same right. Perhaps he had chosen too quickly when he'd decided to ask Anna to marry him. He did not know the answer—only that he was reaping the very unjust rewards of that decision. Perhaps Debbie's death was another unfortunate result of that decision. If he had not married Anna, there would have been no Debbie, and she could not have died so tragically.

He had decided to ignore the invitation to the Thomases' holiday party, but now he was rethinking. The party could briefly take him away from Anna and from their house, which only reminded him of Debbie—his forever gone first child.

• • •

Erin Kelly had decided to attend the Thomases' party on Sunday, if only to escape her husband on an afternoon when he would be off from work and very likely drinking and nasty. Tom worked long hours, sometimes double shifts, and felt he was entitled to do whatever he wanted with his time off—and that meant sitting in his living room chair, glass in hand, bottle on the coffee table, drinking and speaking his mind about whatever was in front of him or moldering in his head.

Erin conceded that Tom could, in fact, rightfully do whatever he wanted with his days off, but so could she, and on his day off this week, she was taking Jimmy and Julie to the Thomases' party.

But when Sunday arrived, Tom shocked her by announcing that he would be joining them and coming to the party too.

• • •

After stopping at the bakery to pick up a box of Christmas cookies, J. J. and Joanne were driven by their father back to the Thomas family home. They were the last to arrive.

Beverages and a bucket of ice were already out on the living room table, and soon, food began to appear. There was a roast turkey—already sliced, with crispy skin and succulent meat—along with candied yams, creamy mashed potatoes, collard greens, fresh cranberry sauce, baked macaroni and cheese, and biscuits with gravy.

J. J. was surprised to see Lou Derico sitting quietly off to one side, while Laurie sat with Julie Kelly. He was equally surprised that Joanne did not immediately rush over to join the girls, given her friendship with Laurie. His sister stayed close to him, near the center of the room. Their father sat between J. J. and Joanne and the rest of the men. What surprised J. J. most of all was seeing Officer Tom Kelly sitting with his wife, Erin, not far from Lou Derico, watching the rest of the guests and their hosts and not quite fitting in. The two men, who knew one another from being on opposite sides of the counter at Dericos' Diner, were perhaps less comfortable without the counter between them.

"I just want to say how sorry I am," Erin Kelly said to Lou. He didn't seem to hear her until she reached out and touched his wrist. Then he looked up and nodded slightly without really seeing her.

Erin looked at her husband and children and corrected herself. "How sorry we all are, that is."

Laurie got up and left the room. Julie Kelly edged closer to her mother and laid her hand on her mother's forearm.

After a moment, J. J. got up and headed for the food, taking a plate, a fork, and a little bit of every food item. He then returned to his seat between his father and sister.

Jimmy Kelly had gone to the kitchen table and sat down with Dwayne, who was bent over a book. Eventually, the two rose together, filled two plates with food, and returned to the table. At the same table were Elly's grandparents—her grandmother clutching a napkin and dabbing at her grandfather's lips while he sat and stared into space. Elly's father sat next to them, but got up now and then to either make sure everyone had what they needed or disappear into the kitchen to help his wife. J. J. could hear Mrs. Thomas's voice along with that of Wanda, the family friend who had been at previous gatherings and was helping out. He assumed Elly was with them in the kitchen.

Elly's father walked by, stopped, glanced down at J. J., and smiled, then continued into the living room. He stood with his hands on his hips and, after a moment, filled a plate and found a seat with the other men.

Those in the living room were seated around the periphery of the room. Wanda and Shirley came in, saw that everyone, including Elvin Jr., was eating, and filled plates for themselves. They took seats in between the cluster of men and Erin, Laurie, and Joanne. Elly was last to take a plate. She sat nearest Joanne.

For a few minutes, there was only the soft sound of cutlery in use. Then Tom Kelly said, "I see things have calmed down a bit now, eh?"

Shirley glanced at him, blinked a few times, and gave a little nod.

"Calmed down?" Wanda asked.

"Well, when your friends moved in, it caused quite a ruckus."

Wanda's eyebrows arched. "They moved in, which was followed by a ruckus, but I wouldn't say it was them that *caused* it."

Tom Kelly's neck reddened. "I guess what I meant was that after the family moved in, the neighborhood went through a rough patch."

Wanda shook her head. "'Tweren't nothing to what this family went through—trust me."

Shirley and Elvin looked at one another.

"Tom's right though," Elvin said. "Things have calmed down some. We do still get at least a few drive-bys every week—kids yelling stuff from cars."

"Least it's just words being thrown now," Shirley mused.

Wanda was not finished. "Having my niece and nephew threatened and their property busted up is more than what I'd call a ruckus."

Erin looked around nervously. "So, Mr. Thomas—" she began.

"Elvin, please," Elvin insisted.

"Elvin. So how are your children getting on now?"

"It's an adjustment."

Erin was clasping and unclasping her hands. "It's got to be hard having your first Christmas in a new neighborhood."

"Christmas is about being grateful," Tom Kelly added. "And we've all got plenty to be grateful for." He cocked his head toward Elvin. "But I've been wondering ..."

"What's that?" Elvin answered.

"Why did you want to move here in the first place?"

The room fell silent.

Wanda was about to speak but was interrupted by Tom. "I don't mean you aren't welcome. Here you are, welcoming us into your home, and you've been through a lot. But why would you want to invite all that?"

Wanda gave a loud sigh and looked away.

Elvin looked directly at Tom. "It's what my family and I decided was in our best interests."

"But look at all the trouble it caused. You must have known some of it was coming. How could you want that?"

"What you mean is," Wanda retorted, "Why would they dare to come into this white neighborhood and stir up trouble?"

Tom Kelly held up a finger; his expression didn't change. "Don't put words in my mouth."

"I wouldn't," Wanda snapped, "if you would say what you mean in the first place."

"Wanda, stop," Elvin said wearily. "These are our guests, as you are our guest. We ask that everyone be courteous to everyone else."

J. J. saw Elly glance his way, then back at her mother, who looked uncomfortable.

"Look," Tom was saying, "I'm happiest when I'm with a bunch of Irish guys. I'm Irish. I'm a man. I like being around other Irish men. That's all I'm trying to say. I want to see everybody happy."

Wanda's expression had gone cold. "And we'd be happiest amongst our own kind. Isn't that what you're saying?"

Tom shrugged. "I'm saying everyone is."

"Getting to know new folks can be a good thing too," Elvin interjected evenly; he laid his hand on his wife's knee. She covered his hand with hers and squeezed.

Tom asked, "But isn't it difficult when everyone's different? We're all pretty different here. We come from different places, we have different music, different customs. So isn't staying pretty much separate going to lead to a more peaceful situation? That's all I'm suggesting."

Wanda rolled her eyes. "Well, peaceful long as the white folks have the best services, cars, homes, schools—"

"Okay, Wanda," Elvin said. "My view is that the effort we put forth in getting to know one another will lead to greater peace, greater understanding, greater community in the long run."

"You know," Tom Kelly said, looking impressed, "you ought to run for office."

Elvin shook his head. "No, thank you. No, no, no."

Chapter 20

Elly accepted J. J.'s offer to help clean up after the party, so J. J. told his father that he would see the rest of the family at home. As he brought plates into the kitchen, scraped them into the garbage, and began washing while Elly dried, a new discussion had begun around them.

"I don't agree," Wanda was saying, "that we are proof that the civil rights movement is succeeding. You moved into a nicer house in a whiter neighborhood—that's all it proves. And as the cop said, it just stirred things up."

"And as Elvin said," Shirley maintained, as she took the cooking pots and pans she had just filled with soapy water and set them on the countertop to soak, "we just had an integrated party. Who else 'round here is doing that? So we didn't agree on everything. So what? Neighbors don't always agree. Friends and family don't always agree."

Wanda pressed her lips together. "I don't buy it. I don't buy that the civil rights movement is getting us much of anywhere."

"Are you kidding?" Elvin was incredulous. "You can walk into some restaurants my daddy couldn't. You can do things my mama couldn't. When you say the movement didn't achieve anything, you're insulting Doctor King's memory. You're insulting James Baldwin and Lorraine Hansberry."

"What she means," Shirley said, as she dumped a pile of used paper plates into the garbage bin, "and I think you'd agree, Elvin, is that there's still work to be done."

"Ah. That's different."

Wanda emptied the garbage bin into a black bag and fit another bag into the bin. "I still think that cop's a racist."

J. J. felt himself flush; he was suddenly acutely aware he was the only white person in the room. Or in the house.

Elvin Jr. was sitting at the kitchen table. Only moments before, his parents had headed up to bed—Makayla's arm curled around her husband's, while her other hand steadied his shoulder. "I think there's a difference," Elvin said, "between cross-burning racists and people who are misinformed and sheltered."

Wanda was shaking her head. "They're getting to you, Elvin."

"You don't think there's a difference?" Elvin was slowly shaking his head. "Most of these folks never broke bread with anyone who wasn't a whole lot more like them than we are."

Wanda's eyes widened. "Maybe there are different kinds of racists, and maybe it's a short journey from being one kind to being the other kind."

"Well, maybe we can help keep them from making that journey." Elvin looked at Wanda steadily. "Maybe, with a little understanding, we can help them make a different journey. Maybe we can even make some kind of journey together."

Wanda looked in amazement at Shirley, who was looking from her to Elvin. "Maybe that cop was right. You should run for something."

"At least," Elvin responded, "I'm not running *from* anything."

Shirley threw up her hands. "And I'm *not* getting in the middle of this."

• • •

J. J. and Elly did not speak while they washed the dishes. He had never liked doing housework or chores, but when the dishes and cutlery were washed, dried, and put away, J. J. wished there were more. Elly asked him if he wanted to watch some TV in the living room. Maybe channel seven or four had a good movie on, or they could watch *The Mary Tyler Moore Show* on channel two. But J. J. knew his father would expect him home, so he let Elly accompany him to the door as he said goodbye to her parents, who thanked him for his help. Elly opened the front door, and J. J. stepped outside, then turned to face her.

"Sorry 'bout all that arguing," she offered, looking at the ground.

"I'm just not used to people talking when they argue," J. J. confided.

"Really? What else would they do?"

J. J. raised his eyebrows, took a deep breath, and let it out slowly. "You don't want to know."

Elly gave him a small smile as he turned away, and she closed the door behind him.

The night air was warm, and moths were fluttering around the streetlights. J. J. heard the footsteps of a group of people, which grew closer but then faded as whoever they belonged to turned down a side street. He let himself into his house and found his mother seated in front of the window. On the sill was a half-empty glass of something clear, along with a slice of lime and some ice that refracted the light from the room. She watched him come in but said nothing. Joanne was standing on the third step of the stairway to the second floor. J. J. could feel rather than see his father, who was on the kitchen side of the stairway and out of his line of sight.

"That's my kitten!" Joanne was protesting. "It's a living thing!"

"Who gave you permission to have a cat in this house?" their father demanded.

"It's been here for months and you never said a thing."

When their father was angry, he moved quickly and with purpose. He suddenly appeared on the other side of the stairs, then on the bottom step. He took a threatening step upward, and Joanne shrank back in fear, then turned and ran up the steps. J. J. heard the door to her bedroom open, then slam shut.

His father turned to him.

"Where've you been all this time?"

"I was— I was helping the Thomases clean up."

"You were helping. When's the last time you did any cleaning up around here?" J. J. could see that his father was already angry and that his anger was searching for an outlet, like water on a roof searching for a crevice.

"Look around!" his father said. "Maybe some cleaning up is in order around here! What'd they have you doing over there, huh? Huh?" J. J. could feel his father's rage building, turned around, and ran back out the door.

As he rushed away from his house, he could hear his father bellowing, "Get back here! Get back here, I said!"

• • •

Erin never realized how much she liked Joni Mitchell. She knew that the artist wrote her songs and that many were recorded by other artists. Her voice was unique and free and glorious. She wiped down the kitchen counters, swept the floor, and checked on the children, who were both in their rooms—Jimmy with a comic book and Julie practicing singing that new Roberta Flack song, "Killing Me Softly." Erin stood outside Julie's door, listening and smiling to herself, then took a towel from the hall closet and went into the bathroom to wash up for bed.

Tom had gone out, and when he came back, he was in one of his moods. She could hear him crashing around downstairs. She assumed he'd been drinking. She heard him come up the stairs, then walk through the hall and into the bathroom. She heard the water running. After a while, he came in and took his pants off.

"Hey," she said, hoping to kill his mood with kindness.

He didn't answer.

"You okay?"

He grunted an unintelligible response. He was sweating for some reason, and Erin could smell whiskey mixed with his sweat. His breathing was quick and ragged, as though his bathroom ablutions had exhausted him.

She started to reach for him, pulled her hand back, frightened, then reached out again and touched his shoulder. He didn't respond, which she mistook for acquiescence, so she moved her hand slowly lower and reached for him again.

He batted her hand away. "Fuck's sake, no."

His words, the disgust in his tone, along with his physical reaction were like an ice pick in her heart.

"Look at yourself," he said, the disgust deepening. "I see prostitutes all day, and some of them look pretty good. But you—" He scoffed, and it was the scoff that drew her tears.

There had been a time—and not so long ago, either—when he had lusted for her. She could have reached for him any time of day or night, and instantly he would be ready. No foreplay needed.

She turned away, her mouth clamped shut, determined that he wouldn't hear her cry.

After a while, she said, "Will you be coming to church with me in the morning?"

He didn't answer for a long time. Finally, he said, "There's something you should know."

She braced herself. "Okay."

"I don't believe in God. I guess I'm an atheist."

She didn't answer because she had no answer. This was a deeper cut even than his disgust.

After a while, he said, "How could there be a God with all the evil I see every day?

• • •

J. J. knocked softly at the basement door on the side of the house, then waited, listening. He heard nothing. He knocked again. After a moment, the door opened a sliver, and he saw Dwayne looking back at him, saying nothing, but not sending him away or closing the door.

"Is your sister here?"

"Just a minute." Dwayne vanished, and, moments later, Elly appeared—her eyes wide with concern.

"Are you okay?"

He had not been prepared for the question. "I just, I just need a place to crash."

She didn't respond at first, but then she opened the door and let him in.

Inside was a dark concrete basement hallway lit by a single decades-old lamp on a wooden table that stood next to a battered gray couch. Another door led to a boiler room of sorts, and there were two other doors that were closed.

"Stay here," she whispered, meaning the couch. "I'll get a blanket and pillow."

It was only now that J. J. considered the trouble he was making for himself; his mother would be unhappy, his father enraged. Elly returned with a fluffy beige blanket and a white pillow without a case. He sat at one end of the couch and laid the pillow down next to him.

Elly sat down on his other side. "They're all upstairs. Nobody's sleeping, but they will be soon." Her eyes wandered; she was thinking. "Can I get you anything else?"

He shook his head, then asked, "Is there a bathroom?"

She pointed to one of the doors. "I'd better get upstairs. I don't want them to come lookin'." She touched his shoulder, a gesture of reassurance, of comfort, then she turned and opened the other of the two doors, which led to the stairs.

J. J. lay down, pulled the blanket up around his neck, and folded the pillow in half to keep his head raised to a comfortable position. He closed his eyes but didn't sleep for a long time. His mind was filled with his father's voice, and the anger behind it. His father had not been as frightening as he'd been on some nights, but there was something about the party that had lowered J. J.'s tolerance for his father's rage.

He pulled his arms around his chest, hugging himself, while his father's anger, voice, and face roiled in his mind. Eventually, he slept.

• • •

"J. J."

He opened his eyes. Elly was standing just inside the door to the stairs. "Are you okay?" she asked.

He thought about the question, then nodded.

"My parents and my brother are going to church. My grandparents will be upstairs. Do you want a spare toothbrush and some toothpaste?"

"That would be great." He sat up, keeping the blanket over the lower half of his body. He was still dressed in his clothing from the day before.

A few minutes later, Elly came back with a toothbrush in an unopened package and a tube of toothpaste.

"They're leaving now. Come on upstairs when you're done."

"Do your grandparents know I'm here?"

Elly shook her head. "Not yet, but they'd be fine with it if they knew why."

J. J. went into the bathroom, washed his face, and brushed his teeth. He looked at himself in the mirror, wondering how he could go back and face his family. What would they say? What could he say?

He heard the front door close, car doors slam, and a car start outside. He walked slowly up the stairs to the hallway that divided the dining room from the living room. Elly was at the kitchen table with her grandparents. J. J. didn't know what to say.

"Why don't you give our guest some milk," Makayla suggested.

Elly went to the cupboard, found a glass, and poured it two-thirds full of milk.

Elly's grandfather said nothing, but his eyes were on J. J. They flicked to Elly, then to Makayla, and then returned to J. J.

"Would you like pancakes?" Makayla added, smiling at J. J. "Elly makes a mean buttermilk."

J. J. wasn't sure why he was embarrassed. "Oh, no thanks. I should be getting home."

Makayla's brown eyes were round with concern. "Are you sure?" She squinted, closely watching his face. "Are you safe at home?"

He wasn't sure what she meant and didn't know what to say. "I— I think so."

She glanced at her husband and then at her granddaughter. "You are welcome here, always. We've taken in a stray or two over the years." She broke into a broad smile.

Gratitude washed over J. J., and he felt a new sense of safety he had not known was missing.

Makayla's copper-colored skin radiated warmth. "Whenever J. J. decides to go, if he does, why don't you walk him home," she said to Elly.

"Yes, Nana Makayla."

Makayla turned back to J. J. "Let's keep your visit between us— unless that is, you need to tell your parents where you were. We can be your safe oasis."

Tears sprang into J. J.'s eyes. He wiped them away and drained his milk glass. "I should go."

Elly got up and brought his glass to the sink, where she rinsed it out. Before they left, Makayla got up and hugged her granddaughter, then held J. J. at arm's length, with both hands on his shoulders, and pulled him to her. Elly's grandfather caught his eye, and something unspoken passed between them—something good.

Elly and J. J. walked back to his home in silence, and J. J. felt no pressure to explain or say anything at all. He worried about what his reception would be when he walked in. Would he be beaten? Would his father scream at him? What would his mother say?

When he arrived at his house, Elly left him with a soft touch on his wrist at the spot where the sidewalk met the walk to his door. He walked in to find his mother seated at the front window, drink in hand, and his father seated at the dining room table, staring into the distance. The only reaction from either of them was his father's eye, which followed him from the moment he walked in the door to when he walked up the stairs to his room.

As soon as he closed the door to his room, there was a knock and the door opened slightly. "Can we come in?" Joanne asked.

"Who's we?"

She opened the door, and J. J. saw that she was cradling Sorry the cat to her belly. J. J. was sitting on his bed; he slid over to make room for her, so she sat down and put Sorry down between them.

Sorry crept over to J. J., climbed into his lap, curled up, and went to sleep.

Chapter 21

J. J. noticed a change in his sister in the days following the Thomas family party. She was more open and assertive, and when J. J. looked for Elly and Dwayne after school, he found his sister with them. The four walked home together. Joanne was also seeing less of Laurie, and J. J. thought he saw his sister walking arm in arm with Mario, one of the school's jock stars—a three-letter athlete in baseball, wrestling, and football.

Christmas for the four families was a private affair. Each family celebrated at home and followed their own traditions. The Dericos usually had a fish dinner on Christmas Eve, then went to midnight Mass. Lou said he didn't want to go, so Anna and Laurie went. On Christmas Day, they usually had several families of aunts, uncles, and cousins at the house, but Lou had asked the relatives to give them privacy this year—a request that was honored. Anna and Laurie visited Ernie at the jail, where they mostly sat silently after catching up on what little news there was. Lou watched whatever was on TV—the programs didn't matter; they were just something to look at.

The Welles family had the same baked ham, mashed potatoes, gravy, and beans dinner they had every year. They ate quietly and did not go to church.

Tom Kelly strung multicolored lights up along the edges and roof of the front of his house and in the branches of a tree in the front yard. The family went to church on both Christmas Eve and Christmas Day and were treated to the choir featuring their daughter, Julie, who sang solos on both "Come All Ye Faithful" and "Silent Night." Tom had a few drinks before and after both services, but these were nothing more than usual. He didn't notice when Erin sat on the other side of Julie and Jimmy, as far from him as possible.

• • •

It was a quiet morning several days after the New Year's weekend, and Lou had taken the day off work. He had cajoled Anna into working today, along with Marshall and Laurie, if his daughter could be relied upon to show up for work. Maria would be there as well.

Lou got out of bed and wandered to the window. He looked out and saw little besides the parking lot and Sunrise Highway on its other side. He went back to the bed, lay down, and covered Erin's hand with his. She pulled her hand away and covered her face with both her hands.

"What have we done?" she groaned.

He watched her, curious to see a woman lying next to him who was so animated. She had been animated from the moment they'd rented the room only two hours earlier, talking nonstop and gesticulating—her hands talking when her mouth wasn't. Her lovemaking had been more active than he had expected too. Her eyes had been tightly shut and her body tensed as a bowstring, and once they'd gotten going, she had built slowly toward crying out in pain and ecstasy—a climax he suspected had been building for much more than the few minutes they had been together.

But now she was a clenched, regretful presence, very likely already immersed in the confession she would force herself to offer, perhaps this very week. He sighed. Was nothing ever as good as one hoped?

• • •

Anna had barely slept since Debbie's death. She had no energy and could barely leave her bed to use the bathroom. She had not cooked or left the house. She had not been to the diner except this one day, when Lou said it was important because he had something he had to do. She could barely find the energy or the motivation to get dressed and brush her teeth, but she did these things knowing she could return home and get back into bed after a few hours.

She worked on autopilot at the restaurant, leaving much of the work for Marshall and Laurie, who came in later. And then she was back home, lying in bed—the TV on, the TV off—light seeping in through the cracks between the blinds, followed by darkness and night.

But no sleep. Her mind, though empty, was restless—a relentless movie she'd seen before, showing her images from her past, from the aftermath of Debbie's death, from TV shows, and of people she had never seen or known as far as she could tell. She was existing without purpose, aware that Debbie was dead, Ernie was still in jail, Laurie was usually with friends doing God knew what, and Lou was usually at the restaurant and barely more capable than she was.

She tried drinking, but vodka made her sick, she hated whiskey of any kind, and beer left her bloated. She had no interest in drugs and doubted a psychiatrist could help her. She was not at all sure she wanted to be helped.

She thought of reaching out to her friends, but she had none that she could remember. She thought of Shirley Thomas, who was a whirlwind of energy. But what would Shirley Thomas want with her? She thought of Connie Welles and tried calling her, but the phone rang and rang, and did not allow her to leave a message.

She'd had something of a friendship with Connie, once upon a time. They'd known one another from when the kids were little and J. J. and Ernie and occasionally Jimmy Kelly, who was younger, had playdates. Connie had complained to Anna that J. J. was a difficult child who was hard to handle, and Anna had confided in Connie that Ernie was nothing but trouble. If there was potential for lawbreaking, fighting, or vexing difficulties in a situation, Ernie would head straight for it.

But now, Anna lay in bed, eyes scanning the familiar walls and ceiling, vaguely pleased that she would not have to shower for another few days.

• • •

Connie Welles sat at her bay window and drank. She was not dissatisfied because she had everything she wanted. She had achieved her goals for the moment—sitting at her window and drinking vodka over ice, some fruit, and a little lime. She tried to remember how much vodka was left in the bottle. About a third. Her memory was not great, but she always made sure to know how much vodka was on hand. She had another bottle for backup—she was quite sure of that.

The most wonderful change had come into her life about a month earlier. Steve's Liquors was now offering delivery for an extra five dollars. When she ran short, she had only to pick up the phone and dial, and a few more bottles would appear at her door.

Life was grand.

John had broken her favorite spaghetti serving bowl two nights earlier over J. J.'s dropped spoon. He'd just hurled the big bowl to the floor, where it shattered and sent spaghetti, sauce, and meat in every direction. John had screamed and screamed—sometimes she could not even make out any words. The screaming left her on edge, and she would become desperate to get away. But where would she go? Once she started cleaning it up, John stopped screaming, so she had not minded cleaning it up.

Later he had said they had to do something about J. J., who, in his words, needed to "get his shit together." She didn't argue, though she thought J. J. was only part of the problem. It was true that he might not graduate. He was smart but paid little or no attention to his schoolwork as far as she could tell. And he'd briefly run away from home—thank goodness he'd come back.

But why worry? What would that do? She had known of many kids who had slipped through the cracks and flunked out, and most were doing just fine. They went to trade school or found jobs that would at least pay the bills. One way or another, J. J. would be okay; she had done her job.

Her thoughts wandered to Joanne but did not linger there. Joanne was doing fine. She was a terrific student—a natural at school. And she had some sense.

The problem now was that John insisted on doing something about J. J., and he would put it on her, perhaps screaming at her, until something was done. Without really considering the idea, she heard herself suggest taking the boy to a shrink. John had stopped yelling, and she could see he was considering the idea. "Do you really think it would help?" he'd asked; she knew he was thinking about his experience with veterans.

"Why not? At least we'll have a professional's opinion we can use at the school."

"But where would we find a shrink who sees kids?"

"I'll call the guidance office," she heard herself say.

And so she did.

Chapter 22

After school on the first Wednesday of the new year, Laurie was at Joanne's house listening to records. Laurie's taste was for the livelier songs, like "Smokin' in the Boy's Room," "Jungle Boogie," and "Rockin' Roll Baby," whereas Joanne liked slower, sweeter, and what Laurie called "sappier" songs, like "Time in a Bottle," the Carpenters' "Top of the World," and "The Way We Were," a song Laurie refused to listen to at all.

The girls sat and listened in Joanne's room. Her parents were downstairs, sitting alone in different rooms, different worlds.

After a while, Laurie perked up and asked, "Where's Sorry?"

Joanne looked dismayed. "I haven't seen her for a few days. She figured out a way to get out of the house." Her voice faltered. "I'm kind of scared she got lost in the snow."

"Maybe the new neighbors stole her," Laurie suggested.

Joanne looked sharply at her friend. "Why do you think that?" she snapped.

Laurie shrugged. "It's what they do."

Joanne looked at Laurie with hard and glittering eyes. "I don't think so."

Laurie was looking at the 45 "Spiders and Snakes," which was still in its jacket. She slipped it out and tried to hand it to Joanne, but Joanne had already chosen Aretha Franklin's "Until You Come Back to Me."

After school on Thursday, Laurie called to see if Joanne wanted to come to her house, but when her mother called her to come to the phone, Joanne didn't respond.

The next day, Sorry the cat appeared, as though nothing had occurred.

On Friday, Laurie spotted Joanne leaving school a short way in front of her and called to her, but she stopped when she saw her meeting up with J. J., Elly Thomas, and Elly's brother, Dwayne.

After that, her calls tapered off and eventually stopped entirely.

• • •

"How are you holding up?" Elvin Jr. cupped his wife's face between his palms as he readied to leave for work.

"Oh, you know."

"I don't. That's why I asked."

"Your father's more or less stabilized. I don't think his cognitive is any worse than it was the last few days. And he's eating and using the bathroom. Nana Makayla helps him with that and to shower, shave, and dress. And you know your mother—she's in her glory when she's helping people."

Elvin's tawny-colored eyes were wide, warm, and compassionate. "I appreciate your report, but I was asking about you."

"Me? I'm fine. Going food shopping."

Her husband brushed her hair back with the fingers of his right hand. "Get yourself something. One of those mini chocolate cake things you love."

She smiled. "And one for you? And for the kids? And for Papa Elvin and Nana Makayla?"

He shook his head, still smiling. "Just for us."

• • •

Connie Welles had come to hate food shopping. The market was forever changing the location of food she regularly bought, and the food companies were forever changing the packaging. How was a person, much less a family, expected to remain loyal to a product or brand? Isn't that what they wanted? Isn't that why they existed?

In recent months, Connie had noticed a change in the demeanor of friends and acquaintances. When she ran into people at the market or elsewhere in her routine travels, she experienced a coolness verging on hostility. The sensation did not enter her consciousness in a way that she was able to quantify or analyze, but she did sense a remove, as though people she knew and who had long accepted her, were now holding her at arm's length.

She hurried around the market, list in hand, eyes darting, head swiveling, as she searched, located, and made a bead for the items she wanted.

She was in the frozen food aisle, trying to find the prepackaged frozen pizzas, which were not where they'd been last week, when she heard a familiar voice.

"Connie Welles!"

Irritated by the distraction, she looked up and saw a familiar brown face smiling and heading her way. Shirley Thomas was pushing a cart filled with items that were not familiar to Connie.

Something was bothering Connie about Shirley, and for a moment she could not remember what it was. She started to greet her neighbor and ask about her family—her usual litany of supermarket greetings—when she remembered what it was.

She brought her cart abruptly to a halt. "Your daughter needs to stay away from my son."

Shirley's eyes widened. Several people passing by glanced at them. "What?"

"You heard me. Your family is stealing my son, keeping him overnight when his place is with his family!"

Taken by surprise, Shirley began to stammer. "He was upset, Connie. It was only a quick thing, to keep him safe until he could get his feet under him. I'm sorry if it offended—"

"Well, it did! You're saying he's not safe with his own family?"

Shirley cocked her head. "Well ..."

"Who are you to talk about who's safe? Why is my family your business?"

Shirley stepped closer; Connie drew back. "Connie, the boy was frightened. He needed—"

"You don't decide what my boy needs! You don't judge my family!"

Shirley managed to maintain a confidential, even caring tone. "I'm not judging. Things happen in every family. Anyone can have a hard time for a night or a day or two."

Connie was nodding vigorously. "And the family is who needs to deal with it. Not some nosy neighbors!" Her head snapped in the direction of her next item, and she wheeled her cart away, leaving Shirley stunned and humiliated. Other shoppers, all of whom were white, went out of their way to wheel their carts around her, giving her a wide berth.

• • •

J. J. didn't know where to turn. He went to school and even occasionally attended class. He walked home with either Elly or Jimmy Kelly, after which he stayed in his room and watched TV—usually Abbot and Costello or cartoons. He kept an ear out for his father, whose footsteps coming up the stairs invariably gave away his mood and allowed J. J. to prepare for whatever was to come. His mother drank at the front window, and his sister was out every afternoon and evening with Mario the jock. Schoolwork came so easily to her that she was not expected to work on her homework in the afternoon or evening as long as her grades were good and the teachers' comments on parent-teacher nights were positive.

Being with Mario the jock gave his sister entrée into that rarified clique of admired girls who rarely deigned to say much of anything to anyone except one another. J. J. noticed that a few of these girls were now acknowledging him with subtle nods.

Saturdays, J. J. typically rode around the neighborhood on his bike, seeing what there was to see and catching up on what news was available to a passerby on a bike—who had a new car, whose brother was buff from training and was perhaps out in the street throwing a football, whose sister was suddenly hotter than the pimply skinny kid with braces everyone remembered.

But this January Saturday, J. J.'s father told him in his no-nonsense tone to get in the car.

"Where're we going?"

"To see someone about you."

"To see someone? What do you mean?"

"Never mind. Just get in the car."

173

J. J. did as he was told and noted that his mother was in the passenger seat, looking out the window with the same non-expression she wore when looking out the living room window.

But there was a difference. His mother turned around and looked at J. J. with an intensity that took him by surprise. She was not angry but focused in a way he had not seen in a long time.

"We're taking you to a psychologist."

"What?" He looked from his mother to his father and back again. "Why?"

His father glared at him in the rearview mirror. "To find out what's wrong with you."

"But there's nothing wrong with me!"

"We'll see," his father said.

• • •

They drove north to an upscale Westchester neighborhood and parked on a hilly, tree-lined street where the homes were multistoried with dormers and extensions, well-tended, sloping green lawns, and driveways paved with imported stones.

J. J. and his parents waited in a drab faux-wood-paneled room whose windows and door to a yard were covered with blinds that were not entirely closed. While the air outside was cold, the heat in the room and its lack of ventilation left J. J. feeling overly warm and slightly faint.

The psychologist, who was introduced as Warren Cluckman, asked J. J.'s parents why they had brought J. J. in today. His mother didn't answer, but J. J. was surprised at how loquacious and prepared his father was. He took several sheets of paper from his left pants pocket and began to read a long list of J. J.'s misbehaviors—examples, dates, and times of his backtalk and acting out.

Cluckman then spent the remainder of the session, which was a very long ninety minutes, grilling J. J. as to what caused his misbehavior.

J. J. had no answers. He had never thought of his behavior or speech as misbehavior, though he nearly always knew beforehand and as events were unfolding that nothing but trouble would come from whatever he was doing or saying.

But he would not have characterized these events as misbehavior. He thought he was being himself—not so different from any other kid. He knew his father was stressed and unhappy, though he didn't entirely understand why. He knew his mother stayed apart from the family and took her drinks to the living room window, from which she watched the world go by in her way.

At the end of the session, Cluckman demanded a promise from J. J. that he would mend his ways, change his behavior, and make his parents proud. J. J. agreed. Both he and Cluckman wanted to make J. J.'s father happy, though their reasons may have been very different. After the session, the Welles family, minus Joanne, drove back to Valley Stream and resumed their lives.

J. J. had long lived with a sense of deep loneliness, and now its depth increased into a chasm—a void that could not be traversed in any way that he was aware of.

He did find an answer in an array of stained wooden cabinets in the living room. It was a bar of sorts—a collection of bottles of various sizes, shapes, and colors, which, J. J. found, could help him find relief from his loneliness and pain. After a few drinks, his father's rages became more manageable; his inability to understand algebra or high school chemistry shrank in importance. Even the emptiness in his life where Elly had been was a little less empty because of this simple little cabinet and its contents.

Chapter 23

A fruit-and-flower basket arrived at the Welles home on Monday after-noon, unaccompanied by a card. At first, J. J. was unaware of it because he was laughing at Costello's whining complaints to his pal Bud on the TV. His father paid no attention to its arrival, except to answer the door, accept the package, hand the delivery boy a small tip, and set the basket on the dining room table for Connie to deal with. Connie had been sitting right there at the window as the delivery boy came up the walk, but she paid no attention to it at all.

She became more interested once John had set the package on the table, and she came over to inspect it. The package was a beautifully arranged and decorated basket of mixed fruit, flowers, and sweets. There was no indication as to why it had come or who it was from. She inspected it, turned it around on the table, and wondered if she might eat some of the chocolate. She liked chocolate, and this chocolate was very good chocolate indeed.

But she didn't. An idea was occurring to her as to its source.

After dinner, she picked up the phone and dialed a number she had all but forgotten.

"Hello?" came the familiar voice.

"Yes, hi. This is Connie Welles."

"Connie! I'm so glad you called. I hope you received the delivery okay."

Connie hesitated, infuriated but not wanting to embarrass herself. "I'm sending it back."

"Why? Just enjoy it. Or, if you prefer, forget it. But don't send it away. That would be a waste."

Connie's anger was gathering steam. "What would be a waste is you trying to buy my friendship with food the way you've done with the whole neighborhood all these months!" Shocked at her own words, Connie held the receiver away from her face and looked at it as though it had offended her. Then she hung up.

• • •

J. J. lived in a precarious universe of chance. His day-to-day experience depended upon his father's mood, his mother's presence or absence, and whomever he came across while in school, walking the local streets, or riding his bike.

This was true, as far as he could tell, for not only his daily life but his future. How would he cope with the intimidating world of high school and teenage nightlife? What did his future hold? How would he earn a living? Would he marry and have children of his own? These questions were beyond him to ask or even consider. Though he had been told how important planning for the future was, the future was, to J. J., another language entirely.

His priority was clawing and scratching his way through each day and the inevitable night that followed.

• • •

Jimmy Kelly was riding his bike along Piccadilly Downs, a north-south street that ran the length of the Yorkshire section of Lynbrook, dividing that village from the Village of Valley Stream to the west. He saw the jock, Mario, riding bikes with his friend J. J.'s sister, Joanne. Jimmy watched, following at a distance as they rode up to Scranton Avenue and then west and south again on Horton Avenue, toward Joanne's house, which was just around the block.

Once in front of her house, Joanne got off her bike, threw her arms around Mario's neck, and kissed him. Mario let her kiss him but seemed embarrassed and didn't kiss her back. As Jimmy watched, the couple spoke for a few minutes, then Joanne walked her bike up her driveway toward her garage, and out of sight.

Mario turned, noticed Jimmy Kelly watching, rode his bike to him, and asked his name. He asked if Jimmy knew the family that lived in the house whose yard Joanne had disappeared into, and Jimmy said that he did, but didn't offer anything more.

Mario went on to talk about himself—about some of the kids he hung around with at night, about the sports in which he had lettered.

Jimmy nodded but said nothing until Mario asked if he was ever out riding his bike after school at night or on the weekend. Jimmy said he was.

Mario grinned, pushed Jimmy's shoulder, and said, "Hey, then I'll see ya 'round."

• • •

If J. J. Welles lived in a rickety world that stood on flimsy legs in a shaky universe, Jimmy Kelly lived in a universe built on solid ground with his parents as foundational pillars. His father, Tom, in particular, had instilled in him the notion that hard work, a competitive mindset, and a keen eye for opportunity would pay off in a good life and that having, aiming at, and achieving goals were worthwhile endeavors.

Jimmy was not a great student, but he had learned the simple value of doing his homework. If he did his homework, he had learned, the grades would follow—and so they did. Not spectacular grades, but passing grades and perhaps a bit more.

What colored his otherwise spartan world with sunshine and sweetness was Lucy. Every day, his best friend waited for him, wanting little more than his company, his attention, and perhaps a treat.

Lucy embodied a core value that Jimmy's father had instilled in him: loyalty. And Jimmy showed the same loyalty his father demanded and his dog so willingly gave him to his own friend, Ernie Derico— whom he visited every month at the county jail and whom he looked forward to seeing once he was released, which was perhaps only a few months away.

Like J. J., Jimmy Kelly had little thought of his future, but unlike J. J., he had always assumed he would follow in his father's footsteps and join the police force.

• • •

Ernie never admitted it, but he was terrified in jail. He put on a stoic face when Jimmy visited and somewhat less so when Joanne Welles did—visits that were less frequent than Jimmy's at first, but perhaps more meaningful to Ernie.

In jail, anything and everything could lead to a fight. A cigarette, a word, a look, a perception. Fights and beatings went on all the time, and Ernie was afraid of the bigger, tougher guys, and those who were members of gangs or groups whose members were more intimidating and menacing because of their numbers.

In a strange way, Ernie's fears led to his saving grace; once a week a guard went around to all the cells, wheeling a cart loaded with books that were there for the taking. So Ernie took a book a week, and while he'd had no interest in school as a student, his fears and loneliness led him to read and eventually to study subjects that interested him.

He began by reading novels but soon moved to biographies. Imaginary people did not interest him, but reading about actual famous people who had transcended their struggles and pain to achieve greatness in any number of fields was enthralling and inspiring.

He was fascinated by his circumstances—not from a place of ego, but as a puzzle, a maze from which he was determined to find an exit.

He found and read books about philosophy, sociology, the law, and addiction. He read spiritual works about tending to others, and his awareness of his own terror informed a newfound willingness to learn, work, and administer to others. He was deeply attracted by the notion that his own pain could somehow help others in similar circumstances.

He began studying to become an alcoholism and substance abuse counselor, and while he didn't understand everything he read, he was determined to learn, to find a program once he had his freedom, and to make the most of his opportunities.

He shared his excitement with Jimmy Kelly, who was happy for his friend but did not fully understand Ernie's attraction to something that to Jimmy was essentially schoolwork. Ernie barely noticed; when Jimmy visited, he had an audience, and Ernie pontificated and lectured, trying out his newly learned ideas in his own voice with a little flavor of his own.

• • •

During much of the previous year, Joanne Welles had spent much of her free time with Laurie Derico, but she had come to see Laurie as judgmental, particularly of the Thomas family, whom Joanne had come to know through her brother's influence. The more she got to know the Thomas family—particularly Elly Thomas—the more she liked them. While it was probably true that she'd originally categorized them in her mind by their most noticeable characteristic—their color—she ceased doing so as she got to know them.

Because she was a naturally good student, Joanne had a lot of free time. Her homework rarely required more than a half hour after dinner, after which she would go out. The time she had spent with Laurie, she now devoted to Mario the jock. She didn't know Mario, even now that she was, by virtue of the ID bracelet he had given her, technically his girlfriend. She didn't need to know him. He looked terrific, and she could bask in the glow of his three-letter jock status, which raised her social profile exponentially.

She knew that walking home with Elly and Dwayne was a head-wind socially. The racist taunts and verbal assaults had died down, but some social snubs remained and extended somewhat to Joanne. She was protective of her brother, and his friendship with Elly meant that her protectiveness naturally extended to her and her family.

Her relationship with Mario consisted entirely of being seen by his side at night. He was old enough to drive, but for some reason preferred riding around on his oversized Sting-Ray bicycle. She was confused by his reluctance to touch her—to hold her hand or to put his arm around her. She had kissed him only once, and he had not returned her kiss and had never tried to slide his hand down her blouse, into her bra, or into her pants.

Her confusion was compounded by the fact that he claimed to want her as "his girl"; that was the way he put it. She was "his girl." And yet …

One day she noticed him talking to Dwayne; she saw the looks in both their eyes, their body language, their eager smiles—and she knew.

Mario liked boys. More specifically, Mario liked Dwayne, and apparently, Dwayne liked Mario too.

Well, that was fine with her. She didn't want anything from Mario besides the social status being seen together conferred upon her. He wanted their relationship to continue because it hid his true nature; she wanted the status. So they continued their subterfuge, each enjoying its particular fruits.

During Joanne's visits to the jail, she was deeply impressed by Ernie's transformation. She had always found him attractive in a "brother's friend" sort of way, and she liked that he was a tough, experienced "bad boy." Relationships to Joanne were very much about the social status they conferred. Being with Mario the jock conferred a kind of status, and being with Ernie did too, albeit a different sort of status—that of being with a "bad boy."

But what she saw unfolding during her visits to Ernie at the jail was much more substantial—the genuine maturing of a young man who was finding his place in the world, a meaningful place where he could grow, contribute, and flourish. And this was more attractive than any schoolgirl crush she'd ever known. Within a month or so, Mario the jock was forgotten; Joanne was falling in love.

• • •

Shirley went to the mall instead of going home; she felt cramped and vulnerable and wanted to be around people but in a more open environment than at the market or in her home. At the mall she felt she was on display; she saw no one who looked like her, no one who *was* like her. The Green Acres Mall had been an open-air mall until about five years earlier, when a roof had been added, enclosing the space. That was how she felt now; enclosed and alone—trapped in someone else's universe.

She had thought she was on her way to accomplishing something—making Nana Makayla proud by swimming upstream against a powerful, old, and ingrained current. Now she could see how foolish she had been to believe that her little self could make a dent in a way of life that had been in place long before she, or Nana Makayla for that matter, was born.

She was exhausted. She had worked much of her adult life to model her beliefs and behavior after those of Nana Makayla, but she now felt so much more like her own mother, who had grown up with familial echoes of Jim Crow oppression pressing down on even recent generations—subtle and not-so-subtle bigotry that had probably contributed to the illnesses and early deaths of both her parents and her only sister.

They had capitulated, whereas Shirley had insisted on rising. She didn't know how or with whom, and then she'd met Elvin and his magnificent parents, especially his mother—who was a true modern queen who seemed utterly untouched by racism or the patronizing looks and comments that Shirley experienced every day.

She arrived home and breezed past the children, who were in the living room—Dwayne reading and Elly writing. She climbed the stairs to Papa Elvin and Makayla's loft, where Makayla sat in a chair next to the bed where Papa Elvin lay, eyes closed, under a multicolored quilt. She had his left hand in her right and was rubbing the back of his hand with her other hand as she hummed some familiar tune.

She looked up at Shirley and smiled, but when she saw her daughter-in-law's expression, her smile vanished. "Ohhh," she said, reaching up with her left hand and cupping the side of Shirley's face.

The dam broke, and a sob burst from between Shirley's lips, and then another, until she had reached the end of her breath but was still pushing out sobs. She began to gasp, eyes wide with panic at not having enough air.

"Shh, shh, shhh," said Nana Makayla as Papa Elvin opened his eyes.

"Little girl," he muttered gently, the first intelligible syllables he had uttered since his stroke. Nana Makayla looked at him, startled, then blinked. Her mouth made a perfect circle, and she smiled a smile of pure love. Then she remembered and turned back to Shirley, who had by now caught her breath and was whining like a little girl.

"I don't want to have parties anymore!" She was crying again, her head in Nana's lap.

"Oh, *mtoto*. Okay. Okay. If you don't want to, you don't have to. But remember, you were only going to put your best food forward, and that's what you did. In fact, you did much more, mind you. Yes, you did! The results aren't up to you. The results were never up to you, and no one said the results would last some length of time. The results are always up to God."

"But Nana!"

Nana Makayla touched a finger to Shirley's lips. "Shh, now. And remember this: no one is saying that any backward steps will last either. No one knows. No one knows."

Chapter 24

Connie was staring at a wall of individually wrapped seeded Italian breads. She had been perusing the shelves in this aisle because she needed butter, milk, and cheese—dairy items that were at the far end of the aisle—but the bread had stopped her and, for some reason, had brought on a sadness that was nearly too much to bear. Her eyes had started to tear, and she swallowed and looked down at her shopping list, which she clutched in her left fist while holding a pen in her right. She'd been crossing items off the list—chicken, chopped meat, corn, broccoli, peanut butter, apples, bananas, and now dairy.

What was happening to her? She felt as though she were falling apart. How was it possible that she had never been aware of how badly John frightened her? He had been this way since she met him, only six years after the war, and she had understood on some level that he, along with all the other boys, had been damaged by what they'd been through—what they'd seen.

She'd been seduced into believing she and John were very good parents because Joanne was such an easy child. She was good at just about everything, needed no extra help with her schoolwork, hadn't been in any trouble that Connie was aware of, and had never been pregnant, as far as Connie knew.

But then came J. J., who was an unexpected handful. He had a quick, smart mouth and would say whatever came into his head— which could be just about anything—to anyone. He could not seem to show up regularly for school and was failing at least two of his classes.

Where had they gone wrong? What could they have done differently?

Blinking back her tears, Connie hurried down the aisle, eyes darting from her list to the space in front of her cart to make sure she didn't crash into anyone. As she arrived in front of a display of vitamin-fortified American cheese, she felt someone looking at her and saw, out of the corner of her eye, a woman watching her. Connie looked up angrily and was about to give the woman a piece of her mind when she realized that the woman was Anna Derico.

"Connie Welles?"

Connie's features softened as she remembered some of what had happened in Anna's life. "Anna."

"How've you been?" Anna asked.

"Oh, fine. Fine. And—" Connie stopped herself from asking Anna how she'd been or how her family was; Connie knew. "You look well," Connie said, deeply aware that this was a lie; what she'd meant was *You look well, considering.* She was embarrassed because Anna knew it was a lie too.

Anna's forehead creased, then her eyes lit up, and she touched Connie's wrist. "Let's go to the diner for coffee."

"Okay," Connie said, surprising herself. That someone was inviting her for coffee was so unexpected that she had no ready answer except to say yes.

They drove separately, and when Connie arrived, Anna was already seated beyond the rotating cake stand, in a cool, blue vinyl booth near the back of the diner. Once they were seated and their coffees had been served, Anna folded her arms on the table in front of her and said, "So, how've you been?"

"I don't know," Connie said with some embarrassment. "My life seems to be falling apart. I don't think I ever knew my husband, and my son's been difficult. We tried to get him some help, but I don't think it did any good. My daughter's never around, and I'm— I just don't know who I am anymore."

Anna's eyes softened; she covered Connie's hand with one of her own.

Connie's eyes filled, she shook her head and looked away. "And look who I'm telling this to!"

Anna looked steadily back at her. "You're telling this to a friend."

"How do you … How do you deal with it all?" Connie was aware that her hands were shaking.

Anna didn't answer but sipped her coffee. Connie did the same. After a few minutes, Anna said, "Let's go to the movies."

• • •

They saw *The Sting* at the Studio 1 theatre, and the clever plot, along with Paul Newman and Robert Redford—the film's handsome stars—carried their minds away from the problems of the moment. Afterward, Anna suggested they go to a bar; Connie countered by suggesting ice cream, which Anna agreed to. They took Connie's car. While Connie drove, Anna started to talk.

"Running into you was kind of a godsend, Connie."

"Really?" Connie was astonished. "Me?" No one had ever called her a godsend before.

"No one talks about anything in my family. My parents didn't talk. They were focused on having enough to eat every day." She glanced at Connie. "The Depression."

Connie nodded. "Mine too. My problems are nothing compared to theirs."

"Well," Anna said. "Your problems are your problems." They sat at the ice cream shop's counter, their voices low, heads bent together. Anna had a scoop of vanilla ice cream; Connie splurged and had a butterscotch sundae.

"My son's in jail for robbing a liquor store, my one daughter's dead, my other daughter's doing God knows what, and my husband thinks I don't know he's having an affair." Anna spoke evenly, as though reciting a shopping list.

"An affair?" Connie breathed.

Anna didn't answer right away. Two spoons of ice cream later she said, "And I know who with."

Connie waited, and when Anna didn't answer she said, "What are you going to do about it?"

"Do? What can I do? He wants to make a fool of himself after twenty-two years of marriage. I say let him. I'm going to live my own life, like we're doing right here."

· · ·

J. J. crossed Mill Road and was walking home along Roosevelt Avenue. An algebra problem was stuck in his mind. His eighth-period math teacher, Mr. Worrell, had gone over the problem with the class twice, and J. J. had stayed after school to see if he could find out why the problem was so baffling. And he'd made progress. The first time around, his answer was different from the teacher's and the class's. But then he learned that algebra had an order of operations Mr. Worrell referred to as PEMDAS: parentheses, exponents, division, multiplication, addition, and subtraction.

And J. J. had seen a glimmer of light, but just a glimmer—a fleeting spark of hope in his lifelong losing battle with math. The glimmer quickly flickered out as he went over the problem in his mind and arrived at a new and different answer.

He turned left under the railroad trestle, then crossed Rockaway Avenue and continued along Brooklyn Avenue. Staying after school to talk to Mr. Worrell had caused him to miss the group of friends he usually walked with, but that was okay. He hadn't been feeling very friendly these last few days, and he was fine with walking alone.

He passed the Brooklyn Avenue School—an ancient, forbidding, austere-looking building—and the dark apartments across the street where he knew you could buy certain drugs if you knew the right tenants.

He thought he saw his sister up ahead, alongside Jimmy Kelly, Elly, Dwayne, and someone else; they were approaching the firehouse at the fork in the road. He hurried to catch up.

Joanne and Jimmy Kelly were walking on either side of Mario the jock, who was riding some kind of enhanced Sting-Ray despite being at least seventeen and eligible to drive.

"Hey," J. J. said breathlessly as he drew even with the group. Mario the jock and Jimmy Kelly were talking about music—a song called "Rock Me Gently" that J. J. had never heard of. He listened to their conversation for a few minutes, surprised that Jimmy Kelly had any awareness of music at all. He had never shown interest in much besides his dog, Lucy, and tagging along with the older boys.

Jimmy was walking on the sidewalk side of Mario the jock's bicycle, and Joanne was walking on the street side, looking at once faintly amused and faintly annoyed.

Elly smiled, and J. J. could see she was delighted to see him.

"Hey," she said, and J. J. smiled back. Dwayne was half buried under an armload of books and said nothing. J. J. thought about talking to Dwayne about the math problem but was diverted by a powerful urge to confide in Elly.

As the group took the right-hand fork southward onto Forest Avenue, J. J. veered left and north on Brooklyn Avenue, and Elly veered with him. The two walked in silence—the sounds of Sunrise Highway's traffic rising and falling constantly from the left, along with silence from the right.

J. J. looked down as he walked. He was near to bursting with fear and remorse and angst but had no words to put to these feelings. Elly gave him a curious then encouraging look, but soon returned her attention to simply walking.

Someone—probably a teenager or a boy in his twenties—yelled an insult at them from a car, and J.J. twitched and walked just a little bit closer to Elly, who paid the person no mind.

He didn't want to go home. He did not feel welcome there. His father terrified him and did not seem to want to know what was wrong except to claim J. J. was somehow defective and had to be sent out for repairs.

His mother was not really a presence in the house but rather a ghost at a window. His sister was okay, but she was his sister—not a real person.

There was some sort of tension between his mother and Shirley Thomas. He could feel the resentment vibrating from his mother. He had been staying away from the Thomas family—perhaps because of his mother's resentment, perhaps for some other reason. He looked back with longing on the days when he and Ernie and Jimmy Kelly rode around the neighborhood and just watched. Observed.

He didn't know what he wanted, but he wanted something.

Chapter 25

Lou and Anna arrived home from the diner in the same car but as distant as though they'd been across the country from one another. Anna went to the upstairs bathroom, got washed, used the toilet, put her hair up, and went to bed, her back to her husband's side of the bed.

Lou thoroughly washed his hands, but he still felt dirty. He washed his face, then took a shower, but this was a feeling that would not be washed away. He knew he had made a terrible mistake—one he could not undo—and he didn't know what the future held for him and his wife. His family had fallen apart, and he was one of the causes.

He now saw what he had failed to see for so long; Anna was at the diner every day, often for twelve hours or more. She did all of the shopping, all of the cleaning, and washed all of the clothes. She cared for him when he was sick.

What was wrong with him?

After trying and failing to scrub away his guilt and self-loathing, he finally climbed into bed next to Anna, who was lying as far away from him as she could.

He reached for her shoulder but faltered. He could not bring himself to touch her, to be pushed away, to bear the brunt of whatever anger she rightfully sent his away.

"I'm so sorry, Anna," he mumbled.

She said nothing.

• • •

"It's for you," Connie called from the foot of the stairs. Loud music was emanating from J. J.'s room—"Bad, Bad Leroy Brown." Joanne's door, she knew, was probably open.

"It's for you!" she called again.

Joanne's head appeared at the top of the stairs. "For me?"

Connie held out the phone, and Joanne came down, took it, and stretched the cord up the steps.

"Joanne?" It was Laurie's voice.

"Hey," Joanne ventured cautiously.

"Hey," Laurie's tone was cocky, cavalier. "Guess what I did?"

"Um, got your driver's license?"

"Better. I just did it with Ricky Taylor."

"Really?" Joanne found this hard to believe. "You *like* that guy?"

"Who said I like him? I did it with him. But I can't stand him."

"I don't get it."

"Who's cooler than Ricky Taylor? Who is cooler to have fucked than Ricky Taylor?"

"But he treats everyone like shit."

"That's how cool he is—too cool for anybody else. He hardly even talks to anyone." She laughed, delighted with herself and her accomplishment.

Joanne was confused. "So you can't stand him, and you fucked him?"

Laurie laughed. "Well, really, I didn't fuck him."

"What? I don't—"

"I fucked *at* him."

The words echoed in Joanne's mind. "You fucked *at* him?"

"Yep."

"Okay."

"Did you know that Bonni Bird wrote and recorded a song about my sister, Debbie, called 'Songbird'?"

"Can I hear it? Can you play it by the phone?"

"Hang on." Joanne heard shuffling sounds on the other end of the line, then a guitar strumming softly and Bonni Bird's lonely voice singing about the songbird that was Debbie Derico.

• • •

J. J. was spending as little time as possible at home; he didn't feel welcome there, so he'd begun spending time with the older boys who hung around behind the high school, at Mill Pond Park, and at Hewlett Bay Park behind Gibson Station. His mother had begun asking questions about what he took to be insinuations and mistrust. "Where are you going?" "Who are you going with?" "I don't like the look of those boys."

He was surprised that his presence was tolerated among the older boys. He had heard that to be allowed entrée to this group of boys, you had to submit to a beating. If they knew you or you had a brother who was part of that crowd, the beating wouldn't be too bad, but if you were a stranger or a member of a minority, or if you talked back during your interview, your beating could be much worse. The beatings were administered to the person's behind with paddles that were shorter but wider than baseball bats, while one or more of the group held the person, who often clenched his wallet between his teeth to muffle his screams.

After hanging around for two weeks, J. J. was brought down by Benny Boone for an interview. Benny gave him pointers for answering questions, and later he would wonder whether those answers were planted so that he would walk into trouble. Benny had suggested he be sure to sound tough and stand up to those performing the interview.

When J. J. did as he was told, he was labeled a disrespectful wise guy during the interview, who deserved extra shots, which is what the individual strokes of the beatings were called. Existing members of the crowd were allocated two shots, with the four biggest guys and the fraternity officers allocated sendoffs, which were shots with running starts.

As soon as the shots began, he began to scream—he screamed the entire time, his wallet between his teeth. J. J. endured fifty-two shots, the worst of which occurred at the very end, on the backs of his legs, which he somehow covered with his hand, whereupon his hand was hit.

He was not immediately aware of the injury to his hand because he was having so much trouble walking. He had to walk in tiny steps, and two of the participants walked a few blocks with him and held him under the arms to keep him from falling, but they eventually grew impatient and went on their way.

When he finally stumbled into the house, everything was as it always was; his father was at the kitchen table, staring into the past, while his mother was at the living room window, staring into the distance. No one commented on his appearance or the way he was walking, and J. J. slowly crept up to bed.

He stayed home from school the next day. He couldn't walk, and his legs were purple and blue and yellow. The pain from his hand was still less than that from his behind and the backs of his legs, so he was unaware of that injury until he went to the bathroom and found that his hand was frozen in a claw-like position and his nails had been driven into the skin, with black blood crusted around them. One of the nails had been partially torn off. The hand throbbed, and he went back into his room, gingerly lay down on his stomach, and buried his face in the pillow. He cried a little bit, then went downstairs and approached his father.

"I did something to my hand."

His father raised an eyebrow and examined J. J.'s hand, turning it over twice as J. J. winced and tried to pull away.

"How'd you do this?"

"Playing ball. Got hit with a bat."

"Why are you walking like that?"

"Got hurt. Pulled a muscle or something."

They drove to the family's doctor, who x-rayed the hand and pronounced it broken in several places. He drilled small holes in several fingernails to relieve the pressure and allow the blood to seep out.

His parents asked no more questions about his injuries, and after a few days, J. J. went back to school, walking slowly and deliberately, and sitting down carefully. He was so focused on getting from one place to another and on coping with the pain that he did not notice that the older boys, into whose midst he had supposedly been initiated, were now turning their backs on him. Only Jimmy Kelly and Elly Thomas were kind enough to invite him to walk with them, and both slowed their walks home to accommodate his disability.

At the end of that week, he had a pleasant surprise: he had passed his algebra midterm exam.

• • •

Elly was lying in bed, her eyes drawn to the window, where a nearly full moon was illuminating her family's yard and much of the street. She heard her grandmother in the hallway.

"Nana Makayla?"

Her grandmother's warm and comforting presence appeared beside her and sank into the bed next to Elly, warming one side of her body. "What do you do if you have a friend who's scared and you don't know how to help him?"

Nana Makayla looked thoughtful, then looked down at Elly with kind eyes. "Anytime I don't know what to do, and many times when I do, I ask for guidance."

"Does he answer?"

"Always, child. Always."

"But how do you know? I sometimes ask him what to do but I don't hear anything back."

Nana Makayla laughed. "Sometimes his answer is 'No,' sometimes his answer is 'Try me again later,' and sometimes his answer is 'You have to come up with your own answer.'"

"I'm afraid, Nana Makayla."

"What are you afraid of, *mjukuu*?"

Elly thought about this. "I don't know. I guess I'm afraid of what could happen. How do I not be afraid?"

Nana Makayla smiled her special smile and said, "It's okay to be afraid. Everyone's afraid."

"Even you?"

"Yes, even me. I just don't let my fears run the show. I tell them to sit down in the corner and be quiet!" She shook her finger as though scolding.

Elly laughed.

"What I suggest is for you to talk to God. Tell him you love him, then tell him what's on your mind. He will be your friend—your very best friend. And he will help you to find people who are kind and who will be your true friends. They are out there. Ask for help in finding them. Seek and you shall find."

Several hours later, when the moon had risen to its apex in the night sky, Elly heard a tapping on the window, which was impossible because her room was on the second floor. She heard it again, so she went to the window and peered in all directions, then opened it and leaned out.

J. J. was standing below, looking up at her.

"Are you okay?" she asked.

He nodded and beckoned for her to come down. Since he was a very real manifestation of a very specific prayer that she had only begun to pray this very night, Elly put on a robe and quietly crept downstairs, whispering along the way, "Thank you, God. That was fast!"

Chapter 26

Tom Kelly walked into his house on Friday afternoon and bent to pet Lucy, who had greeted him enthusiastically at the door. He stood still in the living room, his hands on his hips, listening and trying to figure out who was in the house. Jimmy didn't seem to be there. He could hear Julie playing her tape-recorded singing lessons and singing her exercises—her scales and arpeggios. He had worked a four-to-noon shift, plus two hours of overtime, and he was famished. Dinner should have been cooking, but plainly it wasn't. What was going on?

He looked at the refrigerator, the usual place his family left notes about where they were or what they were doing, but there was nothing. He went into the bathroom, but Erin's makeup was still in its case. No tissues dabbed with foundation or blush had been tossed into the waste basket, and yet her purse was missing.

He went to the bottom of the stairs. "Jimmy! Jimmy!" He went up to Julie's room and knocked.

"Come in."

Julie was standing beside her desk, her posture erect, shoulders and back straight, a finger on the Play button of her little cassette deck. Her eyebrows went up when he came in.

"Where is everybody?"

"Jimmy took the bus to the jail to see Ernie Derico."

"And Mom?"

Julie shrugged. "Don't know."

Tom gave her a suspicious look, though he was sure she was telling the truth. The look was his default when he received an answer that displeased him.

He went back outside, walked from the front door to the sidewalk, and looked up and down the street, thinking hard. He was hungry and wanted his dinner, which had not yet even been prepared, much less put in the oven to cook.

He squinted, still thinking. It wasn't his birthday or his anniversary. Christmas had been weeks ago. His wife's and children's birthdays were no time soon.

Where is she? he wondered.

He got into the patrol car and began driving around the neighborhood, looking for the family's wood-grained 1972 Ford Country Squire. It was not in any of the neighbors' driveways. He drove to the supermarket, assuming she would be there and feeling a little bit foolish. She was probably buying him a steak, which she would bring home and cook, and he'd probably complain about it!

But she wasn't at the market. He kept driving.

He supposed she could be at the mall, where he would have trouble finding her, if he could find her at all. The parking lots at the mall were enormous, but what would she be doing there? Clothes shopping on a Friday afternoon when she should be home, preparing dinner for him and the kids? He wove through the mall's lots, then headed back through Gibson Station, past the church the family attended.

And he saw the car, parked on a side street several doors from the church.

What was she doing there?

The big, oak front door to the sanctuary was unlocked. He walked in and looked around. The sanctuary was empty and dark.

But there was a sound—a sort of whooshing. He walked toward the front of the sanctuary and saw a little movement. A blonde head moving just above one of the front pews. He stopped and watched.

Erin was praying. He couldn't hear what she was saying, but she was praying, her eyes closed, whispered words rushing from her. He could not make the words out, so he came closer until he could.

"I confess to you, Lord, that I have broken my marriage vows, both to you and to my spouse, and have caused untold pain, and I am so sorry Lord, and I repent of all my sin and the evil consequences of my weakness. Lord, I confess that I am weak, but that is no excuse, and I ask that in the power of the Holy Spirit, You would help me to turn away from my evil sins. Help me to overcome temptation and not to fall prey to the enticements of the flesh. Help me to run from sexual sin as the Bible says, and to break free from any sexual soul-ties that I have made. Please keep me, I pray, from being tempted to make any further contact in this regard. I ask that You help me to resist all temptation and to help me to make a complete break from this ungodly part of my life. Purify my heart, I pray, and enable me to turn away forever from this weakness, which I know must be called for what it is—ungodly sexual sin and adultery. Help me to no longer live for my own gratification, but rather I pray that I may be enabled to change my whole behavior toward my spouse and to live in marriage union with my spouse, as You have outlined in Your Word. Dear God, please give us both fresh, new love for each other, and may this evil that I have done not become a stumbling block in our marriage but the start of a new, closer fellowship with each other, and with You. This I ask in Jesus's name. Amen."

She rose and turned, and did not seem surprised to see Tom standing only three pews behind her. He stepped forward, took Erin by the hand, and led her out of the church, saying nothing about what he had seen, heard, or now knew to be true.

Tom and Erin had both been raised to be strict, traditional Roman Catholics, for whom divorce was not an option. Erin continued to go to Mass regularly, even daily—cleaving to Jesus and seeking his love and forgiveness while surrounding herself with the comforting accoutrements of her local church. The prayers, hymns, confession—even the architecture and the smell of polished wood—would remain comforts for the rest of her life.

While Jesus grew to be both savior and personal friend to Erin, Tom sought comfort with his own best friend, the bottle—most often alone. With the aid of his friend, he regularly communed with his father and other aspects of his imagination. Eventually, the couple's wounds became scars, and Tom and Erin were able to move forward in the same uneasy peace that had always been the basis of their marriage.

• • •

As Friday night turned into Saturday morning, J. J. and Elly sat several feet apart on the Thomas family's living room couch. They were drawn to one another despite the distance between their families and now sat on either side of a small stack of novels Elly had collected from shelves around the house. The novels were *To Kill a Mockingbird* by Harper Lee, *Native Son* by Richard Wright, *To Be Young, Gifted and Black* by Robert Nemiroff, adapted from Lorraine Hansberry's play of the same name, and *The Grapes of Wrath* by John Steinbeck.

"Sometimes," Elly said, "I read a book, and it takes me away and changes everything." Her brows knitted as she concentrated on what she was saying, and her eyelashes fluttered. "Or maybe the book changes me."

J. J. looked at each of the books and decided on *To Be Young, Gifted and Black*, while Elly chose *The Grapes of Wrath*.

They read together for several hours, until Shirley came downstairs to make coffee, saw her daughter with J. J., stopped, and watched them for several minutes until a corner of her mouth turned up and she went back to making coffee.

J. J. came away from the book feeling as if he knew Ms. Hansberry. He'd had none of her experiences. He was a white boy in a middle-class suburban neighborhood. Much of the book's magic grew from the author's ability to transport him into life experiences that were very different from his own—those of a Black woman who grew up in a Chicago ghetto, navigated a system rigged against people like her, developed her own transcendent artistic voice, and eventually became ill and died—all before the age of thirty-five.

J. J. had forgotten about whatever was on his mind. His heart ached for Ms. Hansberry, and he earnestly related this experience and his feelings to Elly, whose only reaction was a nod and a shy smile.

He went to the shelves in the Thomas living room, which took up all of one wall—from waist level to just below the ceiling. He ran his fingers over the titles. He turned to her. "What should I read?"

She made an "I don't know" face and watched as he continued to peruse the titles. Then she was next to him, tapping his shoulder and gently guiding him to one side. Her eyes had lit with purpose, and she touched the spine of a book called *Johnny Got His Gun*, written by Dalton Trumbo.

He took the book and turned to Elly. "I'd better get home. My father's gonna have it in for me. If he comes here, don't say I was here, okay? I don't want you getting in trouble. Tell your mother too."

Elly shrugged, went back to the couch, and took up her book again. As he walked to the door, she gave him a cheerful smile and held up a hand in a little wave.

. . .

Ernie's first month in jail had been an exercise in turtling up—protecting himself by closing himself off from other inmates and exposing as little as possible. He became a nearly nonexistent target, and yet, trouble still found him. Trouble found everyone, and you had to be willing to fight, because if you weren't willing to fight, you'd be mercilessly victimized. So he fought. He quickly learned to hit fast, hard, and repeatedly, and to do whatever he could do to stay on his feet. If you went down, you would probably be kicked in the face, gut, or groin, and possibly stomped—which could deliver lasting injuries.

For two months he turned down all services, including medical, mental health, nursing, substance abuse treatment, social work, dental and vision care, discharge planning, and reentry support. He was visited often by Jimmy Kelly, who said he was praying for him. Ernie didn't know what to say to that. He didn't believe in God. He didn't pray, and he hated church, where he had been bored almost to tears. His favorite in-church pastime had been looking at girls and imagining them naked.

He was also visited by Joanne Welles, who suggested that he partake of some of the services the jail offered, if only to make the time pass more quickly. He took her suggestion and was surprised to find that he enjoyed some of the offerings. He had never thought much about what he would do when he grew up, because he had little intention of growing up. He had always done whatever he wanted to do, lived by knee-jerk reactions, and worried more about how he was perceived by others, especially certain cool kids, than about any facts of his own life or his future.

He learned to look at his own life and realized that he had spent an awful lot of time finding and taking drugs of various kinds—particularly marijuana, crystal meth, and Valium. He would go through the medicine chests at friends' homes and take a few pills here and there, but not so much that he thought they would be missed. Of course, he didn't know for sure if they would be missed, but who would suspect a boy who was there one day out of every few weeks?

Gaining some perspective about his behavior and activities led him to learn, with the help of a therapist, about the feelings behind his activities. He slowly realized that he felt quite a lot of fear, and his ideas about himself and others began to change. While he still refused to wear his heart on his sleeve or to allow others to know what he was thinking or feeling, he slowly became less concerned about the opinions of others. He remained resistant to vulnerability—but in jail, that was simply common sense and self-protection.

He realized that just about everyone else thought and felt these same things, and as he felt better and better about himself, he became intrigued by the idea of helping others to feel better about themselves too.

He worked with the discharge planning and reentry support team to fashion a plan for his release. With their help, he decided to attend a county-wide program supported by the National Council on Alcoholism. Several years later, he would go on to enroll in a state-supported community college program to get his CASAC—Credentialed Alcoholism and Substance Abuse Counseling certification, a new degree that would be first available in 1979.

As he progressed in his discussions and planning, he shared everything with Joanne, who became his cheerleader and biggest support. Every time she saw him—which, by the time of his release, was several times a week—she told him how well he was doing and that his goals were in sight.

And so they were. He absorbed pamphlets about the program he would embark upon when he got out, and he became determined to succeed.

On the day of his release, he was given civilian clothes and a small amount of cash, and after shaking hands with the support team, he was ushered into a waiting room, where he was embraced by Joanne Welles and Jimmy Kelly—a free man.

Chapter 27

When he wasn't in school, Jimmy Kelly often went to church with his mother, waiting in the rear of the sanctuary while she prayed, usually about a half hour, but sometimes longer. He sometimes prayed too, his mind skimming the surface of the prayers he'd been hearing and saying all his life. They were familiar, and repeating them was like greeting a kind, old friend. He knew that some people—his father, for instance—thought that God was punishing and angry, but he didn't believe that. Jimmy Kelly's notion of God came from his mother, who believed in forgiveness and grace and God's love. He felt bad for people who got tangled up in wondering how there could be a God when there was so much cruelty, sickness, war, disease, and hurt in the world. That the world was so filled with these things was why God was here, he believed. So many of these bad things were caused by people, not God. God allowed people to do whatever they wanted, and sometimes what they wanted was to murder and go to war. He had learned that the very first week of Sunday school.

He also learned a lot about God from Lucy, who had so many traits Jimmy Kelly thought that God must have—traits his mother had as well, though she believed that everyone was what she called fallen—in other words, sinners. He didn't argue with his mother.

He had begun walking home from school with Dwayne. The more he walked home with Dwayne, the more he liked him. Dwayne was not like anyone he'd ever met. He hardly spoke at all, and he didn't seem to understand what people meant when they talked to him unless they were very specific. Dwayne loved math, but it was more than that. Math was Dwayne's language. To Dwayne, everything was math—angles and shapes and formulas and probabilities. These were all Dwayne thought about or talked about, when he talked at all.

Dwayne never hurt anyone, never said he'd do something and then didn't do it. Dwayne kept his word and never made fun of anyone. And when he was picked on, Dwayne just took it. In his own way, Dwayne was the toughest person Jimmy Kelly knew. He could take a beating without crying like no one Jimmy Kelly had ever seen.

When he'd first met Dwayne, the new boy had been happy, but after a few months of kids picking on him, he'd grown silent, and now he was silent most of the time.

Just a week before, Dwayne had invited him into his room. He hadn't said anything but just motioned him in with a wave of his arm. And then Dwayne showed Jimmy Kelly his ant farm.

After that, the two boys would meet after school, go to the Thomases' house, and spend hours watching the ants. Nothing stopped the little insects. They had their tasks and their complicated little lives, and they just kept at whatever they were doing.

Like Dwayne.

• • •

J. J.'s book was about a man who had been terribly injured in war and wakes up not knowing where he is or much of anything else. Slowly he realizes that he's been grievously wounded, but nearly everything in his circumstances remains hidden from him. He exists only in his own mind.

J. J. read about the man's prior life, which is vividly described in every other chapter. The man's memories and dreams are of a life fully lived—a life of love and adventure and fun. A very real and wonderful life.

Between those chapters of dreams and memories are the man's current experiences, which are portrayed as a frustrating, confusing, horrific puzzle. He realizes that he cannot see. He has been blinded by the war, and this knowledge devastates him. He reminds himself of the wonderful sights he has seen and those yet to be seen and is keenly aware that he will never see them. The beauty of a rose, the face of his beloved—all of life's rich visions are now lost to him because of his injuries.

He realizes he cannot hear and is devastated anew. He thinks of the great music he will never hear, and the luscious, sweet sounds of birds singing, of whispered tenderness, of the wind through the trees.

J. J. was immersed in the book, and he was horrified. It was as though he was experiencing the loss upon loss that is this man's plight.

The man strains his senses to somehow connect his consciousness to his own condition and to his surroundings—to examine himself with whatever is left of his senses—and he realizes that he has no face. He can feel the torn edges of nerve endings where his face had been, and he can feel that they end where his face should be. There is only a crater.

War has left this man with less than nothing—he has lost his senses and his identity. He is left with the acute awareness of his conditions and the knowledge that they were caused by war—senseless, unnecessary, useless, catastrophic war.

And yet, there remains hope in the tender caress of a nurse who strokes his hair and with whom he learns to communicate by tapping his head in Morse code.

The book left J. J. breathless the way horror movies did when he was too young to understand that they weren't real. The reality of the battlefield is made real through the horror of the man's mountain of losses.

He thought of his father and suddenly understood the explosive, awful reality that was locked and hidden away—what he had seen, what he had done. J. J. was awed, and he was moved.

• • •

The two women strolled into the diner and were shown to their table by Wes, the owner, who had by now seen them several times.

"Ladies." He dipped his chin in a deferential semi-bow and smiled politely. The women ignored him.

Anna Derico was small and olive-skinned, and her sad eyes critically examined every aspect of the diner, whose operation was her expertise, her life's blood.

Connie Welles was larger and less subtle, a whirlwind of a woman, whose blonde hair swirled around her head and whose distant blue eyes saw only what she had to see to make her way in the world, whose nuance and detail were beyond her.

They sat and began looking around for their waitress, a fortysomething woman with tied-back dirty blonde hair, big brown eyes, and a kind face. The woman saw them, nodded in recognition, and held up two fingers, confirming that she was to bring two coffees right over.

Anna wrung her hands, which clutched one another as though each one saw the other as a lifeboat and was attempting to clamber on board to save itself. "I'm so tired, Connie. I just don't know what to do! It's all too much—too much!"

Connie covered her friend's hands with her own and stroked the space between Anna's thumb and forefinger with her own thumb. She looked deep into Anna's eyes with what she hoped was a look of validation.

"I know, honey. It is too much. You know what? Let's have dinner this time."

"Dinner?" Anna was thrown. "What will my family do?"

"Who cares?" Connie declared with a wave of her hand. "Maybe they'll starve."

Anna began to laugh. The notion of her family starving!

They ordered pasta with chicken cutlets, meatloaf with mashed potatoes and gravy, poached eggs on toast, two sides of bacon, and a double cheeseburger—all of which they shared. Then they started on desserts.

"You know," said Connie, between mouthfuls of some kind of yellow cake with black-and-white icing, "I had to give that Shirley Thomas a piece of my mind. My son spent the night over there without my knowledge and is still making time with that daughter of hers."

Anna sat back, chewing thoughtfully. Her eyes traveled over the remnants of food that lay, like figures on a battlefield, all over the table. "You say the daughter's a bad influence?"

Now it was Connie's turn to think. "Honestly, I've never met her, and everything I've heard about her parents has been good."

"Maybe you could meet her before you prejudge."

Anna's suggestion had been made without malice or accusation—it was a simple observation, and so Connie could hear it without feeling that she, or her son, was being threatened. "Honestly," Connie said, "my John scares the hell out of that boy sometimes. Out of me too. Only one he doesn't scare is Joanne, and that's at least partly because she's not around." She tipped her head to either side. "Also because she's his little girl."

"Well," Anna observed. "The war ..."

Connie agreed. "He once told me a little bit but started to cry—sobbing like a baby. I felt so bad. I didn't know what to do. I think he was ashamed, and that was that. He never talked about it again."

"It must have been awful."

Connie smiled faintly. "I thought he was exciting, dangerous. Now I see he was just screwed up by the war."

Anna looked at her. "And J. J. went to the Thomases' house because his father scared him?"

Connie nodded. "I guess he felt safer there than in his own house."

Anna's eyes narrowed, and she folded her hands in front of her. "Well, you do what you want, but in my family, everyone did whatever they wanted, and it got out of control, and my family went *berpft*." She pursed her lips and made a little burping noise, bubbling her lips.

Connie pressed her lips together. She was thinking hard.

• • •

Jimmy Kelly saw that his new friend's differences were just facts, like his curly black hair, his math abilities, his brown skin, and his reluctance to speak. Dwayne rarely spoke, and he was extremely organized. He focused on one task at a time. He walked home. He ate dinner. He watched his ants. He did his schoolwork—one subject at a time.

For Jimmy Kelly, Dwayne was much easier to understand than most other kids, since he was not a bully, nor was he involved in any of the social groups that Jimmy found so confusing and difficult to navigate. And he didn't drink or use drugs.

Jimmy Kelly had noticed that Dwayne finished everything he started. He never left anything for later, and he wasn't afraid to let other people see him fail or make mistakes. Jimmy had never met anyone like this. It was as if Dwayne was missing the piece that made him feel bad when he made a mistake.

They talked about all sorts of things. Trees, for instance, were very interesting when you stopped to think about them. They were alive. Their age was apparent in the rings—the outer layers they grew each year. Dwayne was pretty sure they could communicate, but he didn't know how. He believed there were all sorts of things that science had not yet figured out. How trees talked was just one of them.

When the two boys were together, there wasn't much to say. They watched the ants build their tiny civilization, which Dwayne had received for Christmas just weeks earlier. The ants had immediately set about working together to build their world. They dug tunnels and scoured their environment for food, which Dwayne supplied in the form of sugar water and honey. They protected plant life. They divided up chores.

"Ants communicate by smell and motion and touch," Dwayne explained. "Each colony has its own smell. They lay trails made of their smell leading to their food. They also move their bodies in certain ways and use their antennae to communicate by touch." He said all of this without taking his eyes off the ants. Jimmy Kelly was impressed by how much Dwayne knew, and by how much his friend's ant colony grew in complexity each day. The ants knew their jobs and worked hard, and the changes were quickly evident.

"I like that they're all on the same team," Dwayne explained. Jimmy liked that too.

"Ants are eusocial," Dwayne continued.

"What's that?" Jimmy asked.

"It's the highest level of social development."

"Higher than us?" Jimmy asked.

Dwayne nodded. "Some of what makes ants eusocial is that they have child care for the baby ants, they have different groups in ant colonies that have different jobs, and they can't do each other's jobs."

They went on watching the ants for a while, then went outside to walk around, though it was January and the temperature was hovering right around freezing. They decided to go to the deli for tuna hero sandwiches. On the way back, they talked about baseball. Dwayne liked the Mets, while Jimmy Kelly liked the Yankees.

When he went home that evening, Jimmy was thinking about how the Yankees were like ants—each had his job to do. The pitcher had his, the catcher his, and each of the fielders had theirs.

Learning about Dwayne's ant colony stayed with Jimmy for days. Wherever he went, whatever he did, he thought about what his job was and what everyone else's jobs were. The ant colony changed Jimmy Kelly in ways he did not yet understand.

Chapter 28

Shirley pulled into the Sinclair station on Rockaway Avenue and waited as the young man filled her tank. Facing her, on the other side of the pump, she saw Connie Welles smiling at her. She looked away. She heard the car door open and inwardly cringed. *Ugh, no.*

"Hi, Shirley! So good to see you."

Now she had to look.

"Can we talk for a sec?" Connie was grinning down at her as the pump clicked and the attendant removed it from her gas tank and re-placed its cap. Connie's hair reminded Shirley of a small beige animal, coiling atop her head, ready to pounce.

Shirley looked directly at Connie without smiling. "No," she said, and drove away.

When she arrived home, she went directly upstairs; she needed to see Makayla, but Makayla was seated beside Papa Elvin, who was lying in bed, groaning.

She went downstairs and made herself a cup of tea. She had to get out of this town. Her old friends had been right when they'd said she was crazy for wanting to move to an all-white town. While Elvin was right to want to improve the family's quality of life by moving to a better neighborhood, and his willingness to be the first Black family in the vicinity was admirable, the reality of the situation had worn her down over time. The racist diatribes, both subtle and not so subtle, had, as she'd hoped, diminished, but what was left—J. J.'s mother's disapproval of Elly's influence—was too infuriating and painful to bear.

She heard Makayla's voice from upstairs, followed by the sound of the closing of a bedroom door. Makayla soon appeared at the bottom of the stairs, weary but happy to see her. She came and sat beside Shirley at the kitchen table. She took Shirley's hand.

"What is it, child?"

And just like that, all of her pain and frustration poured out—Elly's friendship with J. J., Connie's disapproval, the months of latent and overt racism directed at everyone in the family, Papa Elvin's illness. Makayla was squeezing her hand as she choked back tears.

"I don't want to live here anymore," Shirley said. "We should never have left. We should have stayed with our family, our friends. Oh, what are we going to do?"

The kindness in Makayla's eyes and the warmth of her smile calmed Shirley and brought her back to the moment. "First of all, whatever you decide to do will be the right thing. Know that. We will all be with you. We will all be together. You and Elvin have been so brave to have brought our family here. Give yourself credit for that. And think about this: we have survived it all. The children survived at school. We have survived the neighborhood. Be proud of that. Makayla tickled the inside of Shirley's arm with a fingernail. "I think maybe it is this woman, Elly's friend's mother's judgment, that is hurting you. But you know what? Her judgment is her problem. Not your problem, *mtoto*."

Shirley looked up at her mother-in-law's shining face and smiled.

• • •

J. J. did his homework after dinner in his room, then he came downstairs and saw that his father was seated at the head of the kitchen table, staring into space. His mother was out. She'd been out quite a lot recently, which was different. She hadn't sat in front of the living room window with her drink in nearly a week.

He went to the kitchen table and sat down beside his father. He said nothing, just sat quietly. His father looked at him just once but otherwise maintained his strange vigil.

J. J.'s mind was far away. He had been astonished by Elly's kindness. He had never, as far as he was aware, been offered such care and kindness. It was as though this girl communicated in a language that had been unknown to him.

• • •

After filling her car with gas and being spoken to so rudely by Shirley Thomas, Connie drove home to find J. J. sitting at the kitchen table with John, both of them staring into space. On the way home, an idea had come to her, and she wanted to run it by Anna. She dialed the phone while running water into a large pot in the sink.

But Anna was at the diner; she should have realized that. So she put the pot on the stove to boil, took out a box of spaghetti, broke the noodles in half, and dumped them into the pot. Then she opened three cans of tomatoes and one bottle of premade sauce, and spooned them into a pan, sprinkled in spices, and turned on the burner. Then she spread a pound of ground beef into another pan and set it on medium heat.

A half hour later, Joanne arrived, talking excitedly about Ernie's transformation into a diligent student and budding drug counselor. Connie found this a little hard to believe and perhaps convenient, given the young man's recent prison stint. She was afraid for Joanne, who, though smart, sometimes displayed a disturbing lack of judgment, especially when it came to boys. Maybe, Connie suggested, she and Ernie should take it a day at a time. This was met with the predictable impatient sigh and a whining, "Mommm!"

An hour later, the family had dinner together for the first time in Connie didn't know how long. The experience wasn't too bad.

She went upstairs after dinner, opened the door to J. J.'s room, and was stunned to find his room cleaned, his bed made. She went back downstairs, turned on the TV, and watched episodes of *Happy Days, M*A*S*H,* and *Hawaii Five-O.* When *Barnaby Jones* came on, she called Anna again and finally reached her. Anna was too tired to talk but perked up when Connie told her about her idea. Anna liked it. They spoke for twenty minutes. Now her idea had become a plan.

• • •

Ernie Derico had never been a good student. He had never been much of a student at all. He'd enjoyed woodworking, metalworking, and gym, and he'd successfully done his best to avoid most of his other classes. If he wanted to be an alcohol and drug counselor, he had to change; he had to attend classes and pass those classes. He had to stay clean and sober; whether or not he went to AA meetings was up to him. He didn't like the meetings, which ran counter to the jailhouse maxim,

"Never let anyone know what you're feeling." In AA you had to be aware of your feelings and share them with a sponsor, if not the whole room. He preferred to stay away from alcohol on his own—and he did.

He found his classes surprisingly passable if he really tried. Ernie realized he had never really tried to do much of anything related to any kind of work. The schoolwork centered him. When he was focusing on his schoolwork, the squirrelly part of his brain, the part that got him into trouble, remained quiet. He never thought about going drinking, getting into fights, or cruising around the neighborhood looking for trouble when he was doing his schoolwork; and the more he worked, the less he cared about any of those things.

Ernie Derico was growing up.

He worked a half shift three evenings a week at the diner; Laurie worked the other four. He enjoyed seeing customers he hadn't seen in years, and while his parents kept their heads down and didn't say much when asked about their son's time "away," Ernie was so delighted to have his freedom that he readily spoke about his incarceration when anyone asked.

Joanne Welles had visited him when he was at county, as had Jimmy Kelly. He didn't see Jimmy around much anymore—for whatever reason—but he saw a lot of Joanne, who came into the diner for coffee on the days he worked and who often walked him home. She told him she was proud of him for getting a degree and working toward a real career. He wasn't sure how he felt about that. Something about a person being proud of him left him feeling as though they were talking down to him. Your father and mother were proud of you—but a friend? But any real discomfort he felt about Joanne's support was dissipated by their easy relationship. He enjoyed their time together; after being away in a place where there were no women, he welcomed the company of a nice-looking girl who liked him and wanted to be around him.

Joanne spoke about the future as though they were going to be together—as a couple. She didn't use the word *marriage*, but he could see that was what she meant and saw in their future. He would smile and remain smiling when she talked about their future this way. He had learned to be prudent; to say little and to keep his options open.

He was surprised to see that his father had begun going to church on Sundays. His father asked him to come along, and after saying no a few times, he agreed and began going, if only to keep his father company.

Ernie had little interest in church; while he thought of himself as a Christian, he didn't believe in religion or in much of what was taught at church. He did enjoy the greetings, both by the pastor, Father Charles Donaldson, and by those seated around Ernie and his father, most of whom were regular attendees who sat in more or less the same spots each week.

He enjoyed the hymns. While he didn't believe the words, he liked to sing—it felt good, and made him think of his sister Debbie, whose death had left a painful hole in his life. He had both loved and admired his sister. Debbie had been the achiever of the three Derico children. She had talent and the drive to develop it; she would have been successful at whatever she did. He couldn't think of Debbie without becoming unbearably sad; somehow the hymns allowed him to think of her and to accept her death as part of life.

Most of the hymns were sung by the entire congregation to organ music played by Melissa McGill, who had been a friend of Debbie's at school. One of the hymns, "How Great Thou Art," was sung by Julie Kelly, a small, quiet girl with strawberry blonde hair and a clean, clear voice he could listen to all day. He began looking forward to "How Great Thou Art" every Sunday. It became the highlight of his week.

Chapter 29

J. J. couldn't stay away from Elly's house. Some of this was because he had come to treasure the time he and Elly spent together; she truly saw him as he was. He had no other explanation for their friendship, which was genuine, and without guile or manipulation or hidden motives of any kind.

He thought often of Debbie Derico—not so much about her death but about what he imagined to be her purity in life. If he was being honest with himself, he would have to admit that he did not really know her—she was barely an acquaintance and certainly not a true friend— but he held her up in his mind as a shining light that both beckoned to him and guided him. Perhaps this had little to do with Debbie herself and more with an emptiness in J. J.'s life that he imagined she filled. She was for J. J. an angel of sorts. On some level, he believed that she guided him toward the Thomas family as a healing force in his life.

The Thomas family welcomed him into their home as an equal, as a friend, and very nearly as a part of the family. He also enjoyed watching Mr. and Mrs. Thomas, who so openly loved one another. He'd had no idea that parents shared this kind of love, which he'd thought of as the territory of teenagers and young adult couples. The family was kind to J. J. and expected nothing of him—a new and joyous experience.

J. J. knew his mother disapproved of him spending time at the Thomas home, so he didn't mention his visits, and when Mrs. Thomas asked if his mother was okay with him visiting, J. J. nodded and looked away. He suspected that Mrs. Thomas knew he was lying, but he thought the lie was permissible when the upside was spending time with Elly.

When Elly asked him what he wanted to do when he grew up, J. J. laughed and said, "But we are grown up!"

Elly smiled her playful smile and asked, "So, what's your job?"

"Job?" he asked.

"See? You're not grown up. You have no job."

"So," he replied, "if you don't have a job, you're not grown up?"

She ignored his answer and said, "I was going to be a writer, but now I'm not so sure."

J. J. looked at her then and noticed how beautifully serious her eyes were. "What changed your mind?"

"My grandfather." Her eyes filled with tears. "He's so sick. He can hardly do anything. He needs Nana Makayla's help to get dressed, to shower, to go to the bathroom, to eat—to everything." A tear spilled from her eye and ran down her cheek. "But he's still Papa Elvin, you know? Still wise and strong, but in here—" she tapped her chest. "I want to help people like him, but not just old people—anyone who needs help."

J. J. thought about this. "So, do you want to be a nurse?"

Elly shook her head. "I'm not sure, but medical school? I don't think so. Maybe social work."

J. J. smiled. "You'd be good."

Her eyes flashed with a spark of something. "What about you?"

J. J. shook his head. "I have no idea."

Elly smiled. She began to laugh, and then she pushed his forearm with her fingertips. "You can do better than that."

J. J. shrugged sheepishly.

• • •

Connie and Anna were shopping together—Anna wheeled the cart while Connie scouted the aisles for items on their list.

"What's first?" Connie asked.

"Well, first would be the wine, but I'll buy that."

"Actually," Connie said, hesitantly, "I'm trying to stay away from alcohol right now. Is that okay?"

Anna smiled. "Of course it's okay, but in this case, the alcohol will cook off. The finished coq au vin will have zero alcohol content."

"Okay then." Connie tapped the handle on their cart.

"We need chicken thighs and drumsticks," Anna said, glancing at the list in her hand.

As they began wheeling their cart toward the supermarket's meat section, Connie asked, "So, are you going to forgive Lou?"

Anna stopped and stood very still, then she slowly turned to Connie. "Do you really think I should?"

"I didn't say that. But think about how you'll live going forward if you don't. Do you think he'll do it again?"

Anna shook her head. "He's swimming in guilt." She started walking again. "You know, you've got some forgiving to do yourself."

Connie said, "What I'd really like is for Shirley to forgive me. By saying that her daughter corrupted J. J., I was insulting her family, and that's not going away so fast."

"No," Anna agreed. "It's not."

"But this—what we're doing—is what I can do. It's what she did for the rest of us. The healing can begin with me. And do you know what?"

"What?"

"The results of this thing aren't up to me. With your help, we're going to have a seriously delicious party—and it will be a valentine to our neighborhood. All about love."

A smile broke out on Anna's face. "Where is all this coming from?"

Connie was too excited to stop and explain. "No, the results aren't up to me." Her cheeks were rounded by her smile; her eyes were shining. "No, they're not."

They arrived at the meat section, and Anna examined different packages of chicken thighs and legs. Finally, she chose four of each and put them in the cart, then she turned to Connie. "I didn't know you believed in God."

Connie wrinkled her nose. "I don't know what I believe, but why not hedge my bets? I guess I could put what I'm saying another way: I'm not sweating over the results. I'm going to do my thing with a good heart and let the chips fall where they may."

"Chips!" Anna exclaimed. "They're not on the list, but chips are always good!"

"How can you argue with chips?" Connie agreed.

"Next is chicken stock, then bacon."

"We have both at home."

"Then onions, carrots, and garlic—probably all in produce."

As they headed toward produce, Connie continued her train of thought. "I learned I need to take care of myself, even before I take care of my family. What does Connie need? I need to take care of that. Then I need to relax a little bit. Go easy. My mother taught me to always push, push, push—and she meant well. She wanted me to work hard for whatever I wanted. But I learned if you push too much, you get burned out. So I needed to learn to take care of myself and to relax."

Anna looked at her friend with new respect. "Where's all this coming from?"

Connie gave a self-effacing, twinkling grin. "Oh, I've got some new friends I spend time with sometimes.

"Well!" Anna didn't know what else to say. "Maybe I'd like to meet them sometime."

"Maybe you will," Connie answered.

• • •

J. J. began going to the library. He filled out a form and was given a library card, but he had no idea which books to read. His English class was reading Kurt Vonnegut, so he read *Cat's Cradle* and *The Sirens of Titan*. He asked the librarian what books he ought to read, and she asked him some questions about what he liked and didn't like—questions to which he had no real answers since he had never considered such questions himself.

He went home with *The Autobiography of Malcolm X* by Malcolm X and Alex Haley, Joan Didion's *Slouching Towards Bethlehem,* and *I Know Why the Caged Bird Sings* by Maya Angelou.

When he walked into his house with the books, passing through the living room and within sight of the kitchen table, he could feel both his parents' eyes on him, along with some of their bewilderment.

He closed the door to his room, lay down on his bed, and began to read. He read, and he read, and he read, and he came to hear the cadence of great writing in his mind, to visualize the memories and the visions of some of America's great authors and thinkers, and to hear the clarity of their voices.

He read for himself, and he read for his English classes, and he managed to pass both math and science, both just barely. He talked to Elly about what he read, but mostly he just kept reading.

And something inside him came alive and fell in love.

• • •

After church, Ernie waited just outside the front entrance until Julie came out, and then he walked her home. He did not ask if she was okay with him walking her home, he just showed up and began walking, assuming that she was too shy to object. He was right.

At first, they said nothing to one another. Ernie kept thinking of the song "How Great Thou Art," which she sang near the end of the service each week. He had come to adore the song and to think of it as referring to Julie, whose voice was ethereal and too good, as far as Ernie was concerned, to have come from the mouth of this quiet human being.

Julie's mother, Erin, was at church each week and had apparently said something at home after Ernie had walked her home that first time, because the following week, when Julie exited the church and found Ernie waiting, she excused herself, found her mother, who was inside talking to the pastor and a few of the stragglers, and asked if it would be okay if Ernie Derico walked her home from church. Erin came outside then and asked Ernie about his intentions. He politely answered that he wanted to make sure that Julie got home safely. When Erin said that she was perfectly capable of seeing to it that her daughter got home safely, Ernie said only, "Yes, ma'am," and then went silent. A good answer.

Ernie did well to ignore that fearful look that people reserved for ex-cons who wanted to spend time with their daughters. From that second Sunday on, Erin Kelly walked behind Ernie and Julie. That was her condition—the stipulation that the couple walk in front of her, always in sight, and never hold hands. Ernie was fine with this. He was giddy to be in Julie's presence and was too tongue-tied to speak.

They walked past a small crowd of boys who were congregated on a Rockaway Avenue street corner. The boys were laughing and bouncing the little pink Spalding balls they used for stickball in local schoolyards. The boys stopped laughing and stared at Ernie's little procession; one of them called out, "Whipped!" and Ernie kept his hands at his sides but surreptitiously extended the middle finger of the hand facing the boys. They laughed then.

Ernie was managing the schoolwork that would one day form the foundation of his CASAC program. Assuming he passed his exams, he would eventually be required to pass a high school equivalency test, get his diploma and later, complete approximately six thousand hours of supervised fieldwork at a job to be determined by program supervisors.

He expected to pass his high school equivalency test without too much difficulty. It was the work experience that concerned him, and how he would earn a living at the same time. He was welcome to work at the diner but wasn't sure how much of his family he could take. Everyone in his family seemed to have changed in ways he didn't understand and for reasons he couldn't fathom.

His father had gone from being a welcoming, effervescent restaurateur to a silent, brooding, aging version of himself. His mother had gone from being a hard-working, quiet woman to this vocal, spiritually centered guru of sorts. And his sister was, well, she was still his sister and ever the pain in the ass.

He talked about all of these things because thinking about the future made him anxious and because Julie herself made him nervous. She was beautiful the way a statue or a painting is beautiful—and she was just as silent. So Ernie talked.

They passed the deli, just as the door opened and Joanne came out, shielding her eyes against the winter morning's sun, and stared at him, her mouth open. She had been buying cigarettes, and she tapped the top of the pack with one hand against the opposite hand, opened the pack, took out a cigarette, and lit it, blowing a cloud of smoke in his direction.

Her expression said, "What the fuck?" and left the rest of the sentence hanging.

Chapter 30

"I'm pretty sure we'll be moving after the school year."

J. J. watched Elly's face, waiting for her to say more, but she was silent, waiting for his reaction.

"Why?"

"My father said it was a good idea—moving here—but it's just been too difficult. He said the neighborhood's not ready for Black folks to be living here."

J. J. felt oddly insulted and compelled to argue in defense of the neighborhood, but he stayed silent. Elly's declaration was like a physical blow.

So he told her about his father, and how frightened he was of him, about his father's rages and the beatings and the screaming and how awful it was for him. He had not intended to say any of this; it just poured from him, like sand from one side of an overturned hourglass to the other.

And then he told her about the book—about *Johnny Got His Gun*—and how the book had helped him to understand his father a little bit and to pity him, though *pity* was not quite the right word.

"Compassion," she told him. "The book has given you compassion for your father, and J. J. nodded that she was right. She was exactly right.

As she said this, she looked into his eyes with a merry intensity that was so unique to her that his heart was swept up in the moment, and he kissed her.

And she kissed him back.

It was a good day—a very good day. Until he remembered that Elly and her family were moving.

• • •

"J. J.!"

He came to the top of the stairs to see his mother standing with one foot on the bottom step, holding the phone out to him. He descended the stairs, took the phone, and sat down on a step about halfway down.

"Hello?"

"My grandpa died!" It was Elly and she was crying.

"I'm—"

But she didn't let him finish. "He knew it too. He called us all in yesterday, one by one—it was awful! First Mama, then Dad, then Dwayne, and me, and Nana Makayla was last. We all said, 'No, you're not dying. You're just sick,' and we thought it was the stroke, you know, affecting his thinking. But he knew, J. J., he knew!"

He didn't know what to say, but it didn't matter, because she wasn't finished. "Don't you want to know what he said to me?"

"Well, of course—"

"He said to me, 'Ellygirl'—that's what he calls me, 'Ellygirl.' He said, 'You're the heart of this family now.' And I said, 'No, Papa Elvin, Nana Makayla is!' And he said, 'No, there's a transition goin' on, you best believe it. You're the heart, and you need to believe that you're worthy. Believe it, deep down,' he said. So I said, 'How do I do that?' And he said, 'Picture yourself as a little girl, but like you're seeing yourself from the outside and maybe from above; then just love yourself. Love that little girl and say to yourself, "I love you, and you can do anything." Just say that over and over.' So I said, 'What if I try things and I fail?' And he said, 'There ain't no failing. Just try. Do. Failing is succeeding.' Now what does he mean by that, J. J.? 'Failing is succeeding'?"

J. J. opened his mouth to say something, but she kept right on talking.

"So, he told me. He said, 'You can try, and if you fail, you can figure out what you did that made you fail and try again if you want, or you can try something else. You can, you know, decide maybe that thing is not for you. But the thing to do is to believe that you're worthy of happiness, that you are worthy of doing whatever you want to do, and that you're good enough to try and to be happy with just trying and doing your best. That's the ultimate success!'" And then she was sobbing into the phone.

Later, he wouldn't know why he said it, but he said it. He said, "I love you, Elly." And that shut her right up. She said nothing for a good long minute. Finally, she said, "What?"

He wanted to hang up then. He didn't know what to do, except that he knew he had said it and he knew he didn't want to say it again, so he said something stupid. What he said next was, "Well, you know."

And Elly Thomas started to laugh.

And it was the best sound he had heard in quite some time.

• • •

J. J. hung up the phone and saw that his mother was still standing at the bottom of the stairs in much the same position as when he'd taken the phone from her. She said, "Well?"

J. J. said, "Elly's grandfather died."

And J. J.'s mother's mouth had set and her face had taken on a grim determination that he didn't understand until many years later after he'd learned that his mother had called all of the local funeral homes until she found the one handling the Elvin Thomas funeral, and she'd gotten all the particulars from them. Then she'd set about making her phone calls.

The next day, when J. J. and his parents and sister arrived at the funeral home, they saw that the parking lot was filled with cars. They entered through the rear door, which faced the parking lot.

Inside, the viewing room was packed with people, about two-thirds of them white—all of them were people with whom the Welles family was acquainted. The Derico family was there, and the Kelly family, and many others from the neighborhood and from outside the neighborhood, the families of people he knew from school and their children, J. J.'s friends and acquaintances; his mother had called them all.

He could see that Elly's family was stunned by the turnout. They had not expected strangers to intrude at the time and place of their grief. But Shirley Thomas saw them come in, and went right to J. J.'s mother and embraced her, tears streaming down her face.

"Oh my Lord," was all she said, and she said it several times.

"Shirley, Shirley," was what J. J.'s mother said.

His father, who had always had an unspoken rapport with Elly's father because they had both served, approached the bereaved son and now the family patriarch, and put out a hand. And when Elvin Thomas Jr. shook his hand, John Welles gripped Elvin's wrist with his other hand, and the two men stood together, hands and arms locked together, in a kind of spiritual solidarity.

Both of J. J.'s parents next went to Nana Makayla, who looked frail and diminished, and took her in their arms, and in each case, she nearly disappeared, she was so small and frail. They then hugged Elly and Dwayne and even Wanda, who, along with some other family, was there to support Makayla, Elvin and Shirley Thomas, and Elvin Sr.'s grandchildren.

Jimmy Kelly was sitting with Dwayne, and Ernie Derico was sitting with Julie Kelly, who was called upon to sing "How Great Thou Art," by which time everyone present was in tears.

• • •

J. J. opened the front door and was about to leave the house when he heard his mother's question.

"Where are you going?"

He turned. "Out."

Her hands went to her hips; never a good sign. "Out where?"

He sighed, thinking he might as well get this over with. "To Elly's house."

He could hear her breathing as she stared at him; he knew that she had so recently been angry with Elly's mother. Was she ready for him to return to the Thomas household?

"J.J," she began.

"Let him go," his father's voice came from the kitchen.

"I was going to, but I'd like him to be home at a decent hour."

J. J.'s eyebrows went up.

"Go, J. J. But be home by ten."

As he was leaving the house, he heard his mother say, "There's something I want to discuss, John. Anna and I are planning a party for us, the Dericos, the Kellys, and the Thomas family. We'd like to have it here."

"Here?" His father was incredulous. J. J. could feel his father's anger welling up—an unreasonable storm.

Not wanting to hear more, J. J. slipped out the door.

Anytime there was conflict at his house, and especially when he was involved, what J. J. felt was a kind of trauma that froze him in his tracks. He would not know what to do or say, nor how to act or behave. He would desperately need to escape. So, while the argument—if that's what it was—at his house was not so bad when compared to other conflicts over the years, it was more than enough to drive him from the house.

As soon as he sat down in Elly's living room, he remembered that her family was moving, and where he had been frozen by the trauma at home, he was now unfrozen, but deeply, deeply sad. He felt as though weights were pulling down on his face from the insides, and his stomach was filled with a solid, heavy weight. A soft moan escaped his lips.

Elly was sitting next to him. She said nothing.

"You're really going?" J. J. asked.

Elly nodded somberly. "My father says he looked before he leaped, whatever that means. He said we never should have come here."

"But the parties—" J. J. protested, meaning that parties had soothed and calmed the volatility that followed the Thomas family's arrival.

She gave a shrug and a smile that was both bleak and slightly derisive. "We tried."

He took her hand and held it loosely. She gave his hand a single quick squeeze.

"What are you going to do?" J. J. asked, and he meant, "What will the Thomas family do now?" But what Elly heard was, "What are you, personally, going to do with your life?"

"I've always thought I would become a writer—maybe write for magazines, or write a novel. But now, I don't know. I've been paying attention to all that's been going on, the way people around here have treated us, and I want to do something—not that I really think I can." She'd been looking toward the afternoon light that was coming in the front window of the living room, but now she turned to J. J. "But what, I don't know."

J. J. thought about this. "What do you think caused all this trouble?"

A quick flash of anger lit her eyes. "Don't say us moving here!"

"No, no, no. That's not what I meant. Look, three families came to your parties, and all three of us kind of got to know your family, and didn't things get better?"

Elly winced. "Not everything."

"But between us four families—I mean, it hasn't been perfect, but it got better because of the parties."

She nodded. "So, you're saying I should go around having parties when there's trouble in neighborhoods, to help people get along better?"

J. J. laughed; it was a big laugh that came right up out of the tension in his belly, opening his lungs and his heart. "No! I'm not saying that! I don't know what I'm saying."

They sat quietly for nearly twenty minutes, gently holding hands.

Then Elly said, "I know."

Chapter 31

Ernie was sitting next to Julie Kelly on his couch; both his parents were at work. He had no idea where his sister was.

He had been telling Julie—pale, white, silent Julie—about his plans, about his studies, and what he'd been told to expect from the on-the-job training that was waiting for him down the road. He had talked for quite a while—not only about the details of his studies and his up-coming training, but about his feelings about it all, his hopes and dreams for the future, and for the life he would build and how much better he was sure it would be than the way he'd been living. He even told her a little bit about what jail had been like, and how the sad, sometimes frightening stories he had heard from other inmates had motivated him to find some way of changing, some way of avoiding a future like that for himself.

He thought of Julie as so good and pure and sweet—very much the physical embodiment of her voice, which was so clean and clear. He assumed her insight into all he was telling her would be similarly clear and very likely inspiring. He would understand if she wasn't up to speed, if this was all a little bit too much for her since it was very nearly too much for him.

What he wasn't prepared for was—nothing. She did not react at all. No words. No facial expression. No turning toward him with encouraging body language. No throwing herself passionately at him. He had not expected this last one, but it certainly would have been nice. It would have been something.

He had thought of this moment—he had thought of pouring his heart out to Julie, of showing her how worthy he was of her singing.

He thought of her flawless performances, week after week, of "How Great Thou Art," and he wanted to show her, to convince her, that he was great too!

After a few moments of her nonreaction, he fell back, however unintentionally, on his backup plan, which was to take her in his arms and kiss her, and if she encouraged him at all to go further, to gently touch her neck, allowing his fingers to creep slowly downward, until… Nothing. Again, she did not react. Nothing.

She allowed him to kiss her, yet she did not kiss him back.

She allowed his hands on her neck, and then on her breast, and then to begin to slide into her pants. He suspected she would have allowed him to go all the way, but he knew enough, after a few moments, to stop and straighten his clothes.

The rest of the short time she was at his house, she said the equivalent of nothing, until, saying nothing, she got up and left, without a word.

The next day, he called Joanne.

• • •

Joanne was surprised to hear from Ernie and was cautiously pleased.

"What about your church girl?" she asked, her tone surly and churlish.

"Aw, I'm done with her. Not right for me. Let's not discuss it."

And just like that, Joanne and Ernie were an item again, though she refused to let him do any more than kiss her until their third date.

Joanne had been impressed with the change in Ernie and his new plans since he first told her about them, which was about the time he had made the plans. She hoped that he had changed, that he was done with the crowd with whom he had robbed Steve's Liquors. But she knew enough to be cautious. Doing time had, he claimed, pushed him away from that wrong-side-of-the-tracks lifestyle, and yet, the fact that he had lived in a way that had led him to that point concerned her. She was not immune to the attraction of supposedly cool people who gravitated toward trouble with the law.

But she was willing to give Ernie the benefit of the doubt, for now. He was sober, he was going to a program that would eventually enable him to become an alcohol and drug counselor. She had been fighting with her parents for weeks, claiming that she wanted to go away to college, but they said that going away to school was too expensive, especially if she had no clear plan of where she wanted to go or what she wanted to do afterward.

So her parents were stunned when suddenly Joanne changed her mind. She suddenly wanted to live at home and go to community college. Her parents did not know what to say at first. "So, is that okay?" she asked. "Can you pay for community college next year? I've done well on all my tests …"

"Sure," her father said, with barely a glance at her mother, who nodded, and said, to Joanne's surprise, "I'd like to hear more about it."

Some people around town would always condemn Ernie—once a criminal always a criminal. But that didn't bother Joanne. Some people around town still refused to accept the Thomas family's presence. To hell with them. She was with Ernie now, and she was proud of him.

• • •

Sorry the cat was now a fully grown, independent feline who had the run of the neighborhood and considered herself its queen. She kept watch over the Welles, Thomas, Kelly, and Derico homes, and the animals and people who lived in them. As far as Sorry the cat was concerned, the well-being of the neighborhood was a reflection of her influence and oversight.

• • •

Sorry the cat had influenced Laurie Derico to change. She had loved that cat and had come to realize that she had never really liked Joanne very much, despite the time they had spent together those last few years. She had enjoyed taking Joanne's brother's virginity, but to Laurie, Joanne was a bit of a snob who thought she was better than everyone else, perhaps because she was smart and because schoolwork came easily to her. Her visits to Joanne's house had a lot to do with visiting Sorry the cat and otherwise ignoring Joanne's pronouncements about her schoolwork.

Sorry the cat had planted a tiny seed in Laurie's heart—a seed of love, a seed of compassion, a seed of caring for others. Luckily, the seed did not need much tending, because she was not aware of it. The seed grew on its own into a firm, strong, young idea—of love and of caring for others. Caring for Sorry inspired Laurie, over time, to want to care for others.

Her idea was nearly fully formed now, and it inspired her to start making phone calls and, eventually, to enroll in a year-long program that would enable her to become a registered nurse.

Laurie had long had an energy inside her, an energy she first tried to exorcise with men. The energy had felt sexual, but sex had not gotten rid of it. After a half dozen men, when she was just about all sexed out, the energy remained, only now she regretted her actions, hating the men and at times hating herself even more.

Laurie had to get out of this town and away from these people. She would do it by putting her head down and working hard, becoming a nurse, and devoting her life to caring for others. She was startled by the completeness of her idea, which was now nearly a fully charted course for her life. She knew it was the right course.

She had to do something, so she threw herself into a nursing program an hour east of her home, in Suffolk County, and developed, nurtured, and grew her sense of self and her self-esteem by doing esteemable acts. Eventually, she would go on to be the chief nursing officer at a major hospital on the north shore of Long Island from the mid-1980s through the late 1990s, caring for thousands of people, savings lives, and helping others to become competent, successful caregivers as well.

• • •

While Connie and Anna set up for the party, J. J. arranged the furniture for a gathering of sixteen, bringing extra folding chairs in from the garage. Anna had assured Connie that others would bring desserts, but John got up from the kitchen table and said he would drive to the bakery and pick up a cake. Connie was speechless, and watched him walk out the front door and across the lawn to the driveway and the car.

Connie had laid out the ingredients and began handing them to Anna at the proper times. She read the recipe out loud, and Anna, who, after all, made her living in a kitchen cooking for the public, did the actual cooking.

Anna poured the wine and chicken stock over the thighs and drumsticks, while Connie prepped the vegetables. Anna cooked the bacon in a skillet and set it aside once it was crispy, then removed the chicken from its wine marinade, dried it with paper towels, and began placing it in the pan, skin side down.

Anna seared the chicken until it was golden on both sides, then removed it from the pan, and poured leftover marinade into a separate heat-proof container. She then added sliced onion and carrots to the pan and let everything brown, added garlic, and cooked the mixture for another minute.

Connie watched all of this with something between awe and admiration.

Anna added the vegetables to the pan, followed by several tablespoons of tomato paste. She cooked the pan's contents for several minutes, then added the remainder of the marinade, and laid the chicken in the pan, sprinkling it with thyme. She placed the cover on top and smiled at Connie. "Now we let the magic happen." She wiggled her fingers over the top of the covered pot as though she were playing an invisible piano.

Anna then sautéed mushrooms, which she added to the pot, along with some pearl onions. She mixed her *beurre manié*, which was a small mix of flour and butter, removed the chicken, and stirred in the mixture, which would thicken and enrich the sauce. She added a dash of salt and pepper, laid the chicken back into the pan, and topped it with the cooked bacon and mushrooms.

Side dishes had been prepared earlier and included steamed basmati rice, roasted root vegetables, braised kale, Swiss chard, three boxes of pasta, and a thick, crusty bread John had picked up from the bakery.

Chapter 32

Guests began arriving, and, as Anna had suspected, everyone brought dessert. The Thomas family brought homemade brownies Elly had made; the Kellys brought an apple cake. Connie noticed that Erin sat at the far end of the room with her daughter, Julie. The two women folded their hands in their laps and alternately watched the proceedings and looked down at their hands.

Tom Kelly arrived in uniform and walked around the room, shaking hands effusively with all of the men, regardless of age, and hugging all of the adult women. He waved to Elly and Joanne, who had come with Ernie, whom he took aside and spoke with quietly for several minutes. With a slap on the back and a grin, he sent Ernie back to the living room while he looked over the food and asked Connie whether she had anything stronger to drink than the soda that was out on the living room counter.

After a pause, Connie led Tom back to the living room, where she opened a cabinet and took out a bottle of whiskey and another of vodka, and placed them alongside the soda bottles, the cups, and the ice bucket. Tom thanked her, poured a half glass of neat whiskey, drank it, poured another, and took a seat near John Welles and Lou Derico, who looked as though he'd aged fifteen years in the past three months.

Connie and Anna, both in colorful aprons, clustered around the Thomas family, who, along with Wanda, were still standing just inside the front door. They were quickly joined by Erin and Julie Kelly and Joanne Welles.

Everyone offered the family words of heartfelt support and comfort.

"We're so sorry for your loss."

"He was such a good man."

"If you need anything …"

Everyone was hugging Makayla, whose head was shaking up and down with exhaustion, overwhelm, and perhaps some new medical condition. They hugged Shirley and Elvin, who looked embarrassed.

John Welles stood up and was looking at Elvin with a faint smile. Elvin came over to him, and John put out a hand. "Glad you could come, Elvin. Real sorry about your dad."

"Thank you, John." Elvin poured a little bit of vodka into a cup and sat down near John and Lou, who nodded woefully and silently put out a hand, which Elvin shook.

. . .

As the guests were offering comfort to the Thomas family, J. J. had beckoned to Elly, and the two disappeared into the backyard. The temperature was slightly above normal for a February afternoon, and two robins were chattering in a maple tree. The birds might have been the first two arrivals of the season, or, like some robins, they might have stayed all winter long.

Elly still wore her coat; J. J. wore a gray football Giants sweatshirt. They sat next to one another on a picnic bench.

"So, I know what you should be," J. J. said excitedly.

"What I should be? Don't you like what I am now? You want me to be something different?"

"No! I—" He realized she was kidding, pressed his lips together, and gave her a playful shove. "A guidance counselor. I don't think I ever mentioned it, but I had this guidance counselor, Mrs. Palley, and somehow, whenever I saw her, if I was having a hard time, she always knew what to say to make me feel better."

Elly was very still for a long moment, then looked at J. J., her eyes bright. "Yes!" she agreed.

J. J.'s expression was exuberant. "Right? And when kids are in trouble or starting fights or hating on people—"

Elly's expression turned thoughtful. "Of course, I'd have to know that there's a problem in the first place."

"Right. Right. Of course. But maybe you could help them figure out what they want to do and then help them do it."

"Well, yeah!" She was smiling, and they leaned close to one another, their shoulders touching.

The back door opened, and Dwayne and Jimmy Kelly came outside, saw J. J. and Elly, and turned around to go back in.

"It's okay, guys." J. J. beckoned, and they came back out and sat together on the bench on the opposite side of the picnic table. Jimmy Kelly was talking, and Dwayne was nodding occasionally.

Moments later, the door opened again, and Connie leaned outside. "Come on in, guys. Shirley Welles wants to say something."

The young people came back inside. Tom had sat down next to Lou and was whispering to him. Elvin was talking to John Welles, who was nodding. Anna and Connie were in the kitchen. Erin and Julie had returned to their seats to one side; on the opposite side of the room were Ernie and Joanne, also alone. Wanda was sitting nearby.

Laurie Derico, J. J. noticed with some relief, had not come.

Shirley was standing at the head of the room just inside the doorway, holding hands with and perhaps holding up her mother-in-law. At a signal from Shirley, Elvin got up and stood beside them.

Shirley waited for quiet. "First of all, thank you. Your support at this difficult time has meant the world to us."

"Yes, Lord," Makayla echoed.

"I don't know how to approach the subject, so I'm just going to say it. Our family has decided it would be best if we sold our home. While we are grateful for the friends we've made at our parties and we hope we will remain friends going forward, we've decided as a family that this is what is best for us. We have, in fact, had a pretty decent offer from someone a realtor introduced to us just yesterday. So maybe we can think of this as a sort of farewell party."

A dissenting clamor arose and filled the living room.

"I appreciate that," Shirley said, "but this is what we've decided is best for our family."

"Now just a goll-darned minute!" Wanda had stood up and was glaring at Shirley. "I moved to this all-white town to be near you," she said; her tone was firm and forceful but not angry. "And now it's my home. It took a little while for the people in my apartment building to get used to a Black face, and I wasn't too happy about that, and maybe they weren't either. But, I kept quiet and I waited. And some of them still aren't too happy. And you know what? Tough! Because some of them are okay. I learned from my best friend, Shirley Thomas, to put my best food—yes food!—forward. And that's what I did. I baked and I cooked and I made friends. Food can be good for that. Yes, it can!" She had begun to smile, but her face clouded over, and she pointed to Makayla, Shirley, and Elvin. "Let me tell you something!" she said, her tone no nonsense. "You are not going to leave me the only Black face in this town. Don't even think about it!"

Elvin walked over to Wanda and put his arms around her. "Let's go out back," he murmured, and he and Shirley and Wanda stepped through the kitchen and into the backyard, while Connie helped Makayla, who had grown frail since losing her husband, to a seat, and brought her a soda and a small plate of appetizers.

Ten minutes later, Elvin, Shirley, and Wanda returned. Anna was looking at Shirley, who gave a nod, and Anna announced, "Dinner is served!"

Two card tables had been added to the dining room table, which was now laid out banquet style. Everyone found their seats and took salad, which was in a large wooden bowl in the center of the table. Anna and Connie each brought out a platter of the coq au vin, which the women portioned out, along with sides, which John, Joanne, and J. J. helped to bring out from the kitchen. Everyone agreed that the meal was one of the very best they'd ever tasted, and enjoying it with friends made it even better.

"Dad?" Dwayne was looking at Elvin, who raised his eyebrows. "I'd like to join the Army."

Shirley turned to stare at her son and was about to say something when Makayla spoke first. "I think that's a terrific idea. You'll be a credit to our country."

Shirley was looking hard at her mother-in-law. She mouthed the word *Vietnam.*

Makayla held up a hand. "Later," she said.

Tom Kelly was looking at his son. "Are you planning on joining the Army too?" he asked.

Jimmy shook his head. "Nope. I'm going to fashion school. Me and Dwayne talked about it. It's what I've always wanted."

Tom blinked several times and looked stunned.

Elvin rose from his seat. "I'd like to make an announcement—well, it isn't exactly that, because I don't have anything to announce, except to," he chuckled, "take back our earlier announcement."

A cheer went up around the table.

Elvin cocked his head. "I'm not saying we're not moving. I'm not saying that. What I am saying is that our friend Wanda means a lot to us —as do you all; as do you all—and we're not making any hasty decisions."

"That sounds wise," John Welles said.

The dinner continued with the clatter of cutlery and plates and the pleasant drone of friendly conversation.

"I realized that nothing's final yet, but perhaps," Connie said, "instead of a farewell party, we might think of this as a tentative welcome-back party for our neighbors, the Thomas family."

THE END

Dear Reader: Thanks so much for reading The Neighborhood.

I hope you will join my mailing list to learn more about my next

books at:

https://www.davidefeldman.com/books.shtml

If you enjoyed this book, I would be grateful if you would

post a review online.

See you again soon!

-DF

9 798218 117962